T0209072

THE
PSYCHIATRIST

ELENI TRIGAS

authorHOUSE®

AuthorHouse™ UK
1663 Liberty Drive
Bloomington, IN 47403 USA
www.authorhouse.co.uk
Phone: UK TFN: 0800 0148641 (Toll Free inside the UK)
*   UK Local: 02036 956322 (+44 20 3695 6322 from outside the UK)*

Published by AuthorHouse 06/23/2021

ISBN: 978-1-6655-9092-1 (sc)
ISBN: 978-1-6655-9091-4 (hc)
ISBN: 978-1-6655-9093-8 (e)

Print information available on the last page.

Any people depicted in stock imagery provided by Getty Images are models, and such images are being used for illustrative purposes only. Certain stock imagery © Getty Images.

This book is printed on acid-free paper.

CHAPTER 1

It was 10 o'clock in the morning, the day of the 22nd of August in the year 2005. The sun was already high in the sky and was burning the earth below. The sky was clear and you still could not see any clouds that would bode a rainy day. You could not put up with this heat wave and if it would be possible to speak to the Rain-God, you would beg for a rain shower without waiting a second. At the time we already had 32 degrees Celsius in the shade and as it seemed it would only get hotter during the day. The sweat was running from my forehead down to my neck, down to my back. You can surely imagine where it was running down then. I tried desperately to set the damn air conditioner in my old Ford Dodge so cold air would come out of it. But of course instead of cool air, hot air came out of it. The damn thing was in the shitter again. I got the air conditioner fixed a number of times but every time it only worked for a few weeks before it broke again. I believe, no, I am certain, that it was time to buy a new car. I have the Ford for a long time and so far I couldn't separate from it, we have a long history behind us. Slowly, but surely I had to take the matter "new car" very seriously. To get some cool air I opened all the windows so the cool coast air could flow in. It felt really good to get the fresh air blown into my face. On the news they had announced rain for the afternoon, perhaps that's why it was so oppressive. I had the impression that the air stays still in this area. Hopefully it will rain soon to cool down. I love rain more than anything. Summer or winter, for me, it is the most beautiful spectacle in the world. Especially when I sit in the front deck of my house, on the swing, with a cold glass of beer, watching the rain. Then you can see all the lightning in the sky shooting down and hear the thunder that's announcing the next lightning. I really love rain. There are people that with the slightest thunder hide in their houses waiting for the storm to pass. For me, this was never a problem. Even as a little boy I loved it, to walk in the rain, jump in the water puddles and roll in the mud like a small piglet.

I am on my way to Florida, to the military base Ford Creek. The base is located near Cape Canaveral. I had just closed my latest case when my superior called me in his office. His name is Jack Osborne and even though he is constantly screaming around, making my life difficult, he was a good boss. I had just arrived in his office, when he pressed a file into my hands, which I had to study fast. It was about some deaths on the base in Ford Creek. The deaths themselves were not so extraordinary. They seemed like normal deaths. A drunken soldier was killed in a car crash. Another committed suicide. Basically, normal deaths, but the extraordinary about these deaths was that the victims were young women. As I was going through my file, I noticed, that the victims all died almost within a year. My superior did not believe that it was a coincidence, so I had to look into them. To be honest, I must say, that as soon as I read the file, I had a strange feeling in my stomach area. I could always count on this feeling and most of the times I was right. But this time I did not want to tell my superior, because my plan was, to start my well deserved vacation. It has been two years since my last vacation and I was really looking forward to a few days to rest. I had some really hard cases behind me that cost me a lot of time. Among those cases was one that was a little bit tricky. It was about a soldier that was stealing guns from the armoury and was selling them to terrorists. The young man's name was Thomas Good and he was a professional soldier. He had really well planned the sale of the guns, which were not regular shotguns, but were Stinger-Rockets among others. I needed eight months to solve this case, because it was a hard one to solve. I had to disguise as a soldier and sneak into their troop. It was not easy for me but in the end I earned his trust. We became friends and he talked to me a lot about his family. He had everything so well planned; he even faked an attack on himself so that nobody could suspect him. One night we were on duty by the armoury, when suddenly several men broke in the armoury and surprised us. They knocked us down, tied us and gagged us with no mercy. That night they took everything from the armoury and left nothing behind. This incident messed with my head, because from the beginning

I had a funny feeling in my stomach. Since I met this young man I didn't like him and if my stomach is rebelling, I can count on that. To make the long story short, I will tell you how I caught him. It was about two weeks before, that when we sat one night at officers quarters drinking beers, he had a few more beers than usual and was not in the best mood. When I asked him what was wrong with him, he stood up and paid our beers. He wanted to get some fresh air, but since he was drunk, I didn't want to leave him on his own. So we walked to the car and drove off. Luckily for me, we had a flat tire and stopped to change it. We got out of the car and I went to the trunk to get the spare tire. As I lifted it to get it out, a magazine of bullets fell in front of my feet. I picked it up and inspected it thoroughly. I memorized the number on the casing and put it back in the trunk. The next day I found out that it belonged to the stolen magazines of the armoury. A few days passed and after a bit of more research, the case became clear. The thief was caught. To tell the truth, I felt sorry for the not. When I found out why he did all that, I felt terrible. He needed money for his six year old daughter that needed a heart transplant. The medical bills were so high he could not pay them anymore. The soldier stood before the military court and got sentenced to a few years of jail on probation. At the same time he was dishonourably discharged and he had to forget all about his compensation. He got off with a slap on the wrist. That is the best example on why I am not married yet or started a family. You never know what the future holds for you. It is not that I haven't had any women in my life, but I haven't found the one I want to spend the rest of my life with. But this is another subject.

I complained to my superior and asked him to send someone else for the new case. Jack didn't want to hear a thing; he clearly said I was the best man for this. And yes. I am no bad investigator; so far I have solved almost all my cases. I was just not in the mood to start a new case. This new case looked like a lot of work, weeks, maybe months before I could solve it. After a lot of pressure I said yes and I am now on my way to Florida. They booked me a first class so I could arrive faster on the base. But fortunately I could persuade my boss to take my car and drive there. After a fifteen minute discussion he gave in and reluctantly agreed to my idea. It was a two day drive, but at least this way I could get some time to myself. Which I really needed. At noon I arrived in Ford Creek. I stopped at the gatehouse and took my badge at of my shirt pocket, holding it in my hand. A soldier came out and saluted me. He asked about the reason of my visit and I told him that I have been expected by the general. The soldier took my badge and went back to the gatehouse. He probably would call the general's office to confirm my arrival. He talked a few minutes on the phone, nodding a few times. Unfortunately I could not hear anything but it was of no importance anyway. He hung up the phone, wrote my name in the guest book and returned from the gatehouse. I took back my badge, putting it back into my pocket. After a short salute I got on to the base. It was a pretty large military base and all the roads had signs. On the way to the headquarters I passed a lot of barracks and as I drove on I passed the armoury after a few kilometres that were located across the military hospital. The guest house was located another three kilometres away from the hospital. I inspected the base thoroughly and almost lost my way, hadn't I seen the road sigh to the headquarters, in the last minute to turn right. I parked my car in the parking space in front of the headquarters. Before coming out of the car, I quickly grabbed my suitcase to get a can of deodorant spray. I sprayed myself head to toe, because after the drive I was sweating all over and must have smelled really bad. It was no pleasant feeling and I so wanted to take a cold shower, but it had to wait until later. I got out of the car and didn't even bother to lock it. Who would steal a car off a military base? Slowly, I walked up the stairs to headquarters, greeting the guards standing in front of it. We saluted and one of them opened the door for me. I entered a reception area and introduced myself. My name, the reason of my visit and my appointment with the General. The secretary looked at my credentials and showed me the way to the second floor, where the general's office was. He kindly gave me back my badge and I made my way up to the second floor. Again, I entered another reception area and saluted. I stated my name and waited to be announced to the general. The secretary picked up the phone and spoke quietly to announce me. After he hangs up the phone he informed me that I could enter the general's office. I thanked him, went to the door and knocked. From inside I heard a "Enter" and opened the door. I stood in front of the general's office and saluted as it was proper.,,John Man, reporting for duty.",,Leave the formalities and sit down, soldier. Welcome on my base, even though the cause of your visit is not quite clear." As long as he was welcoming me, I had the chance to look at him carefully. He must be about sixty years old and had gray hair. For his age he must still look very attractive for the female population, he was pleasant to look at. He was quite tall, about 1,90cm and well build. I had a leak in his file before coming here. He was in the Vietnam War in 1976 and the gulf war from 1989 to 1991. Through the Vietnam War he was awarded many medals and trophies. In his file was stated, that he is a fair man and was always giving a second chance. The most important thing was that he made no distinction between white and black and this is important if he wanted to be respected by his men.,,General" I started the conversation.,, I was sent here to do a small investigation. I would like to see the files of the death and talk to the witnesses. In my opinion it should not last longer than a few days. My boss finds the time distance between the deaths odd, and most of all, that every victim was female.",,What are you saying ?" asked the general surprised and widely opened his eyes. "You think that there is someone here who kills young female soldiers? Does he have something against women in the military? If that is the case, I want him caught and locked up as soon as possible.",,Yes, my General", I answered and saluted.,,Today evening at 21:00 o'clock we will meet here again in my office, so you can give me all the information about these cases. I want the whole story to end before someone gets wind of it. If there is really a lunatic that goes after young women soldiers and the news hear about it, then it will get really crazy.",,Yes, my General. You are absolutely right. I will give my best, to solve the case as quick as possible. In my opinion, it is just an unfortunate coincidence, but as I said, my boss wants me to study the files a little bit closer. As soon as I am through with them, I will inform you. Then we will see if we have a case or not." He nodded, picked up the telephone and called his secretary into the office. A few minutes later the door opened.,, Fuller, here is a list of names. I want you to pull out these files and hand them to the detective. When this is done, you will show the detective to the guest house. It might be that he will be our guest more than a couple of days.",, Yes, General Sir. I understood!" I stood up and saluted the general, as our conversation was over. Fuller and I exited the general's office and closed the door behind us. We didn't speak a word to another and he silently did what he was ordered. He sat behind a desk and took some files out of one of the drawers. I was surprised that these files were stored here and not in the file room, but I was sure that my boss contacted the general and informed him about his suspicions. As I was thinking along, Fuller made a call and a few minutes later he hung up the phone. He took the files and handed them to me.,, I reserved a room in the guest house in your name, but I didn't inform them about your profession in purpose. I hope, you agree with me. The guest house is located opposite the shooting range. It is easy to find, every building is marked with signs. If I can do anything for you, don't hesitate, to call me." We saluted each other; I thanked him for his help and promised to get him back on his offer, if needed. I put my sunglasses on and went back to the ground floor. The door was opened for me and I thank the soldier with a nod. With slow steps I walked to my car. It was already two o'clock and the sun was burning on the ground. I opened the door, sat on the driver's seat and was looking forward to drive to the guest house and take a cold shower. I started the car, got out of the parking space and drove half way back looking at the road signs. With approximately 30km/h, I passed several big buildings and stands and observed the surroundings. I passed in front of the airborne school and saw how soldiers learn how to land on the ground, jumping of a high tower with their parachutes. After that I drove pass the military infantry academy. Finally I reached a sign that pointed to the guest house and turned into the road. A couple of minutes later I parked my car in the last spot of the guest house parking space. I grabbed my bag and the files and closed the car door. From the lack of parking spaces I concluded that the guest house was fully booked. As I walked to it, I curiously looked through the parked cars. On every car there was a coloured sticker on the side. Each colour stated the rank of the officer or soldier, or the different people visiting the base. The blue sticker meant the car belongs to an officer. The red meant the car belonged to a civilian that worked here on the base and needed permission to do so. I walked up to the reception of the guest house and stated my name. The receptionist saluted me and gave me the key to my room. My room was in the second floor and again I needed to climb stairs. I put the key in the keyhole, opened the door with a yank, turned the light on and closed the door behind me at the same time. I threw my bag on the carefully made bed and left the files carefully on a small table near the window. Then I opened the window and next the shutters, so the sun could shine into the room. I closely looked at my room. It was a small room and was only equipped with the bare essentials. A bed, a dresser and a closet. It was painted in the standard military green and even the curtains were in a shade of green. It must be a pretty old building, because from one of the back corners of the ceiling, the plaster had fallen down. Exhausted, I sat on the bed, took off my shoes and threw them next to the dresser. Automatically I looked at my watch and noticed that it was two thirty in the afternoon. I took my clothes off leaving them on the floor and went to the bathroom to take a cold shower. The ice cold water ran down my back and was really healing in this heat. I immediately felt better and relaxed. After the shower I quickly put on a clean uniform and put the dirty one in a green bag to bring it to the laundry. Meanwhile it was three o'clock and I thought I could go to the mess hall to eat something. After I left the bag for the laundry next to the door, I grabbed the files and headed to the mess hall. It was not so crowded of that time, so I had no problem finding a table in a quiet corner. I sat down and left the files on the table with the front side down of course, so that nobody would see the names on them. Already after a few minutes, the waitress came to my table to get my order. I ordered a steak with fries and a large green salad. With the meal I wanted an ice cold beer. The waitress took my order and smiled at me the whole time. I smiled back, not too much, because I didn't want to get her hopes up for something I didn't want and had no time for. I needed to think about my case and this was the most important thing right now. Either way she was not my type. When she left my table I started reading my files. The first victim's name was Jane Olson and she was just 25 years old when she died. She had a bad car crash on her way home and was killed on the spot. Empty bottles of alcohol were found in her burned down car. The autopsy showed that she had a blood alcohol content of 0,350. According to the file she had just served two years on the base as a soldier. Approximately one month before her death she applied at the parachute school to get further training. In order to get that training she needed to get an evaluation of the psychiatrist on the base. She had to pass a certain test in order to see if she was fit for the training, physically and mentally. The procedure was the same for every training. She had to visit the psychiatrist a few times to talk about random things in order to understand if she was a threat to any of her colleagues. Jane Olson died on the 20.03.2005. I searched the file for the psychiatric evaluation but I couldn't find it. Only after I turned every single page at the file, I held the evaluation on my hands. The name of the doctor was written on the top left corner of the page and on the right corner was the date the evaluation was issued. As I read through the file, I noticed that the girl had passed all the tests. While as was reading the waitress came with my order. She left my meal on the table and I thanked her. She smiled back, left the table and my eyes followed her walking back. This is when I noticed a woman sitting at the table next to me. I was so focused reading the files, that I didn't realize her coming in and sitting at the table next to mine. I could see her clearly from where I was sitting, so I stared at her. I did it in a way she could not notice me doing it. She must have long, blond hair that she had styled to a tight knot at the back of her head. I noticed that when she turned around to talk to someone that just came in. She wore a white uniform that looked pretty good on her. Her upper body was well build and I assumed that the part of her body under the table looked as good to. Damn good. Suddenly she turned around and looked at me. Surely she noticed that I was staring at her. For the first time in my life my face turned so red from shame and I nodded embarrassed. She must have noticed my red face and smiled back at me. I saw the waitress stop leaving her change on her table. The cute blond, that's what I named her, took the money in her hand and put it in a small black purse. After that she stud up and walked to the exit. She gave me no further glimpse. Great. The first woman that I liked in months had no interest in me. Maybe I was already too old. I watched her walk out the mess and turned to my meal. My thoughts where already back to the file of Jane Olson and I thought about the case. I had to make a list of all the witnesses and compare with the other cases, to see if I could find any similarities. It was possible, that I would find some common facts between the cases. After the meal I quickly finished my beer. I wanted to get back to the hotel to study the other two cases as well. I paid for my food and drove back to the guest house. When I returned to my room I realized that I had no place to work on. Meanwhile it was almost five o'clock and I was hoping that the General's secretary had not finished his shift. I asked the reception to put me through the General's secretary and didn't wait long for him to answer the phone.

„Yes. Here is detective Man. I have a small problem here. To make my job a little bit easier I need a small office because here in the hotel room I have no place at all. Could you help me with this?"

„I am not so sure about this but give me a few minutes to see what I can do. Don't worry. I will find something for you!"

„ Thank you, my boy. Do me one more favour. Today evening I have an appointment with the General, but I am not sure, if I can make it today. Could you reschedule the meeting for tomorrow evening? Let him know that I want to meet with several witnesses and I will not make it tonight!"

„I will do that immediately. In about half an hour I will get back to you, to tell you where the office is located for you!"

I thanked him and said goodbye for now. I sat with the files by the small table next to the window and started reading and making notes. Not even half an hour later the phone rang and Fuller called me back. He informed me that he found a small office for my in the psychology school of the base. He apologized that it is not very large but it should do for the job. Secretary Fuller hat already ordered someone to put some furniture in the room and hand me the key. I thanked him again and wished him a good evening.

CHAPTER 2

With the files under my left arm I crossed the main road of the military base, where all the main building were located. I wanted to walk to my new office to have a look at the rest of the base. I walked pass an area where the brigade was trained. It consisted of a row of large, long buildings for housing. The buildings where made out of wood with the typical military green color. Finally I arrived at the school for psychological operations. A soldier was waiting in front of the school for me. Fuller must have described me to him because he walk right on to me and saluted me.

„ Good evening Sir. My name is Thomas Cassidy. I was ordered to wait here for you and hand you the keys to your new office!"

„ At ease soldier!" I ordered him and saw that he was relaxing his posture.

„ Thank you to make everything happen so quickly. Could you show me to my office?"

With these words we both turned and walked towards the entrance. The soldier held the door for me and I entered before him. We stopped in front of a closed door and the soldier asked me for the key to unlock the door. Automatically his hand reached to the right side of the door and he turned on the lights. He apologized for the office being in the basement, but so quick they couldn't find anything better to help me with. I, on the other hand, apologized to make such an inconvenience. He should not worry about me. I thanked him for his help and we said our goodbyes. He turned around and left the office. When he was gone I closed the door and had a closer look at my office. It was not bigger than 15 square meters. They brought a desk with a chair, a small filing cabinet and a file tray which was left on the desk. They were so thoughtful, they even left a small ventilator next to the desk. I turned around and noticed that there was not a single window in the room. This was not so important, as I surely would not spend more than a few hours in this room. Only until I finished reading the files and formed an opinion about them. As I wanted to sit at the desk, my eye fell on a small refrigerator that was put in the back corner. I put the files on the desk, took of my uniform jacket and started working without wasting no more time. As I had already read the file number one, I continued with victim number two. The second file was the case of Mariah Johnson. She was twenty four years old the time she died and was a nurse in the hospital on the base. If I could trust the files, she had no affairs with any soldier on the military base. She had a lot of friends on base and everyone described her as a friendly and full of life girl, but not in the sense that she would fool around with anyone. With her ex boyfriend she had a good relationship and they stayed friends. She was found dead in her bathtub. She supposedly cut her wrist with a razor blade. Her death date is 01 May 2005. After I read the file thoroughly and made some notes, I put the file on the desk and rubbed my eyes. It was again a long work day for me and I felt completely drained. I ordered from the mess a strong coffee and continued with the other file. I had not even opened the file when someone knocked at the door. Automatically I said 'come in' and the door opened. A soldier entered with a tray in his hands and the smell of freshly made coffee woke me up immediately. I thanked the soldier for the coffee and he disappeared after a couple of minutes leaving me to my work. I drank a big sip from the brown hot broth and it brought great comfort to my soul and I immediately felt better, as the caffeine ran through my vanes. In front of me I had the third file and I started reading it. The third victim was a Sonja Smith. Her nickname was Sonny. She was just one year on the base and was the secretary of the psychiatrist on the base. Sonny died at the age of 26. The more I read through the file, the more attentive I became. She came from a really good and wealthy family. Her father was Admiral in the marines and her mother was a housewife, that dealt with a lot of organizations. Once again a wealthy housewife and mother that did not know how to kill her time. Also Sonny had no problem with her social environment and got along well with everyone. Perhaps because her father was an Admiral she was preferred and paid attention to. Shortly before she died, she got engaged. Her fiancés name was Sam

Neil. It sounds like an actor. But this Sam Neil here is an officer who is in charge of the armory. He is thirty years old, comes from a wealthy family and seems to be an alright guy. It stated in the file that when they found the dead girl, her fiancé was devastated and could not believe that she had committed suicide. The day she died was 01.08.2005. Her fiancé could not and would not understand, how she could hang herself. I read the file to the end, put it aside and started some making notes in my notebook. Then I made a list with the causes of their deaths and noticed that two were similar, as they were suicides. A car accident was not so uncommon, especially if you considered the amount of alcohol in her blood. But two suicides, in a short period of time, was extraordinary. After that I corrected the list and compared the victims with each other. All three were of similar age at the time of their death. None under twenty and none over thirty. None of them was more than three years on the base. Two of them had a link to the psychiatrist, one worked there, the other visited him for an evaluation. The third had nothing to do with him. The only thing she had in common with him was, that they were serving at the same time. I made a note, that I needed to find out if she had known the psychiatrist or if she wanted to do some further training and had maybe come in contact with him for an evaluation. I was so absorbed in the files, that I shook up as suddenly the bugle call was played on the megaphones from a cassette, ordering everyone to rest for the day. Baffled I had a look at my watch any noticed it was already ten o'clock. This was enough work for today and I sorted the papers on my desk. Actually I thought I'd take the notes and files back to the hotel room, but then I changed my mind and locked them in the file cabinet. I took the key, put it on my key chain and put them back into my pocket. I turned of the lights and locked the office.

CHAPTER 3

After a cold shower and a close shave, I went into the mess hall to get a snack and a drink. Fortunately I found an empty table and sat down. I didn't have to wait long before the waitress, an other one this time from the one on the afternoon, came to take my order. It was my first time working on this base, so naturally I didn't know anybody and sat alone at my table. I planned to have one or two drinks and go to bed early. It was a very long day and I needed to go home to get some good sleep. Home? How did I come to think of getting 'home' . Two hole years I haven't been at my home. I didn't even know if my house still stands or if the roof broke down in it. It was time to make the decision if I wanted to continue in the army or if I should file my papers for resignation. I have already 25 years of serving behind me and I am starting to get fed up. After my years of serving I had the right to retire and I would get a good compensation as well. With this money I would open a private investigations office. < Private investigator John Man> that sound not bad, doesn't it? Icould already picture the advertising for the office and I started to like this dream. I was deep in my thoughts, as my cute blonde walked in. This time she wore a pair of washed out jeans and a top with spaghetti straps. Her hair still tightly held in the knot as before. This was a shame. As she stood now almost in front of me I could see her better, and what I saw I liked better and better. What could I do to get in a conversation with her? I needed to think of something. Basically I wanted to get back to the hotel, but I changed my mind and ordered another drink. I could not take my eyes of this beautiful blond and continued staring at her, making sure she would not notice it. It is impolite to stare at anyone. She was talking with two men and I assumed one of them was her boyfriend. The waitress came back with my drink and I took the opportunity to asked her about the cute blond.

„Can I asked you something?"

„What would you like to ask?" she asked me with a smile.

„ Could you tell me, who this blond beauty at the bar is and what her name is?"

I pointed at the bar and the waitress turned around and followed my finger to the blond girl. Then she turned around and answered me.

„This is Sarah. Sarah Connors. She is doctor in the bases hospital. A really decent girl. I don't mean to hurt your feelings but I don't think that you have the slightest chance with her mister."

She kept looking at me and smiled. I was floored by her answer and wanted to know why I don't have a chance.

„ Simply because she doesn't get involved with just anybody. She carefully picks out the men she goes out with. She is picky and makes it hard for men to win her heart. Her nickname is <blond ice block>. An if you allow me to tell you my opinion, you are a bit to old for her!"

With these words she left me there and I felt like an abandoned puppy. I watched the waitress walk back to the bar and could not believe what she had just told me. Sarah Connors. This name clicked in me. I had heard that name before, but at the moment I could not remember where I knew it from. I left a ten dollar note on the table, paid for my drinks and went back to the guest house. I had enough for tonight.

CHAPTER 4

I hang again over the files making a list of the people I wanted to look up, to aked about the victims, when the phone rang. As I was making my notes, I picked up the phone with the left hand and wandered who it could be disturbing me doing my job.

„Hello. This is detective Man. Who is this and what can I do fro you?" I asked in a strict tone. I didn't like to be disturbed while working.

„ I wish you a good morning my friend. This is your boss calling. How are you coming along with the case? I am waiting two days for you to call!"

The good old Jack Osborne. By the tone of his voice I could understand that he was pissed off. I could see him behind his desk snapping at the phone. With this thought I smiled, good that he couldn't see me right now. Otherwise who knows what he would tell me. He would go crazy and I am not in the mood for this right now.

„ Good morning, Jack. I am sorry you had to wait by the telephone waiting impatient for my call. I arrived around noon on base and got straight to work. I didn't have the time so far to get back to you. You just caught me buried in these files working. Today I wanted to get in touch with some of the victims friends, to get a better opinion about them and their death circumstances. I wanted to call you in the evening to inform you."

„My hard working boy. As always working. I am sitting here in agony, feeling sorry for myself, because I want to know, what your opinion is on everything! Tell me, what is going on and how are you getting along?"

„ To tell the truth, I have not found out much. There are not too many facts in the victims cases, this is why I need to get in touch with friends and witnesses, to find out more. I need to get to know the victims more to make a clear opinion about how they died. In one thing I am absolutely certain and no one can get it out of my head. I am sure that the three victims knew each other, even if they had only seen each other. This base is huge but it is not that huge."

„ John, This I would have found out myself. Tell me, what you really think. I am begging you, don't hold it out for me any longer!"

„ Let me finish my sentence, you asshole! Two of the girl knew the psychiatrist of the base. One was his secretary and the other needed an evaluation from him and visited him a few times. What I need to find out is if also the third victim knew the psychiatrist. If she did, we have the link we are looking for. Then we can go on."

„Are there any other similarities between these dead girls?"

„No. Other than the fact that they were all in a similar age. But, one was tall and skinny, the other short. One a natural blond, the other dyed her hair blond."

„This does not help us. Ok, my boy. I will leave you to it then. Don't forget to inform me about any findings. I count on you. You are the best man for the job!"

I didn't have the time to answer, because Jack had already hung up the telephone. Best man my ass. This is how you treat your best man, leaving him work for two years without a vacation? I collected my thoughts and focused on the investigation. I decided, to get in touch with the friends of the first victim. In the file I could see that there were no relatives listed. This meant that I would have to get in touch with some of her colleagues and friends. Fortunately, they were all on the base so I didn't have to drive around in the car on this so hot day. In this heat you could fry eggs on the street. I called the operator to find out where these people I was looking for were stationed. It only took half an hour and in the end I located several of them. They put me through to observation post four as I asked.

„ Observation post four. Private Thomson speaking."

„ This is detective John Man. I need to speak to private Mike Johnson!"

„ One moment please. "

I could hear how he left the phone down and walked away. A minute later I could hear someone coming closer and answering me.

„ Private Mike Johnson speaking. How can I help you?"

„ This is detective John Man. I have some questions about the late Jane Olson and I was hoping you could help me with them."

„ Ok, what do you need to know? But I don't think that I can say a lot."

„ Tell me what you know and let me decide if you helped me along or not."

„ I am quite sure, that I already told the military police everything I know. But if you want to hear it once from me, I have no problem."

„ I don't mind and I would like to hear it one more time from you so I can form an impression of the deceased. How long did you know her?"

„ About a year. We had were in an exclusive relationship, that was going nowhere and so we split up three months after. We stayed good friends."

„ By this you mean that neither of you would have a problem with the other starting a new relationship. Did I understand this correctly?"

„ Of course. Why should we have problems with this?"

„ In the autopsy it said, that they discovered that her blood alcohol was 0,35. This brings me to my next question. Did she use to consume large amounts of alcohol?"

„ No, not that I knew of. We went out a lot together, even after we broke up, but she never drunk more than a bottle of wine. I wandered about that too, when I heard about her car crash. Even more when they informed me that she was completely drunk and had empty vodka bottles in her car."

„ Why is that?"

„As I said, she did not drink more that a bottle of wine. And that rarely. Maybe once a week or even more."

„Did she have any troubles? Maybe she had worries about her military carrier? What would you think could bring her to drink that much and cause a crash?"

„ No, everything was going great in her life and her job. She had no problems with nothing and no one. She was really excited that she had passed all her tests for her upcoming training in the parachute school and everything was looking good."

„ What tests do you mean?"

„ I mean the test she had to take for this stupid psychiatrist."

„ Why do you say <stupid> psychiatrist. Did you have problems with each other?"

„ I am sorry for the choice of words, but for this psychiatrist there are a lot of bad words you can describe him with. Every time Jane visited him, he tried to talk her out of going to the school."

„ What to do you mean by that?"

„ I mean exactly what I told you. Every time he tried to talk her out of the idea of signing up for the training at the parachute school. I remember very well, after the third session they had she called me and started complaining about him."

„ What was the reason he wanted to talk her out of it. Do you remember that? I mean if you can exactly remember what she told you?"

„ He wanted once again to talk her out of going to the school, when Jane had an outburst. She started screaming at him asking what his problems where and why she should not sign up for the training. He answered that it would be better for her to leave the military. She should go, like every normal woman, to get a husband and have a lot of kids. He was basically saying that women belong in the kitchen nowhere else. The men take care of them and the family. Do you know what I mean?"

„ Yes, I understand. Do you know, if she complained about him to any higher ranking officer?"

„ We talked about it, but she only wanted to do so if he failed her in his tests. But he didn't dare doing it and so she passed the tests."

„ When did you last see her?"

„ Two days before she died. You cannot imagine how much her crash affected me. The day I last saw her, she invited me to a party she wanted to have. She wanted to celebrate with friends for passing her tests. She was excited, that she had passed and could move on to her training."

„ You where not at the party. Why?"

„ That night I was on duty and couldn't find anyone to fill in for me."

„ Do you think she went against herself that night and drank so much? What do you think?"

„No, I don't think that. The party had not taken place yet, when they informed us about the car crash."

„ So, you think, that she was alone and had not drink anything. Is this what you want to tell me?"

„I know that she was alone and when she was alone she never drank more than two glasses of wine."

„Ok. I thank you for your information. I have a better picture about the deceased now. If I have any more questions I will get back to you. Thank you very much."

I hang up the phone and started thinking. That what private Mike Johnson just told me, was the complete opposite of what was written in the autopsy. If I can trust his words, then there was no reason why she should drive her car so drunk. In this case something was bothering me, but at this moment I was not quite sure what it was. My stomach started rebelling. This was no good sign for me. I spoke with some other colleagues and friends of the victim but I got the same answers from everyone. No new information. Suddenly I had a thought, to get in touch with the psychiatrist himself and called his office. It went straight to voicemail. I left a message telling who I am and what I wanted to talk to him about and asked him to call me back. I wanted to make an appointment, to talk about the cases Olson and Smith. So I could kill two birds in one stone. After I left the message, I hang up the phone and got up. I went to the refrigerator, opened the door and got a bottle of water I put in there a while ago. The cold water got down my throat and refreshed me. I started to stretch, I was tired and drained, I was sitting at the desk for more than seven hours. As I could not reach the psychiatrist, I opened the file of Sonny Smith. I left the autopsy by the side, because I had more interest to find out about her family and friends. I noticed the name of her fiancé and continued reading about him. His name was Sam Neil and he was a soldier on the base. In the file it said, that he is in charge for the armory. He is thirty years old and, for his age, he had a good carrier and will go very far in the military. According to the report, he was completely devastated to hear about the death of his fiancé. He could not believe that she hang herself. I wanted to talk to him and the family of the deceased. In the file where the addresses and telephone numbers of everyone. I wanted to talk to the fiancé first and then the parents of the girl. I tried desperately to find him on the base, but they told me that after her death he took an unpaid leave. I had another look in the file and noticed that the couple had rented a house outside the base. It was no problem for me to find the address . I had installed a GPS system in my car that would show me the way to even the smallest alley. In this system where uploaded all the maps of America. I just needed to put in an address and it would show me the way anywhere. Before I drove there, I wanted to make sure that officer Neil was at home, so I called. The telephone rang more than twenty times but no one answered. In the moment I wanted to hang up somebody picked up the phone and talked to me.

„Yes, who is there?" I heard a guy asking with a husky voice. He was not that sober as I could understand. He must have had already a few beers.

„ This is detective John Man. I would like to talk to officer Neil if it is possible."

„This is him. What do you want?"

„ I wanted to ask you a few questions about the death of your fiancé. Only if you agree, of course."

„ Come on over then."

He wanted to give me the address but I informed him that I already had it and told him I would be there in an hour the latest. Then I hung up the phone again. Not to waste any time I locked the other files back in the cabinet. With the file o Sonny Smith in hand I left the office and locked the door. I sat in the drivers seat, threw the file on the seat next to me and started the car. I put the address in the GPS and a minute later it showed me how to get there and I left the base. I drone on the George Kennedy Road. It was full of super markets and Nightclubs. Everywhere you looked where bleak spaced that were used as parking places. Every few meters you could see cheap motels, fast food stands and a lot of car dealers. They all promised better prices that the dealer next door. This must be heaven for the soldiers when they were on leave. They didn't have to drive all the way to the city, they hand everything around them. Even the cheap motels were of good use. So they could have a good time when the girlfriends came and they could not get them on base. After around twenty five minutes, I reached the end of George Kennedy Road. The residential area was quiet and nice. The area had no more than sixty houses. They all had well kept lawns and flowers in front of them. Next to the entrance was the garage. I quickly found house number twenty eight and parked on the street before the drive way. I grabbed the file got out of the car and closed the door. With the file in my hands I walked up to the house and stopped in front of the front door. I rang the bell and waited for someone to open the door. The name of the deceased was still standing on the nameplate. Again I pressed the door bell and I could hear the sound of a canary on the inside, what was the door bell sound. A few minutes passed and a rang one last time, but still no one came to answer the door. How could that be? I called announcing my arrival. Slowly I started to loose my patience and I was not sure what to do now. I felt abandoned and lonely and I noticed that I was being watched. In the house across the street the curtains in one of the windows moved. I decided to go to the back of the house in the garden and took the small alley next to the garage. Hecould not have left, I told him I was coming. I opened the wooden gate into the garden and had alook around. I noticed that the back gardens of the houses were attached, separated only by a wooden fence so that everyone could have their privacy. One side of the fence was painted green with big beautiful flowers. In the back of the garden was a typical BBQ grill surrounded by garden furniture, one table with six chairs. A large umbrella protected the furniture from the sun. On a sun bed, I saw a guy lying there with a bottle of beer in his hand. I don't think he noticed me coming in and he brought the bottle to his mouth and had a big sip. As I was watching him drink, I had a closer look at him. He must be around 1,90 m tall and had a trained body, but if he would not stop drinking beer his belly would get bigger and bigger. You could see how much beer he already had to forget his sorrow. He had blond hair, which were a little bit longer now, as was the beard. Who knows how long he had not trimmed is hair or beard. You could see haw devastated he was. He just wanted to leave the empty bottle on the grass to get a new one when I made myself noticeable. He looked at me, surprised that he just noticed me. He tried to get up on his feet to greet me but he was up for it and almost fell. I walked towards him and wanted to help him keep standing but as I wanted to grab him, he declined. Instead he sat back down on the sun bed. With a gesture he showed me I should sit in one of the chairs. I brought the chair closer to him and took a seat. We were sitting now across each other, studying each other. Who knows how much beer he already drank today, to be this drunk so early in the day. I did not know where to begin and was thinking how I can get information out of him. It would not be easy.

„ I am very sorry to disturb you, but I must ask you some questions about the death of your fiancé, if that's ok with you!"

„ What for? Either way you will not reopen the case. I have told everything I know to the investigating military officer at the time. So, what is all the fuss about? Let her rest in peace."

„ If you are up for it, please tell me once again what you told the officer then, that was investigating the case. I want to form my own picture of the deceased. It would be a great help."

„ He was staring at me but, in the same time, not looking at me. He was looking passed me like he was on a trip through time. The time travel began and he sat there for a few minutes in silence. He started talking with a broken voice.

„I still can't believe that she is gone. That she died. I cannot understand and for months I have been asking myself why. Why did she do that? We were such a happy couple. At least this is how I felt about us and, I am a hundred percent sure, that she was happy too. We got along fine between us and had no problems with each other. We had picked out the date for our wedding."

„ It was you that found her, right?"

It was more of a statement than a question that I asked the officer.

„Yes, I found her", his eyes filled with tears.„I was coming home from a night shift around six o'clock in the morning. Her ship was starting at eight, so we still had enough time to have a coffee together before she left for work. I opened the door and,believe me, I had a strange feeling in my stomach. Something was not right in the house. We had planned, the night before, to have coffee together in the morning but in the house everything was still dark. Not even the small lamp we usually leave on at night, was on. I turned the light on when I was closing the door and wandered. I called her name but became no answer and I thought maybe she is in the shower and can't hear me. The only thing I became as an answer was a sweet sour smell that was going through the house. Call it suspicion or telepathy. In that moment I knew she was dead. I ran up the stairs into the bedroom. The smell got more and more intensive. I could not find her there so I ran into the bathroom and saw her in the shower. She had hanged herself. At least this is what everyone says. I don't believe it's true."

„ Why would you say that? It is not unusual for people to get cold feet before the wedding and sometimes there seems as there is no other way out than to do something uncommon. You cannot imagine what some people did in order not to get married or not to hurt the partner by asking for a separation."

„ You cannot fool me. I don't believe a word you said. We were happy!"

He got really upset and his face turned red. He got up and grabbed another beer out of his icebox that stood on the table next to me. He opened it and offered me a bottle but I didn't want one. He slowly walked back to the sun bed and sat down. I could see that there was more he wanted to talk about and I was right. He came so close to my face and started whispering.

„ There is something else, I have to tell you. It is not in the autopsy. The Admiral and I thought that nobody should know about it. Most of all, her mother. She would kill herself too, if she'd found out. Sonny was pregnant!"

This really was news for me. It floored me, like a bomb exploded over my head. I must have made a face like an idiot, when I saw he was making an effort not to laugh.

„ Do you understand what I am saying now?"

„ Why did you not tell he military police that? You should know that the pregnancy is a crucial fact in the case. This brings a whole new light on the case. You must know that!"

Slowly I began to think that we were dealing with a serial killer that was dumping off women. Two cases that, according to the witnesses, were not what they seem. It started to get complicated and I absolutely didn't like that. With this though I felt sick. He must have noticed me, because he looked me in the eye and asked:

„WHAT?"

I had no intention on filling him in on the investigation but I had to say or do something. Somehow he knew from the beginning that his fiancés death was murder. Only, no one believed him.

„ Well alright. I think it is time to tell you the truth. I will only tell you if you promise not to tell a singe person until I solve these cases!"

„ Cases?"

„Yes, cases. The death of your fiancé is not the only one that looks suspicious on the base!"

„ What are you saying? You need to be more specific, because I cannot understand."

I told him about the other two cases and saw that his facial expression was changing. He jumped up and started walking up and down like a tiger. He stopped and turned to me with anger in his eyes.

„So I was right all along that it was murder, no one believed me. What will you do now?"

„ I will return to the base and examine the other cases. I need from you to do as you promised and not tell a single word to anyone. It could harm the investigation. If I have any news I will inform you."

We shook hands and I made him give me his word again that he would not talk to anyone about it. He had to give him my word that I would inform him about the investigation.

Everything around him was wrapped in darkness. He got this prickling sensation in his fingers again. It was time to continue his work. He had already picked out his next victim. For days he has been following and watching her. He was very careful and she hadn't notice anything. From the day he started following her, he always felt sick when he saw her. He hated her guts. Not only her, all of them. He hated all women. Every female creature. This was the reason, he was never married. He would never marry. Even the smallest thought he could have a wife brought him pure fear and he would break into sweat. He sat in the dark and he felt sicker and sicker. He started shaking and couldn't stop it. He couldn't make himself feel better so he jumped up his armchair and ran to the toilet to throw up. He got there just in time. From the outside you could hear the retch and that something is falling in the toilet. After throwing up, he stood up and looked in the mirror. His face was red and sweat was running down his forehead. With the right hand he took a tissue out of his right pocket and cleaned his mouth. He made a grotesque face. How he hated her, SHE was the reason he got sick. Every time he thought about her. He opened the door and sat back down on his armchair to calm himself down and think. He needed a few days to complete his plan. She could not escape from him. He just needed to decide which way she was going to die. It must be a slow death, she must suffer. She needed to pay for his suffering. He was lost in his thoughts and sat there still in the dark when the phone rang bringing him back to reality. To hell with women!

CHAPTER 5

As I arrived on the base I drove straight back to the guest house to take a shower and put on a fresh uniform. At nine today evening I had the meeting with the General. So I had a quick shower and made a plan to eat something before I went to see him. When I arrived in the mess hall I sat at a quiet table again, where I could collect my thoughts on the cases. I took the file of Sonny Smith with me and wanted to read it thoroughly one more time, while I was waiting on my dinner. I read it one more time from the beginning to the end and had a closer look at the crime scene photos. There were a lot of different pictures with the different positions of the dead. I saw a young woman that must have looked very beautiful before she died. I laid the photos in order on the table. Around her neck she made a noose that she tied around the supporting rod of the shower. I examined the pictures carefully but I couldn't find anything unusual. Basically it was unusual to hang yourself in the shower using the shower supporting rod. Most of the suicide victims choose something else, for example the living room ceiling or jump off a bridge. In the living room they tie the rope on the ceiling lamp and stand on a chair that they knock down after. It was easier to jump off a bridge. You tie the noose around your neck, jumped and that was it. I could barely believe that you could hang yourself in the shower, above all, if the neck has to break. The space between the legs and the ground was not high enough. How did she do that? I read the autopsy report again. It said that she didn't die directly. When suicide victims hang themselves they wriggle around for a few minutes. Most of the victims only then realize what they are about to do and wriggle in hope to cut themselves loose. But in the end they all die. But there was something else I was interested in. I searched in the report if they found some bruising or wounds on her that were caused before her death. The doctor had stated no such thing. The only bruises and marks the dead woman had, were caused after he death. In the report, it was written, that on her body you could see the outlines of the tiles. Thos happens when the blood begins to clot and the body hasn't been moved for hours. The same happened to Sonny Smith. It was written that the time of death was between nine o'clock in the evening to two o'clock at night. It had to be someone who knew that she would be home alone and nobody would come back to disturb his work. He must have broken in to the house but how did he manage to get her in the shower without struggling? Maybe he drugged her. But in the report there was no mentioning about a toxicology analysis even being asked for. As it seemed no one asked for it because they were dealing with suicide. I needed to exhume the body. Maybe we find something in the remains that would help us get further. It was worth a try.

I was on my way to the General and had another half an hour for our meeting. I sat in my car for a while, smoked a cigarette and thought about the cases. You must know that you never go earlier to a meeting with a General or a military high ranking officer. It looks as if you do not have nothing better to do with your time and don't do your job to heart. It is always better if you come a little bit later to a meeting, but never later than ten minutes, because then you have a problem. I had just put out my cigarette and made my way to the Generals office, when it clicked in my head. You know what I mean. When you want to think about something important but you are just talking to someone about something meaningless and try to remember to think about it later and then, hours later, it clicks in your head and you have the thought back you wanted to think about. This was what happened to me now. The thought that popped into my head was that the murderer didn't have to break into the Smiths home. Maybe it was someone one of the couples friends that knew that Officer Neil was on duty that night. Maybe one of the neighbors saw him and didn't think it was something extraordinary because they had seen him before. I quickly dismissed the thought, if they had seen anything they would have told the military police. As I was lost in my thoughts, I walked up the stairs to the second floor and stopped in front of the General's door. His secretary recognized me and asked me to wait a few minutes, so I sat down on a leather couch just across the secretary's desk. I could see that

Fuller picked up the phone and talked with a low voice. He was probably just announcing my arrival to the General. A few seconds later I was sitting across the General and waited for the discussion to begin. He was looking at some papers and, as I didn't want to waste any more time, I cleared my throat. He looked up, sighed and closed the files he was working on. Then he got up and walked to a cabinet that looked really expensive. He opened the door and took two crystal glasses and a bottle of scotch. The General put a glass in front of me and filled them both with scotch.

„ To wash the poison down our throats. If you don't mind!"

„ No, not at all, sir."

„ So, let us begin then. What did you find out?"

These Generals. They didn't play around much and shoot straight to the heart. So I informed him about talking to witnesses and friends. When I referred to the Sonny Smith case I let him in on the secret officer Neil told me. I could see the General's face get darker and darker and that he didn't like what he heard. On one hand he was glad they kept it a secret, on the other it made him think that this all means there is really someone on the base how has something against women in the military. Or it was all just a big coincidence and the deaths were accidents and suicides as there were stated.

„ If officer Neil had talked about the pregnancy they would look closer into the suicide. Why did the Admiral want to keep it a secret? There is nothing bad about an engaged young woman to be pregnant before the wedding. What do you think?, he asked me.

„ Maybe he thought that the girl should marry first and the get pregnant. But if they wanted to get married later, you would see he belly anyway, after the 12th week you can not hide it anyway. Or not, sir? Tomorrow morning I wanted to get in touch with the Admiral, to talk about his daughters case and see what he thinks."

„ I think it is a good idea. So you are completely sure we are dealing with murders here, right?" he asked with a heavy heart and stared at the ceiling.

It was more of a statement than a question and he sat back on his chair drinking another sip of scotch. He finished his glass and filled his and my glass up.

„ With what I could find out from talking to the victim's surroundings it became clearer. I am absolutely certain that we are talking about murders. It brings the cases into a whole new light. Only one thing I am not sure about jet is what the motive can be for these murders."

„ Do me a favor. I want that you proceed quietly. I don't want the press getting any wind of it! Did you understand me?"

He looked straight into my eyes and I could see he was secretly begging. I nodded and gave him my word. I promised it will all be done quietly and I would report back to him every day.

„ Good. This is it for tonight. If you'd excuse me, I must make some calls. One of them is to the minister of defense. When he called me this morning to tell me that he knew about the investigation I felt sick. How they find out so quickly, I have no idea!"

I told him I didn't know either but it was a lie. I know to good that my superior Jack is not only good colleagues with the minister, they play golf together every week. What a coincidence, right?

He looked at his watch and it was around ten o'clock in the evening. He sat in his car and had binoculars in his hands. For almost a hour he was sitting here, on post, watching her from the window of the hospital. He sucked in every step she made and licked over his dry lips. Sweat was running from his forehead down his cheeks ending on his shirt's collar. All day he was thinking about how he would do it and came up with the perfect plan. He wanted to make it look like a murder in course of a robbery. That was the perfect plan. No one will find it extraordinary, such murders happen almost every day in his state. You could read or hear about them every day in the news. For him, it was the perfect plan and if everything went as planned, she would not survive the next night. After half an hour, he left the binoculars on the seat next to him, started the car and slowly drove home. He had planned to attack tomorrow evening so he needed to prepare so nothing would go wrong.

CHAPTER 6

For the next morning I had planned to contact the Admiral. I wanted to do so early in the morning to complete the Sonny Smith file at noon. When I called the Admiral's house a maid answered and informed me that he was out and would come home around noon. I told her that it was important for me to talk to the Admiral and I cannot delay it. She promised she would get in touch with him. As I hung up the phone, I thought, I would drive to his house and wait for him there. These things are better said in person than on the phone. I looked at my watch and saw it was nine thirty. If I left now for the Admiral's house I would be there around eleven. His house was two hundred miles away from here. They were living a bit outside Florida. I thought about it for a little while and made the decision to drive there.

Approximately two hours later, at eleven thirty, I arrived at the Admiral's house. The grounds were surely two hundred hectares big. I drove up to a big iron gate. The whole property was surrounded by a two meter high wall covered by ivy. Next to the gate was a bell with a communication system to announce you so they would open the door. On the left and right of the gate cameras were installed to see every visitor that comes near the house. I parked in front of the speaker and pressed the bell button. A voice asked me about my name and the reason for my visit and a few minutes later the large gate opened and I could drive on the property. After the gate began gravel road that I followed for another two hundred meters until I arrived in front of the house. In the houses forecourt was a big fountain which bubbled away and some birds where playing and bathing in his waters. I parked directly next to the fountain. As I was walking towards the entrance of the house, I took a closer look at it.

It smelled of money and power and I must really be careful with my choice of words, because they could send me straight to hell. I rang the door bell and a maid opened the door asking me to come in. She showed me straight to the Admiral's office and told me to wait there. The office was furnished really stylish and everything in here was shining from furniture polish. A lot of light came into the room from a large window making the office feel welcoming. I sat down on a big leather armchair and the maid offered me a hot cup of coffee, while I was waiting for the Admiral, which I accepted thanking her. I had just take a sip of my coffee when the Admiral entered his office. Immediately I put down the cup and saluted the Admiral.

„ Please, sit down. I was informed of the topic of our conversation and I must tell you that we are not only talking as Admiral to officer today, but also as a grieving father to a friend!"

„ As you wish", I answered him and I was very surprised by the mild sound of his voice. I think this would be an easy conversation. I just needed to find the right words to get the answers I was looking for. The Admiral was standing behind his desk. He was wearing a blue suit and on his chest he carried his shining awards. As he shook my and I offered him my condolences.

„ Thank you. But, please sit back down and make yourself comfortable."

So we both sat across each other on two leather armchairs that were located in front of his desk. He poured himself some coffee and I was carefully watching him out of the corner of my eye. He had red hair that slowly turned gray and blue eyes. His features were rough and I thought it might be from the exposure to sun and saltwater due to his lifelong carrier on sea. He held his coffee sitting back in his chair nit saying a word. As I have said before, when you are in the presence of a General or Admiral it is not common to start the conversation if you are not spoken too. You needed to wait until you were granted permission to speak. We were drinking our coffee in silence and I knew that the Admiral had no intention of opening his mouth soon. I t was not proper, but I had three cases I needed to investigate and catch a killer so I did not need any delays.

, Admiral, as you know, I am here to talk about the death of your daughter. I hope and rely on that we can work together."

„ you will get from me every interesting fact, although I cannot imagine what this would change. The case was closed months ago and everyone was certain it was a suicide. I don't understand what will be different now and why a new detective is been needed. And now you are sitting here with some more questions."

He was looking me straight in the eyes and I knew, he would give me a true answer to every question in order to help me get along with the investigation.

I asked the classic questions a detective needs to ask. For example, if his daughter was unhappy, when he last saw her, if she had trouble in her carrier or with her fiancé and so on. He answered every question as good as he could and he told me when he last saw his daughter the weekend before she died she seemed genuinely happy. I asked a lot of questions, when he suddenly stopped and looked at me.

„ Why are you asking me all these questions? She is almost dead for three months. We answered the same questions to the military police then. Why are you coming to me now, asking me again?"

This was the moment I needed to be honest and tell the Admiral why I was sitting here. So I told the Admiral about the investigation and the other cases. The Admirals face turned pale and he got completely silent, not interrupting me even once, while I was talking.

„ I want to ask you one more thing. Why did you keep your daughters pregnancy a secret? There are a lot of women who get pregnant before the marriage. It is no shame."

This question dropped on the Admiral's head like and atomic bomb. He looked at me wandering where I knew about the pregnancy.

„ How do you know about my daughters pregnancy?", he said with anger leaving his cuo on the side table.

„ Officer Neil confided in me. Your daughters fiancé."

Angry he stood up and walked up and down like a tiger in a cage.

„ How could he? How could he say this to you? We swore never to tell anyone."

He walked silently up and down the room, then sat back down and didn't say a word. The minutes passed seeming like hours to me and I got restless. He sat straight and said to me.

„What I am about to tell you now, must stay between you and me. As soon as you say anything to anyone I will deny it, of course, and look like

I am just hearing it for the first time. You need to promise me that you will not tell a single word to anyone!"

„I swear!"

„ Good. It is not easy for me, you must believe me. I don't really know where to start."

I sat back in my chair. I was sure he would drop a bomb on me, and I was right. I sipped my coffee and let him speak, not disturbing him once.

„ It was the beginning of April when Sonny was at our door, visiting unannounced. Her mother and I were very surprised, because usually months pass by without her visiting and in the end we always had to invite her to come and visit us. She had a really demanding work schedule and as you know, women in the military and the navy, have a harder time building a carrier. We asked her what the reason of her surprise visit was and she told us that she had a week of vacation. I knew, this was a lie, because they both didn't want to take any more vacation except the two weeks before their wedding and after that for their honeymoon. She was already three days here when her mother accidently caught her in the bathroom. There was it where she could see grazes and bruises all over Sonny's body. My wife was completely shocked and wanted to know what happened. You should know that I am against violence in the family and I swear to you that I have never even slapped my daughter. I am sure that my wife thought that Sam beat her up like that, but Sonny didn't say a word. She wanted to talk only to me, so we sat down here in the office. We were not like father and daughter, more like two old friends who could share everything between them. We knew neither of us would say anything to anyone else. Not to run around the bush, I will tell you what happened. It all began early in April, when she was coming home from work. When she arrived at home someone grabbed and raped her. As this was not enough he beat her up, almost to the death. The only thing she can remember was that she woke up hours later naked in the garden. The next day she came straight here. She lied to Sam telling him that her mother needed to go to the hospital for a week and she wanted to take care of her. I knew that she would heel here and that some day, she would tell Sam about it. After a week she went back home. The wounds were healed and if Sam saw any bruises she wanted to tell him that she fell of the stairs. Everything went well and there were no problems, since Sam was satisfied with her story.

And then, almost a month later she called me and told me that she was pregnant. You surely understand how shocked I was. Sonny didn't want Sam to find out about the rape and all the time she talked to me she cried like a small child. It broke my heart. We looked for an answer, because an abortion is against our religion, but we couldn't find anything and hoped the kid is Sam's. ''

,, What I don't understand, Admiral, is what this has to do with your daughters suicide?''

,, You must know that Sam doesn't know anything about the rape. We kept it to ourselves and Sonny took this secret to her grave. To tell you the truth, I don't know what I was thinking when I decided to hide the pregnancy. I thought that she did commit suicide. That the rape and the child were too much for her. The guilt to hide everything from Sam. I was sure that it was too much for Sonny. But if I suspected, that she would commit suicide, I would personally tell Sam everything and I am sure she would still be alive today.''

,, Did your daughter have a suspicion on who the rapist must have been? Anything that would help us? Didn't she want to report the rape and get an investigation started?''

,, No, she didn't know who the rapist was. She had no problems. With no one. I had contacted General Pilot and asked him to run a discreet investigation. I did that behind my daughters back, because I wanted to get swine in front the military court. Unfortunately, the investigation had no result. Unfortunately.''

,, She never complained about any one, that bothered her with telephone calls or send her threatening messages or something?''

,, No, nothing of the sort. What do you mean? Do you think the rape has something to do with her suicide?''

,, To tell you the truth. In my opinion, yes it does. But I cannot be absolutely certain and this is why I need to asked you for a favor. It is not easy for me to ask you this and I don't if we are going to find anything. But in my opinion it would be crucial for the investigation…''

I was not sure, how to ask the General about this and he noticed that I couldn't find the right words. He couldn't tolerate the silence between us any longer and asked me directly what it is I wanted.

,, What is it? What do you want to ask me?''

„ I want to ask for your permission, to exhume your daughter's body!"

„ What are you thinking? Have you lost your mind?"

„ Sir, I swear. I must find out if your daughter was drugged that night. I am a hundred percent sure, that she didn't commit suicide, but was murdered. If you don't want her body to be exhumed it is ok. Nut you must know, it would be a great help, not only to explain your daughter's death but also the death of the two other girls."

He looked at me and then nodded at first reluctantly, then with complete consent.

„ Alright then. I will give you permission. But I am warning you my friend, if nothing comes out of it, then God help you!"

„ I thank you Admiral. You will not regret this. I will do my best to do everything as discreet as possible."

Three hours later I was sitting in my small office, behind my desk calling my boss. I informed him about the progress of the investigation and asked him to start the process of exhuming Sonny Smith's body. When he first heard about it he was shocked, but when I told him why we needed the exhumation he said he would put everything in motion. I finished the call with my boss and called my friend Thomas. Thomas was the leader of a special unit that have requested in many other cases before. He and his team were the only ones on whose results I could count on. Give Thomas something to investigate and he would put his mind on it like a pit-bull, that doesn't let his teeth go of his pray. He is a criminologist in a criminal laboratory and he has often helped me in complicated cases. I dialed his number and waited for him to answer.

„ Thomas Brain. Who is speaking and what can I do for you?"

„ Here is John Man and I want you and your team to come to Fort Creek!"

„ Hello John, old friend. What are you doing down there in Fort Creek?"

„ I have a job here for you and your team and I need you tomorrow noon at the latest. If you can arrange this of course. What do you think?"

„ You can forget about it. I am in Utah at the moment to solve a case!"

„ But I need you here and this is an order my friend."

He tried to get out of it with several arguments but I didn't let go and begged for his help in the end.

,, Alright. Tell me what it's all about. I am warning you, if it is not that important, I will hang up the phone and you can kiss my ass."

,, You are a real friend Thomas. Listen, what I will tell you now will shock you. And just so we understand each other, don't tell a soul about it. It is a case of great importance and I only want your help."

I informed Thomas about the mysterious cases and told him every last detail, without leaving out a word. He could hardly believe a word I was telling him, but I reminded him that it is a complicated case, that is why I needed his help.

,, When will the girl's body be exhumed?"

,, Tomorrow morning at eight they want to start with the exhumation. I believe she will wait for you on base around eleven. Do you think you can be here by then?"

,, I can make no promises. To come to you I need to make sure and find someone responsible I can leave here in my place. Before that I cannot move from here. I will call you tomorrow morning and inform you about my arrival."

,, Thank you. We'll talk tomorrow then."

CHAPTER 7

When he came home, he took his clothes off and took a cold shower. He needed strong nerves, because tonight was the big night. At last the night came and he couldn't believe it. He was thinking about his next victim and about the murder that was about to happen, when he noticed that his penis was rising and he was standing there with a boner. He could not put up with such excitement and started touching himself. The cold water that ran down his back and the thought that he would soon put his hands on her neck and slowly choke her until she has no air left to breath, was giving him pleasure. The ecstasy. Quickly he finished his masturbation and he spurt everything out, that he had inside him. Panting he washed himself one more time and got out of the shower. He wore his bathrobe and went in the kitchen to eat something. He preferred a light supper; he didn't want to eat anything to upset his stomach. He needed to be in his best shape tonight. Maybe he would fry two eggs and some bacon with a large green salad. When he finished eating he went to the bedroom.

He took the bathrobe off and stood completely naked in front of the large mirror. He turned a couple of times and was so proud of his figure. He had the shape of a eighteen year old and could not find a bit of Ft on his body. Once proudly turned one more time and went to bed. He laid naked on the satin sheets. The satin sheets were always a turn on for him, especially if he was laying there naked. Before he fell asleep he put his alarm on 23:00. He was only sleeping for an hour, when he had terrible nightmares again. He has been haunted by nightmares for as long as he can think. For years he has not slept though a night. The only nights he can sleep through are the nights he could lay hand on these sluts. Every time the same nightmare. He saw his mother in her officer's uniform. She was mad at him again. She took her belt of her uniform and commanded his to pull down his trousers so he would bend in front of her with a naked butt. He begged her not to hit him but she would not hear a word and hit him with her belt. She had no mercy for him. While he was sleeping he could feel every strike on his body. He was sure that this feeling would never leave him. He slept restless, twisting, turning and sweating in his bed. While he was sleeping like this he almost completely took the sheets off the bed. With a scream he sat up on the bed covered in sweat. He sat there for a while to recover from the nightmare and calm his breathing. But then he felt sick and ran into the toilet. When he came back out of the toilet he sat on his bed and looked at the clock. It was nine thirty. Exhausted he laid back in bed trying to sleep. He still had some time before he needed to get up.

CHAPTER 8

I was in the mess hall drinking my well deserved third whiskey after this long day. Since I had made all my calls, putting things in motion, I was feeling satisfied with everything. The only reason I was sitting here was to see the cute blond one more time. But it seemed that I had no luck tonight, because she didn't turn up and I seem to be waiting in vain. After finishing my fifth whiskey, I decided to go back to my hotel because tomorrow I had a big day ahead of me.

He was already waiting two hours in front of the hospital watching everything that was going on. He didn't miss anything. He had informed himself that her shift ended at two o'clock at night. Again he had this tingling in his fingers and was full of excitement. He had the perfect plan and waited for the hour of salvation. This with the robbery was no bad idea. He was not after her money, he was only interested to get his hand at her throat and slowly take her breath away. He wanted to see her eyes open wide in pure fear and take pleasure out of her expression. This was a glorious thought, the fear in her eyes. With this thought he got a hard on again and felt jittery. He had to stay focused and not get distracted. Lost in his thoughts, he looked at the entrance of the hospital and saw two female figures coming out. He looked closely to see if he could recognize her. When he saw it was her, he quickly put on his rubber gloves and stared at her fascinated. The two women talked to each other for a few minutes and then went separate ways. As the place was badly lit and the women were dressed alike he could not surely recognize which was which. He decided to follow the woman that was the right one, in his opinion, that walked towards the shooting range. Why did most of the street lights be out of order tonight? You couldn't see your hands in front of your face. Damn it, he cursed. He started his car and tried to follow her without turning the lights on. He followed her for couple of hundred meters, when he saw her going into a small building where the toilets were located. Immediately, he turned off his car and wanted to get out of the car, when the headlights of another car fell on him. He panicked and forced himself to stay calm. He started his car again and parked a few meters further, behind a big bush, so that he could not be seen. The other car was one of the jeeps here on the base. It parked in front of the toilet building and he saw a man getting out of it, going into the building. He couldn't see who he was so he slowly walked up to the building. He needed to be very silent so that so that no one would notice him. When he reached the building he looked inside from one of the small windows. He couldn't see much, because the light was out. All he could see was the silhouette of the couple that hugged. They kissed passionately. The soldier took off the woman's uniform, put her naked butt on the sink and took her from the front. She started to moan heavily. If somebody would walk passed, he could easily hear them and understand what was going on. Because there was hardly any light he couldn't see the expression on their faces. He regretted that. All women were alike. They were all sluts, fucking with the one and the other. They all needed to be punished, because they are not worthy to stand equal next to men. He watched for another five minutes and then went back to his car. As he heard them moan, he felt sick again and struggled not to vomit. He waited patiently for the couple to finish their love game and never left the toilet building out of his sight. After about twenty minutes, he saw the soldier exit the building and driving off in his jeep. Now he could get in the game. Slowly he opened the car door and closed it behind him without making a sound. He silently walked to the building and looked through the window he was looking before. He saw the silhouette of the naked woman in front of the sink and heard water running. She probably wanted to wash herself before getting dressed. He didn't have to waste no more time. It was the perfect time to strike. He entered the building and come on to the naked woman from behind. He was lifting his arms as if he wanted to hug her. Now was his time. The time for revenge had come.

It was the middle of the night. I had just fallen asleep with a heavy headache, because I must admit, I was not that sober. In the mess I drank more than a bottle of whiskey, I had good company. Soldier Fuller showed up, he wanted to get a drink after finishing his shift before going to bed. We chatted and I didn't even realize how much we drank. Slightly tipsy I got into my room and didn't even manage to get off my uniform. I fell straight in the bed fully dressed and fell immediately asleep. As I said, I had just fallen asleep, dreaming of a small island in the pacific on which the only inhabitants were me and my cute blond, when I heard a ringing tone in the background. It must have rung about twenty times until I finally open my eyes. In the dark I searched for the telephone and finally found it. I didn't even bother to turn on the light.

„ Who is it?"

„ General Pilot speaking. We will meet in half an hour at the toilet building next to the shooting range!"

He sounded pretty serious and I didn't like the sound of that. What did he want at this hour and in my state? I only hope he couldn't hear how drunk I was.

„ What happened?", I asked with difficulty.

„ A woman was found dead in the toilet building next to the shooting range! I will wait for you there and be quick!"

I wanted to ask him something but he had already hanged up the phone. In a second I was completely awake, although I still had a headache and heartburn from the whiskey. I stud up and rushed into the bathroom to have a cold shower, to get back to normal. Then I dressed in a fresh uniform and headed to the shooting range.

CHAPTER 9

Half an hour later I was driving to the south end of the base, I had just passed the shooting range when I could already see the jeeps of the military police in front of a small building. General Pilot was standing in front of the building talking with the military police. The whole place was lit up with extra lightning that was put up. I inspected the place and noticed that six men were positioned in different posts to control the crime scene. Nobody would walk through here undetected. I looked at the shooting range and saw the fog lifting at this time. Then I noticed the targets that looked like silent figures in a game of silence. They were standing there waiting for the game to begin. I turned to the General and saluted him.

„ Did someone search the surrounding area to see if we have maybe another victim and who started the search of evidence?"

„ No. I mean we didn't want to destroy any evidence and I forbid everyone to walk around and wait for you, to give out your orders. Don't forget, you are the investigator here!"

„ Ok then. Tell me what we have here."

„ A soldier, who was on patrol, had to use the toilet and found the dead body in the toilet."

We both walked through a grass spot where you could leave no footprints and walked up a small building that was build with bricks where the toilets were located. The whole area was blocked off. We passed the yellow tape that marked the crime scene. The right door was marked <men> and the left was marked <women>. The door to the men's toilet was open so we entered. The light was still off, so I took a tissue in my hand and turned the switch and the whole room filled with light. At first my eyes were blinded by the light, as they got used to it I could see clearly and inspected the toilet room. They were build very simple and there was only what was necessary. There was a concrete floor, nobody bothered to lay any tiles. In here were two sinks, two dividing walls, to separate the toilettes from each other. Everything looked clean. I was lost in my thoughts wandering, if yesterday a group of soldiers that were on the shooting range and came through here, a cleaning crew must have cleaned up after that. I got that, because I noticed the trash can completely empty next to the sink and there was nothing swimming around in the toilet bowls, as it was often in the men's room. I turned around and walked to the left toilet where the body was found and stopped in front of it. She was sitting in a strange position on the toilet. She was sitting there arms and legs opened and her head slightly to the side. Her eyes looked like she stared into space. I walked towards her and put on some rubber gloves. She was completely naked and sat on the toilet. The only thing she had on was a golden bracelet on the right hand. Her stuff was found under a sink in the right corner. They were just left there, and I wandered if she took them off herself and left them there or if the killer just threw them there. Around her neck was a thin cord that was used to strangle her. The cord was not longer than fifty centimeters, as I could see. The young woman must have been around twenty five to thirty years of age. She had a great figure and firm breasts. She had toned arms and legs. I kneeled beside her and noticed that her skin was beige and slightly translucent. That was common in strangulations. I took one of her hand putting them on mine and noticed that she had lost her pink color and I left it down again. She had no bruising in the face and no abrasions. So far I could see, there were no marks on her body. Looking at her positioning I would think that she was raped before getting murdered. I bend over to look at her genitals but could not find any traces of sperm. Nor on any other part of her body. On her body she had no dirt or blood and by inspecting her hair, I could see that they still looked freshly washed and smelled like it too. I stood back up and examined the neck and face of the dead girl. I could find no trace of stiffening and raised one of her arms again putting my finger in her armpit noticing that she was still warm. Her legs had already taken a dark purple color that was again a sign of strangulation. I didn't need to see the cord to find that out. I put her arm back down and pressed one of her purple legs with my finger. As I pressed my finger down the spot became white and when I took my finger back it became purple again. Now I was absolutely sure that she died about three to five hours ago. I slowly loosened the cord around her neck. The cord left a red blue line on her neck that caused her death. I left her head and went back to examining the legs. I lifted them both into the air. Her soles of her feet were completely clean and I could find any marks. So I was sure that she didn't walk barefoot on the outside of the building or that she was dragged here. From this I could conclude that she was killed here in the toilet room. As I calmly examined the body nobody said a word and so I could hear the birds twittering. I sun would rise soon and another day would begin. I left the body and turned to the General.

„ Who found the body?"

„ Soldier Kacy."

He called for soldier Kacy and ordered her:

„ Come in and give Detective Man a full report!"

„ Yes Sir General, Sir. I was on patrol and was on my way to station four, when I needed to go to the toilet. I parked the jeep next to the building and entered the toilet facilities. In the beginning I couldn't see anything so I turned the lights on and then I could see her legs. I found it curious to see bare legs so I walked to her and found her like this. Immediately I checked her neck to feel her pulls or the heartbeat. After that I wanted to see if she was breathing, but I found out that she was already dead."

„ What did you do next?", I asked her.

„ I went outside to my jeep and called for help."

„ You didn't touch anything, did you soldier?"

„ God no, Sir. I exited the same way I entered. The only thing I touched in here was the light switch. Nothing else. I didn't enter the building again after I went outside to call for help."

„ Do you have to report anything else other than what you just said?"

„ No, Sir. That was all I had to report!"

„ Thank you."

We saluted each other and soldier Kacy left the room leaving me alone with the General. We too exited the building and looked for a quiet spot where we could talk. We looked at each other and started talking quietly, so no one would hear what we were talking about.

„ I do not like all of this, Detective. How could that happen here on base? Do you have an idea what is going on or what should happen now?"

„ I have a few theories running through my head, but we must wait for the autopsy report, to make sure. Before that I cannot say anything certain!"

„ why do I have the feeling that you have already ordered forensic team without informing me. It is so, isn't it?"

„ Yes, Sir. I ordered a team yesterday and they are on their way from Fort Knox, Columbia."

„ Really good, soldier."

Fort Knox was located in Columbia, approximately four hundred kilometers North West of Fort Creek. The laboratory there was one of the best, equipped with the newest technologies. They were in charge for the cases in the whole northern America. Only the best worked there and you can be certain, that they solved all of their cases. They went wherever they were called to go. There were hardly any important cases in the military involving murder. There were quite rare so there was no problem sending any men out here. I looked at my watch and realized that I needed to hurry. So I told the General:

„When the forensic team arrive, would you please tell them to have a look at the whole area here."

„ Where do you want to go?", the General asked and I shouted back at him, already leaving:

„ Don't you remember? I have another dead body to welcome today!"

Now I sat in my office next to a big pile of file I needed to process. I waited for the coroner to file their report of the last victim and for Thomas to arrive. Although I watched Sonny Smith's body being exhumed this morning they still haven't send the remains here jet. I want to know what is taking them so long. Until I could decide what I wanted to do, I started reading the file of Maria Johnson. It was the only case in which I hadn't talked to friends and family. According to the file she was an only child from a perfectly normal family. The victim's parents were divorced. Her father worked as in engineer in Panama. It must be hard to get in touch with him. So I decided to call the victim's mother. The address and telephone number I found in the file. I dialed the number and waited for an answer on the other end of the line. After a few rings someone answered.

„ Hello. Johnson's residence."

„ Good morning. Here is detective Man. I am working on your daughter's case. If it is alright with you, I need to ask you a few questions."

For a few seconds she was silent but then I could hear a sigh. Then I could hear the voice of the crying mother.

„ She was so young! How could she do that? I still cannot believe it. How could she do that to me?"

I heard the woman cry, the mother, and I felt sorry for her. I didn't want to push her too much so I waited a few seconds and started the interrogation.

„I am really sorry for what happened to your daughter. It is really important for me if you could answer some questions, so I can close the case. Do you understand me?"

„ Yes, I understand! I cannot tell you much. I hadn't seen my daughter in two years. We really only talked on the holidays. Christmas, Easter or Thanksgiving. Do you know what I mean? I didn't know anything about her personal life really. I think you can tell me more about her than I can tell you."

„ Do you want to say that for two years you didn't really know what was going on in your daughter's life?"

„ That is correct!"

„ What can you tell me about your daughter?"

„ The only thing I can tell you is that she was always a very confident girl. When she told me she wanted to go to the military, I tried to talk her out of it nut I didn't make it. I was not sure she could handle it. But she did, as she always did when she was determined to do something. She could always put up with anything and anyone. This is why it was so hard for me to understand that she had committed suicide."

„ Did you know if she had an affair with anyone at the time?"

„ I cannot tell you that, I hadn't talked to her in month!"

From the discussion with the victim's mother, I understood that she knew less than me. I asked her about her ex-husband, if he had contact with her daughter and maybe she talked to him more often. But she made it clear that her daughter had completely no contact with her father since she was six years old. I really couldn't get any new information, so I broke off the conversation soon. Disappointed I sat back on the chair. How could it be, that a mother didn't know what happened in her daughter's life. But alright. On the one hand working in the military was not an easy job, because it was no nine to five job. With all the seminars, the exercises and many more things. You couldn't get a vacation easily and so was the military the whole life of a soldier. But even so, you could find ten minutes to talk to your own mother. I could not understand that.

Again, I looked at the list of friends and lovers of the victim. Well, she had a lot of lovers and most of them where here on the base. She was really busy. I searched for the name of her last lover. They broke up approximately one week before she died. I tried to find him on the base and located his in the laundry. I asked him the same questions. He told me that she must have been a little slut sleeping with almost everyone here on the base. Anyone she laid her eyes on. She did not have a bad character but she was not what you would refer to as a <good> girl. As I understood she was the kind of girl you would not get into a serious relationship, let alone marry. He could not say, why she would kill herself. I ended the phone call quickly. My God. What a waste of time. Couldn't anyone give me some information about the girl? I had already give up hope, when the name Sarah Connors popped in my eyes. A bell rang in my head. I had heard this name before, but I was not sure where. Then it hit me! Could it be the name of my cute blond? Well, Connors was a common name, but with the name Sarah it could not be a coincidence. I checked the file; Sarah Connors was the victim's best friend and colleague. Sarah Connors was chief of staff in the base's hospital and was working closely with the victim. She was the right person to get information from about the victim. I called the hospital asked for her and got her straight on the phone. I asked her if she could be in my office in ten minutes to ask her some questions and she immediately said yes, promising me she would be here the minute she found someone to replace her. I looked at the clock and noticed I was good with my time today. I called the coroner to ask of Sonny Smith's remains had arrived, he said no and told me it would take at least two more hours. So I still had enough time to find out more about Maria Johnson. Later I wanted to drive to the apartment of our last victim to examine it. Someone knocked at the door and I answered with a <enter>. The door opened and in that moment, exactly in that moment, when I saw her, I thought she looked like the beautiful morning sun in September. She had her hair again tight in the back and she was wearing a white uniform, a white short skirt and a white jacket. My eyes stared at her from top to bottom and I noticed she was wearing white heels that complimented her long toned legs. She took my breath away. She had a timid smile on her lips. Fortunately she turned her back to close the door behind her so I had time to get my breath back and collect my thoughts. She must have remembered me because as she walked towards me her smile got larger, so I smiled back at her.

„ Please, have a seat!", I told her and stood up offering her the chair in front of my desk. She sat down gracefully and crossed her legs. I was ready to start the interrogation, when the phone rang. I excused me for the interruption, sat back down on my chair and answered the call. From the corner of my eye I could see her how she was examining me as I was talking on the phone. Cold sweat was running down my back, I liked this hot-blooded woman.

She closely examined him from top to bottom. She had seen him many times in the mess hall and he was always sitting on his own. Then she could not look at him directly because she didn't want to get noticed that she found him attractive. She immediately saw that he looked good for his age, but up close, he looked even better. He must be quite tall because his long legs peeped out and he had trouble sitting comfortably at this desk. He must be around 1,90 m tall. He had black, short hair and ocean blue eyes you could get lost in. Automatically her eyes fell on his hands and delighted she noticed that he had no ring on. She got goose bumps. He turned while he was talking on the phone and so she could see the right side of his face. She shook up a little bit because she saw a scar from his ear down to his chin. She asked herself how he got such a big scar. But somehow it added to his attractiveness and masculinity. She was so lost in her thought that she didn't even realize that had ended the phone call and was talking to her.

„ I am sorry. What were you saying? I was just thinking of something."

„ I noticed that. I told you that I wanted to ask you a few questions about your colleague Mari Johnson, if that is alright with you!"

„ Of course. What would you like to know?"

„ You must know, I talked to some of her friends and couldn't find out a lot about her. Her mother knew less about her than her friends. Since I saw in the file that you were friends and colleagues, I thought I could ask you. I can imagine that you can tell me more about the dead than anyone else. Am I right?"

„ That can be. What do you want me to tell you?"

„ First I want you to describe me what kind of person she was."

„ So. Well. Maria was a lively girl. She never took anything really seriously and if she had problems with anything or anyone, she sat down and tried to solve this problem."

„ Do you want to say that she had problems with anyone? Personal or work problems?"

„ No, this is not what I meant; I said IF she had any problems. As far as I knew she didn't have any. No work and no personal problems. She was a great nurse. She took care of everything and everyone. I could count on her. She had a lot of affairs, with a lot of men, some in during the same time, but that was not such a big deal. I had talked about it a lot with her and offered to go with her to a psychiatrist but she declined."

„ Why should she see a psychiatrist?"

„ To tell you the truth, it was my idea. I didn't like the fact that she had affairs with different men at the same time. This could cause trouble. In her private and in her professional life. Maybe she had a psychological problem. But don't ask me, I am no psychologist. You should ask an expert. I am just stating my opinion, that's all."

„ Are you sure that she didn't go without you to the psychiatrist, to start a therapy?"

„ Yes, I am absolutely certain. Why would she keep it from me? I was the one telling her to go together for support. She knew she didn't have to be ashamed by me, because we were friends."

I turned the pages of the files and said:

„ It says here that you were the one that found the body. Tell me about it."

She cleared her throat and I could see she was trying to concentrate. Her expression became serious, I could understand, it is not easy finding your best friend dead. Although, I had seen a lot of dead bodies, in my twenty five years on the job, I must say, every time my stomach turns. You cannot get used to seeing dead people.

„ So, it was like this. We were both on duty that day. I was called in the hospital earlier, around three at night, because a soldier came in with severe abdominal pain. As it turned out he needed to get operated right away on his appendix. When I arrived at the hospital I realized that we still had an hour before we would normally start our shift. I prepared the patient for the operation and you must know that I am not doing any operation if I do not have a second nurse by my side. When I finished preparing the patient, I realized that she was almost an hour late. She had never done that before. She was never that late. As the patient needed to be operated I quickly found another nurse and went on with the operation. From the minute I finished the operation I started calling every half an hour at her house, but she wouldn't answer. After I finished my shift, around two in the afternoon, I drove to her place, wanting some answers. You must know that I had covered for her at work so she wouldn't be in any trouble. I pushed the bell button at least thirty times but no one opened the door. I saw her car in the garage so I was sure she was at home. I started having a bad feeling and I remembered that she had told me before she keeps a second key in one of the flower pots. She used that key sometimes when she had forgotten hers. I took the key and opened the door. As I knew my way around her place, I went straight upstairs to the bedroom but I couldn't find her. I started calling her name. I just wanted to leave the bedroom as my eye fell on the bathroom door. She was closed. That felt odd, she never does that, she like the breeze coming from the open windows of the bedroom and the bathroom. So I went to the bathroom door and knocked at first, when I got no answer I opened it. At first I didn't see her; the bathtub is just behind the door. I went in the bathroom and there she was, in the tub with her wrists cut. You can imagine what went on then. I touched her to see if she had a pulls, hoping it was not too late, but I felt no vital signs. She was dead."

As she was talking to me she started to shiver and I could notice that all of this still affected her. I gave a few minutes to collect her thoughts and offered her a cigarette which she declined. She asked for a glass of water and I turned to the refrigerator, took out a cold bottle and poured some water in to a plastic cup. She drank up the water quickly and seemed to feel better.

„ What did you think finding your friend like this?"

„ Why she would do it?"

„ Can you not imagine why she would do something like this?"

„ No. I could think of no reason."

„ well. You said that she didn't have any trouble with anything and anyone. Her private and professional lives were perfect. Could you imagine that a bitter lover could have had anything to do with her suicide?"

„ What do you mean?"

„ That maybe she had a disappointment? A love affair gone wrong or something like that?"

„ God no. She may had a bewildering love life, but she would never kill herself over a man. You can be sure about this."

We sat there a few minutes in silence following our thoughts. I needed to think about everything and clear my head. Suddenly the phone rang and I excused myself again to her.

„ Yes, here is Detective Man. Who is this? Oh, yes Doctor Martin. How are you? You have the preliminary results of the examination of the dead body? Yes, please tell me!"

While I was talking on the phone, I looked at the doctor the noticed that she was all ears listening to what was being said.

„ So you could ID the body. So, yes. Her name is Pamela Simpson. Did you run the toxicology tests? What you don't say. She was drugged with ether and then killed…"

I didn't have the time to say anything more with the doctor, when the other doctor fainted in front me and dropped of her chair. I just shouted in the phone that I will get in touch with him later and dropped the phone of my hands. I went around my desk and kneeled next to her. I picked her up and put her upper body on my knees. She was lying half on the floor and half on my knees. I tapped gently on her cheeks, to get her conscious.

As I was holding her and my head was close to hers, I smelled a scent of lavender. The smell went through my body and I got goose bumps. She slowly opened her eyes and I could see she had beautiful green eyes. With small gray dots on the green. When she completely opened her eyes, we sat there looking in each other's eyes for a few second and the time seemed to stand still. At that moment I knew I had found the woman of my life. I looked to her lips that at just a hint of lipstick and looked so luscious I felt the urge to kiss them right then. I noticed that she felt a little embarrassed lying like this in my arms, but I couldn't let her go.

„ You can let go off me now, if it is ok with you."

„ Are you feeling better? Do you want me to call a doctor?"

She started laughing and, I must admit, she had a contagious laughter that I felt damn erotic.

„ You must have forgotten that I am a doctor, right?"

„ You are right. It completely slipped my mind."

„ I am sorry. I am really embarrassed but as you were talking on the phone it just hit me. What happened to Pamela?" she asked with tears in her eyes.

„ You know her?"

„ Of course. She is, sorry; she was a nurse at the hospital. We ended our shift together yesterday night around two and then we went separate ways. I went home and Pamela said she had an appointment."

„ Do you know with whom or when?"

I got really curious and I was lucky to have a source of information right in front of me and wanted to get some answers.

„ No, I am sorry. I don't have a clue."

„ And you said you finished your shift together!"

„ Yes, correct. What on earth happened?"

„ Basically I am not allowed to tell you anything about the case, but since she was your co worker sooner or later I would have to question you anyway. What a coincidence, right?" I asked her looking at her.

So I told her about the dead body of Pamela Simpson, that was found in the night before in the toilet building near the shooting range. She took it well and I could see that there was something she wanted to tell me and either she didn't have the courage or she was not sure if she had to tell me.

„ The poor girl. How could this happen here on the base. I don't get it."

„ Well, the ways of the Lord are inscrutable. You wouldn't know where she lived, right?"

„ I certainly know where she lived. She had an apartment in the Kennedy-housing estate with the number thirteen. Why? Do you want to look at it?"

„ Yes, this was my plan. And you are coming with me. You could be a great help for me."

I had taken the key of the victim's apartment, which were in her purse that was found next to her uniform. I just wanted to drive off the base, when I saw my friend Thomas arriving. We saluted each other and then hugged, we were not only good colleagues we were also very good friends. I informed him about what happened here last night and we agreed that he would start without me and we would meet as soon as I came back to the base. I had to take a look at the victim's apartment before the word spread out about her death. Maybe there was someone that needed to disappear something from there and didn't want to risk us finding it. I had been to this area before so this time I didn't need a map to find it. In fifteen minutes we reached the housing estate. Naturally I stepped on the gas pedal on our way here. As I was driving like mad, I noticed, that Officer Connors was not afraid of a little speed, sitting relaxed in her seat.

CHAPTER 10

As me and Officer Connors slowly walked up the driveway of house number thirteen, I asked her:

„ Are you armed?"

She shook her head and said:

„ As a doctor I am not carrying a gun. You know, we save lives, we don't take them!"

„ Good, wait a moment. I am quickly going back to my car, I have a back up gun in there!"

So I went back and took out a nine millimeter glock pistol. I walked back up and handed Officer Connors the gun.

„ You can shoot, correct?"

She nodded and held the gun firmly in her right hand.

„ Good. Wait here for me and don't move. I will enter from the back of the building. If someone is in there that is not supposed to be and comes out the front door you will stop him. Do you understand?"

She nodded silently and I moved to the back of the house through a small alley. Carefully, I inspected the garden and noticed that big glass balcony doors led to the garden. You could hear no sound coming from the house and everything looked quiet, but when it comes to murder you had to be extra careful. I didn't think that the victim was living with anyone but I tried to be careful. With one ear on the glass door I tried to hear anything from the inside but there was nothing. From here I could see part of the living room. Carefully I tried to open the sliding doors and I was lucky. The doors opened easily. I entered the room and inspected it, trying not to make a sound. The hallway was on the right side leading to the kitchen and I slowly walked on, constantly looking over my shoulder. On the other side of the kitchen was a closed door, probably to the basement. Quietly I walked up to the front door and opened it for Officer Connors to enter. She came in and I closed the door behind her. We stood in the entrance for a few seconds and then I made her a signal to have her gun ready and yelled:

„ Police! Stay as you are and don't move!"

To our luck or not, we became no answer. I went to the big closet and opened all the doors almost at the same time. But there was no man in the closet but only coats, jackets and shoes. I searched every room on the ground floor but couldn't find anyone so we moved up to the first floor. Normally, I wouldn't go up s staircase I am not familiar with without a second person there, a person who would not hesitate to shoot if necessary to cover me. Staircases are always a dangerous trap, especially when the wood would make different sounds when you stepped on it. But I was ninety per cent sure that nobody was in the house. Officer Connors waited at the bottom of the stairs for me to call her up. I came up to the top floor where there were three doors; one of them closed the others open. I called again but again I got no answer. Quickly I opened the other door getting down on my knees shouting <police>. Nothing. I looked at the room, it was a bedroom. I shouted once more turning to the other side. I had to follow protocol, even though it might look stupid to yell into an empty room not getting an answer. The other room was a sparsely furnished room and looked more like a guest room. The third room was a bath room. I called Sarah to come upstairs. Somehow it is sad going through a dead person's house, knowing this person would never see her house again. When the investigator searched through the personal stuff and the dead cannot say anything about it. You opened closets and drawers, search trough personal items and read personal correspondence and messages. You go through the refrigerator, bookshelves, make up and food who don't belong to anyone anymore. An invasion of privacy and noting can stop the strangers going through your things. You can learn a lot about the victim. For example, if they were clean or dirty. When you opened the drawers and the clean clothes were sorted you could see that the victim wanted everything to be in order. A dead person cannot show you around the house showing you his favorite pictures and photos. It is sad. I went into the bathroom, opened the mirror cabinet over the sink and inspected it. There was nothing in it that would not be in any other household. The only things in there were a package of birth control pills, ibuprofen, a tooth brush, mint toothpaste, a pair of earrings and two golden rings. Other than a package of sanitary wipes nothing else in there, so I closed he cabinet. We left the first floor and went down into the kitchen. While I was examining everything, Sarah stood next to me not saying a word. I had almost forgotten about her, because I was so focused trying to absorb everything in this house, when she suddenly spoke:

„ Do you want to see anything else?"

„ Yes, I want to take a look in the basement then I thing we are done here! But before we do that I want to take a look in the kitchen and the rest of the rooms on this floor, if that is alright with you."

The kitchen brought us les information than the bathroom. I opened Pamela Simpsons refrigerator and I could see that she was watching her diet. In there were only fat free products, yoghurt, bread and cheese. As I was searching through edibles, my stomach began to complain. The kitchen cabinets were filled up with drinks and on the bottles I could see the labels. They were bought from a store on the base. Here on base you can get the bottles for less than in a regular store.

„ I am pretty sure that every week great parties were held here. Why should she have so many bottles of liqueur in her cabinets? What do you think?"

„ You are right. Every Saturday night she threw a party, she always had a lot of people around her. I have been on that parties many times and, I must say, she really had a talent for organizing a great party."

„ Come. Let us have a look in the rest of the rooms down here", I answered and walked ahead.

We had a look in every one of them. The toilet on this floor was as clean as the upstairs toilet. The only thing in here were two towels to dry your hands, a half finished toilet paper roll and a bottle of cleaning fluid next to a bottle of air freshener. The smell of the air freshener was <ocean blue> as was the smell of the soap on the sink. Last, I inspected the living room. The furnishing was modern and everything was perfectly clean. On the wall were hanging a few pictures of cats with their babies and some other animals. I went to the cabinets and noticed that they were packed with Italian porcelain. My eyes fell on a few books that were placed in a row but not alphabetically. She had a good taste in books, <the three musketeers> by Alexander Dumas, followed by a few books of criminology and then a few books of Steven King. Next to the books was a big pile of CDs and I picked some up to see what she was listening to. I was amazed; it was a big collection of all kinds of music, from Rock and Jazz up to classical music. I put the CDs down and looked at some of the family photos. On two photos she was smiling next to some colleagues, on another next to a much older woman, probably her grandmother. I shook my head, what reason would someone have to murder a woman like that. I couldn't understand. Officer Connors looked at me and must have understood why I was shaking my head and said:

„ She was a sweet girl. There was no day she wouldn't smile and she was always friendly and helpful. She was a good companion and friend for everyone."

She stopped talking and looked me straight in the eyes and before I could answer, she said:

„ I want to help you in this case! You cannot imagine how I feel. Pamela was a friend. I need to catch this guy, I mean of course, you need to catch this guy."

„ Mrs. Connors…" I wanted to answer her but she interrupted me before I could finish my sentence.

„ Miss! But better just Sarah, if this is fine with you!"

„ Sarah. It would be perfectly fine with me if you helped me on the case and we would work closely together. But I must tell you. I am not sure with whom or with what I am dealing here. What I want to say is that I am certain, this case could get dangerous. I don't want you to get hurt. Do you understand me?"

While I was talking I noticed her hanging on my lips, listening to every word carefully. After thinking about it for a few seconds she answered:

„ I don't mind if it will get dangerous, or not. Two of my friends are now dead and I wish, no I want, the guy responsible to get caught. And do you want to hear something else? I will do it with or without your help!"

Now was my turn to hang on her lips. This woman had fire and a will that blew my mind. I was swept of my feet. I was sure; this was the beginning of a great friendship. Sarah came towards me and put her hand on my shoulder. That surprised me. And then she said:

„ Are we ready to solve this case together? Or does it bother you, that I want to help you?"

„ No. It does not bother me and I am sure, we will solve this case together!"

We walked out of the living room into the kitchen and stopped in front of the closed door to the basement. I unlocked it and took a step back

„ Count to fifteen and the yell down the stairs and give me cover. Understood?"

She nodded and began to count, while I went down the stairs. From above I could hear Sarah shout.

„ Police. Hold your hands high and come up the stairs."

We waited a few seconds but no one appeared, from what we could see in the dark. I told Sarah to turn on the light and the whole basement was flooded with bright light. It took a few seconds to get used to it and Sarah was looking in every direction to see if something would happen now. She never left the gun out of her hand and was very tense. Meanwhile, I was sure that no one was here. The basement was a normal room and there were things you would find in a normal basement, a washing machine, a drier, a boiler for hot water and for the heating in the winter. Next to the boiler was a working bench with some tools. Even in here she had hanged some pictures of animals, as she had in the living room. We inspected the rest of the basement but couldn't find anything interesting.

„ I think it is time to go Sarah."

„ If you don't want to inspect anything more, then let's go!"

We turned around and walked up the stairs at the same time.

CHAPTER 11

It was around twelve o'clock at noon. Today he woke up later than usual, because last night was the first night in months he could sleep through without having nightmares. He felt great and he actually wanted to call in sick, he didn't want to leave the bed to go on duty. Not to have any nightmares for the whole night was one of his wishes. He came home around four in the morning and he went straight to the basement, took off his uniform and threw it in the washing machine. Then he went upstairs to the bathroom to have a shower. He was thinking all the time about the slut he strangled. This thought felt great. The water was running down his back and he was standing there with a hard penis, releasing his pressure and excitement with his right hand. He felt sky high and could feel his soul at ease. While he rubbed one out, he could see clear images of the murder flashing by like a movie. He licked his lips and moaned with pleasure. When he was done, he finished his shower and went into the kitchen o get something to eat. He finished his meal quickly and went back upstairs to the bedroom to get to bed. Now it was time to rest and he immediately fell asleep and woke up around eleven he next morning. At first he got a shock that he had slept that long, but then he took his time to get dressed and thought the base could go to hell. He parked his car outside the mess hall and went inside. No one turned as he walked in. As it seemed they were all absorbed in their conversations and didn't care who walked in. Every time he walked in the mess no one really cared, so today was no different. He knew that no one really liked him but they could at least say a good morning. They would all pay for this that they never cared about him. This was for sure. He went to the bar and ordered a coffee to go, to take it to his office. While he was waiting for his coffee, three soldiers came in and stood next to him. They were whispering to each other so he couldn't understand what they were talking about. The waitress brought his coffee and he was about to pay when he overheard some of the soldiers conversation after all.

„ I swear, I tell the truth. She was found strangled and naked in the toilets next to the shooting range."

„ Poor girl. How could something like this happen on base?", the other asked and looked at his colleagues.

They stood speechless for a while not saying a word.

„ Do we know, who she was?"

„ Yes, a few minutes ago I heard her name and I know who they meant. Her name was Pamela Simpson and she was a nurse in the hospital."

He could hear now every single word they said and couldn't wait to hear more, so he ordered a sandwich not to get suspicious what he was still doing here. When he heard the dead girl's name, he lost the ground under his feet. Maybe he didn't hear right? How can that be? Did he really strangle the wrong woman? He tried to calm himself and took a few deep breaths relaxing immediately. Sweat was running down his face into his shirt. Quickly he took out his handkerchief out of his pocket and dried his forehead. His right hand was shaking and he almost spilled the coffee on his uniform. Alright. Relax. It was really dark in the toilet room yesterday and he couldn't see her face clearly. He could only see her silhouette nothing more. But to make such a mistake, was unforgivable. Damn it. Everything went wrong. He grabbed his sandwich and coffee and left the mess furious. He walked though these three soldiers, bumping into them. They snapped at him, telling him to watch it but he just kept walking. He wanted to go to his office as quickly as possible to think about last night.

CHAPTER 12

We just arrived on the base, when my cell phone rang. It was Thomas, who wanted to see me in his laboratory. At the entrance of the base I counted ten big busses that belonged to Thomas and his criminological laboratory team. We drove through a road that was covered with green tarp and arrived at a big tent that was set up at the end of the road. We got of the car and went inside the tent. I could find Thomas immediately and went straight to him.„I must tell you something, my dear friend. Even though it is sad, that this soul died, it doesn't stop the military from doing his normal duties and exercises. I am telling you this because I am examining the area, the shooting range I completely packed doing practice. I am pointing that out, because although the case is unpleasant, it is not that unpleasant like going to war. I am still alive and just a hundred meters away from a girl was found dead. Do you understand maybe, what I want to say? Judging from the look on your face, you didn't understand a word I just said. I want to make it clear. More than forty men walked around the crime scene and helped me a lot. The whole theory of laboratory investigation is that you can rely on the evidence of the murderer and the victim. I had to make shoe prints of at least forty men to rule out the murderer. This makes me so mad that I have the feeling I am having a stroke in the next few hours. Then you can examine my body! This is just a waste of time. I cannot work like this!" I tried to calm him down, saying that, I am sorry that he is the best man for the job and can do anything he sets his mind to. That he was a great help on my case and that I counted on him. That he was completely right to leash out on me because I should have had the idea to shut down the shooting range. After he accepted my apology, I asked him to give me his report.„ So, as I said, the theory of criminological investigation is that there are two points on with we count on, the transition to the crime and the exchange. It is believed, that the perpetrator takes something off the victim and leaves something in exchange that he lays near the victim. Of course, there are cases where the murderer is so clever he doesn't leave any clue behind, even if it is pubic hair or a drop of spit. From what I have seen and examined so far, we are dealing with a pretty smart fella. I am completely certain that he plans his murders before executing them!" If this was true I had to rely on good old police work and spent hours interrogating. That meant, I had to run around intensively looking for the murderer. And if I would find him, I needed to find evidence to connect him with the cases. Thomas stopped talking because a tall, bold man came and gave him a stack of papers and talked with him for a while. My friend was the leader of the investigation and every piece of information his team collected was send to him to have the last look. He was a smart guy, he could immediately see what significance the smallest clue had in a crime scene. He liked playing detective and this is why we worked so well together. We were a great team because we completed each other. Thomas' face was red. This happened every time he saw a dead body and examined it, and was a indication that his brain was working on full speed. He just noticed Officer Connor and I introduced them. They shook hands. I informed him that Sarah wanted to help me solve the case and that it was no ad idea, because every help was welcome.,, Did you find any foot print on the scene?"

,, Yes, of course. As I told you before I took prints from at least forty boots and trainers. But there were not found directly next to the toilets. We hardly found anything near the toilets. It was all too clean, as if the cleaning fairy had just cleaned up. We found a few hairs in the sink and about ten cigarette buds in and around the trash can.",, Did you find any semen on or around the victim?",, I examined the victim for semen and I found traces of it. If you believe me or not, the whole sink was full of it, as were the victim's hands. In my opinion, it is a little strange. I don't know what to make of it. We took samples of the victim's genitals and her mouth. In about an hour we will have the result then we can see from there. We collected fingerprint from the inside and from the outside walls of the toilet. You must know, there are over sixty sets of fingerprints. This makes it a little bit more difficult, but I am sure in a couple of days we will have the results. The chemist took samples of the victim's hair and it looks as if the hairs in the sink are hers. Before you asked me any more questions, I must say, you need to wait until the late afternoon until I have any results in my hands.",, Come on Thomas. Don't play hard to get. You must have found something so far!",, Later John. We will speak again today afternoon." With these words he just left me there and walked away. Every time he did the same. In the beginning he plays upset, then he plays hard to get and when he has something in his hands he says how hard it is to find anything in his lab. We left the tent, walked back to my car and stood there in silence. I looked over the shooting range and not even five kilometers away was watchtower number six. I followed the road with my eyes and saw that there was a blind corner leading right here. Suddenly I remembered Sarah's words that the victim had a rendezvous after her shift. Thomas came over to us and said:,, The cord which the girl was strangled with, I mean the ends of it, where reaching to her hands. Under normal circumstances she could manage to take the cord out of his hands. So I am sure that she was drugged then strangled. She was a trained soldier, judging from her physique. If she was drugged the killer must not even be that strong and had an easy task. I looked at the cord and noticed there was a special knot that you are taught here every day. You wanted to know something about here foot soles, right?",, Yes!",, A hundred percent, she took her shoes off in the toilet room. We found traces of cleaning fluid on them.",, Alright, my boy. So we have sorted out something at least. I was not quite sure about this.",, How did you manage to get this case, John?",, I kissed the wrong ass.",, I wouldn't want to be I your shoes. Especially since I heard that it is not the first murder on the base, isn't it right my friend?",, Even I don't want to be in my shoes, if I cannot catch the guy." He smiled at me and put his right hand on my shoulder.,, If we mess this up, think of a nice place where we could go and enjoy our pension. Did you maybe see the General while you were here?",, I saw him hours ago but the lost sight of him.",, Did he say anything or did he want to know something more?",, He asked for the same things you asked from me. I think the psychiatrist is looking for you. They told me that you left a message on his answering machine.",, I did, yes. Alright. I will go to my office now. We will talk again this afternoon. If you find out anything sooner, you know where to find me."

CHAPTER 13

On the way to my office, I left Sarah at the hospital. She wanted to take a few days of to help me with the investigation. When I arrived in my office, I sat heavy in my chair; I needed a little rest to get it together again. I remembered that the psychiatrist was looking for me, so a called his office. Luckily, I found him behind his desk and he was in a friendly mood. He asked me about the reason for his call and I told him I had a few more questions to close the cases. We decided to meet at six o'clock in the afternoon. I looked at my watch, it was already five and I stretched my feet. I was up for thirteen hours now and I felt beat. Luckily the psychiatrist's office was in the same building as mine so I didn't have to drive around the base looking for his office. I had ordered his file to inform me about him, I wanted to know what kind of a part he plaid in this theater. I wanted to have an opinion before meeting him in person. I had about an hour to read it so I started right away. His name was Thomas Silk. Silk, that sounded like an American cigarette brand. As I thought of that I grabbed my cigarettes lighting one on. I hadn't smoked I hours and longed for it now. The psychiatrist was almost twenty years in the military service. He is forty two years old. He must have started really early in the military and could retire if he wanted in five years. He would even get a bonus as a fair well present. On the top right side there was a picture and I had a closer look at him. He seemed unpleasant. There was something in his face I didn't like and again I got this strange feeling in my stomach. He lived in a house outside the base and was not married. His job was to advise soldiers with psychological issues and write certifications and evaluations about them. The certifications were for the soldiers that wanted to go on different trainings to continue their education. Like, for example, the parachute school. He had not offences and he was good at his job. His offence record was the cleanest I had ever seen and I didn't like it. He must have done something wrong sometime. No one has such a clean record.

CHAPTER 14

The school of psychology on base was a total of twenty five buildings that were build close together. The color of these buildings was gray green so they looked a little ugly. Everything was made out of cement and there was no peace of it where you could see grass or flowers. You could count the trees, located in front of the building, on one hand. What a nightmare. Except one or two buildings was everything already dark. It looked as no one remained in these buildings at this time, they must be the office building. The building with the lights on was the accommodation building. it was not a regular school. It was just named like this. As I found out you were trained here how to use the enemy to your advantage in case of war. This was not achieved of course through fair game rules. You were trained here how the enemy would react to something you could hold against him. I was sure that some of the experiments tried here, no one knew about. It was hidden away quite effectively. I went in one building and looked for the reception, which I found a few minutes later. The secretary saw me coming, stood up and saluted me.,, Soldier, I need you to show me the way to Colonel Silk's office.",, I am sorry, Sir, I cannot do that!",, Of course you can. Let's go!" The secretary didn't move one bit. ,, I am sorry, Sir. Without an authorization I am not allowed to let you enter. You are here in a territory with strict security regulations." Great. The same again. I hated this game. So, I looked at the soldier and told him:,, To make one thing clear. I spoke today with Colonel Silk, on the phone and he is expecting me at six in his office. Could you be so kind and inform him that I am here and I am ready to meet him!" He hesitated at first but he seemed to think about it and changed his mind.

,, Alright, Sir!"

He picked up the phone and whispered something in it without me understanding a word. While he was talking, I looked around, and realized that it really was a depressing building and you could easily get a crisis in here. A few minutes later I was in Colonel Silk's office. I was standing in front of a middle aged man, who wore a gray green training suit. He seemed completely unappealing and he gave me a feeling that I want to punch him straight in his ugly face. But I didn't want to form my opinion based on the picture I saw. But now I am sure, I don't like him.

„ Mister Man?" he asked, although I knew that he was certain who I was and what I was doing in his office. I had told him the whole truth about who I was, what my job was and why I was here. The only thing he knew only from rumors is that I was going to ask him a few questions to close the case files. A voice deep inside of me, warned me about this guy.

„ Yes, Sir!", I answered and we shook hands.

„ I thank you, that you took the time to see me!"

Colonel Silk was forty two years old, but he seemed much older. He had short black hair. A little bit longer than allowed in the military. I realized that he was inspecting me and I was pretty sure he thought about what psychological problems I could have. A shiver went down my back and I tried not to make it noticeable but he must have noticed it, because his lips formed a smile.

„ Colonel Sir. I wanted to see you, to ask you some more questions. It is about two girls that, if I may say so, were murdered!"

A bad start into a conversation, but I didn't come here to make friends with him.

„ Why do you think they were murdered? How could you conclude that?"

„ I only told you what I think about the deaths."

„ I must be honest with you, I have never heard about a murder, here on the base!"

I had no intention of telling him anything more than that and I somehow had he impression that he wanted to play with me. So I wanted to let him think I didn't get that. He could keep his stupid psychology test for his patients and should let me do my job.

„ What happened and what girls are you talking about?"

I took my notebook out of my pocket and opened it.

„ We are talking about your secretary Sonny Smith and a certain Jane Olson, who was you patient, wasn't she?"

More, I didn't want him to know today. I wanted him only to know so much that he knew what this talk was about.

„ You are right, I knew both of them. Sonny worked here for about a year as a secretary. This Jane Olson I saw two or three times in my life. As you may know, she needed an evaluation from me, to continue with her training for the parachute school."

„ How did you get along with them?"

„ What do you mean by that?"

„ I mean, how you got along with your secretary. Did she cause you any trouble? Was she on time for work and did she always do her job right? Talk to me about her!"

While we talked I had the feeling that the doctor was not in his right mind. He was constantly lost in his thoughts for minutes and stared at me. Maybe it was only a trick so I would think so, but I must say it irritated me. I couldn't shake off the feeling that he tried to read my mind. It doesn't happen often, but this man had something about him that made me insecure. He had an evil look and it felt as he could see through my soul.

„ Did you know the two women personally? I mean outside the base? Did you meet them in the mess hall for a drink or elsewhere? Did you maybe have sexual contact with any of them?"

„ How do you dare asking me such questions? I had only professional contact with these women, nothing else. The only thing I knew about Sonny was that she was engaged and was planning to get married. About Jane Olson I cannot say anything, because I didn't knew her."

„ I understand. How did you feel when you heard about their deaths?"

„ I am still shocked! I cannot think of why she would do such thing."

And bla bla bla. I was sure that his pain was only played and he was perfectly fine. I have often worked with psychologists and psychiatrists in my carrier, helping me in many of my cases. The psychiatrists I've met knew exactly what words to use in any case. But the one I had sitting in front of me didn't know at all what to say to get out of the conversation. He noticed that I had stopped listening to his babbling and he shut up and sat there looking at me.

„ Allow me to ask you what you are doing here in Fort Creek?"

„ That is confidential and I am prohibited from sharing any information!,,

„ Aha", I answered, while I was making notes and nodding my head.

„ Do you, by any chance, know Sonny Smith's father?"

„ Yes, I have met him. We know each other only professionally not personally, if you want to know!"

„ Where did you meet him?"

„ In the Golf War our paths crossed a few times."

I asked him some more questions, but I was sure, I couldn't find any more about him. He didn't have the intention of telling me anymore and I was about to tell him the truth about me. I was not in the mood to hear any more of his talk and I wanted to find out the truth. I was certain he lied. When I called and left a message on his answering machine, I told him that I was from the military police and had some questions to close the case. But now was the moment of truth. I took out my badge and threw it on his desk. Curious he picked it up and read it. Shocked and angry he stood up and looked at me furious.

„ What the hell…?"

For a few seconds he looked at my badge and then back to me. I could see that he did not believe what was going in here. If he could kill with his look, believe me, he would do it in second.

„ Sit down, Colonel! As I said, I am examining the deaths of these women. I didn't read you your rights, because you are not considered a suspect. But, I want you to answer every question truthfully without talking around the bush and without lying. Do you understand, Colonel?"

„ You didn't have the right to pretend to be from the military police trying to manipulate me. I will sew you and complain to your superiors…!"

I didn't let him finish his sentence and with a firm voice and a strict face I shouted at him.

„ Please. Sit down and let us finish this interrogation. I have work to do and cannot stay here the whole evening, if you don't mind!"

„ First question…!"

„ I am not answering any of your questions, if I don't have my lawyer with me!"

„ It seems to me as if you watch a lot of TV series, Mister Silk. You don't have the right to an attorney and you don't have the right to be silent.

If you refuse to work with me I will treat you like a suspect and read you your rights, then you have the right to an attorney, if you want. I will kick your butt! Do you understand?"

He stayed silent for a while and thought about his actions. I liked him even less now. Why would he ask for a lawyer, if he is innocent? Now it was time to ask the right questions about these two women, also about the new case we had.

„ I don't have anything to hide, but I didn't like that you snuck in here with a false identity. You must believe me. And just to be clear, I will still complain about your methods. Do we understand each other?"

„ To be honest, I don't give a shit! And now let's get to business! When did you last see your secretary and Jane Olson?"

„ My secretary I last saw the day she died, so about half past three in my office. Jane Olson I last saw when I issued her evaluation. This meeting also was in my office. For the date I need to check my calendar, to tell you the exact day!"

„ Can you say anything about the behavior of your secretary? Did she behave oddly that day? Was she worried or sad? How did she behave in general that day?"

„ No. She was like always. I couldn't see any nervousness or odd behavior. If she had any worries I really didn't notice anything, she must have hid them well."

„ Where is your house located?"

„ What has my house to do with Sonny Smith?"

„ That is not of your concern. Will you answer my question!"

„ I have a house outside the base, on the Victoria Boulevard."

„ Was your secretary not living there too?"

I wanted to confuse him a little bit and see how he reacted to the question.

„ Yes, I mean no. I don't know where she lived!"

„ Naturally. Are you married?"

„ No. I have never been married."

„ Why?"

„ Let us say that I never had a good connection to women and have trouble meeting the right one. Especially, when it comes to the rest of my life."

I had the impression that he didn't have a good connection to anyone!

„ Do you maybe want to tell me that you are gay?"

„ No, for God sakes. I am not gay. I just haven't found the right one to spend the rest of my life with. That's all. Do you understand me?"

„ Tell me. Did you find Sonny Smith attractive?"

„ Yes, you could say that she was a good looking woman and I believe she was not fit for the military. If she had stayed at home, she was probably never have been found dead!"

„ What do you want to say with this? Can you explain?"

„ I want to say, that the place for women is at home, in the kitchen and not on some military base. If she maybe had a different fiancé, she would have not committed suicide."

„ Do you want to tell me that there may have been problems in the relationship and this is why she killed herself?"

„ Can we rule that out? Why would she kill herself for?"

I put my notebook aside and looked at him. Then, I asked him with an innocent look.

„ Did you maybe hear what happened last night here on the base?"

„ No. What happened?"

„ This morning, we found the body of a dead female soldier!"

I tried to read his face but I couldn't see anything suspicious in his stupid face. He made a surprised face but, I was not sure if he was being real or faking it. if he faked it, he was really a great actor. His look didn't give away anything. I was certain he was hiding something, but how could I prove it!"

„ Really? You found a dead body here on the base?"

„ So, so. You haven't heard anything about the find. That is odd, because everyone here on the base is talking only about this body."

„ Yes, that is correct. I didn't hear a thing. You must know I came very early on the base today and had a lot of work to do. A lot of paperwork and I was so absorbed by my work that I didn't even have the time to go for lunch. That's why I haven't heard the news!"

„ The dead soldiers name was Pamela Simpson. Did you know her?"

„ No. I have never heard of her!"

„ Are you sure?"

„ Of course, I am sure. How can you doubt my words."

„ How could it be that you didn't know her? I found out that she was at least three years stationed here on this base."

„ Listen. As you know this is a very large base with a lot of soldiers. Every soldier has their own duties to fulfill, as I see it, it is impossible to know each and every soldier personally. Maybe I had seen her before. Can you rule that out?"

„ So, so. You are stating that you have never met the soldier. Correct?"

„ Yes, correct!"

„ Ok then. I think, that was it for today. I thank you for your help."

I finished the interrogation and told the psychiatrist that if I had any more questions I would let him know. He made it clear that he would help in any case, as good as he could. I put my notebook in my pocket and as I walked out of the office I stopped in front of the secretary's desk. I was not sure what I wanted to do here but I needed to do something, because I had this feeling in my stomach again. As soon as the secretary saw me, he stood up and saluted me.

„ Soldier Stone. I want to ask you. Is there, maybe, a toilet nearby? I was so long in the pffice and cannot hold myself. If you know what I mean?"

„ Of course, Sir. Let me show you the way to Colonel Silk's private toilet room."

He left his desk and showed me to the toilet. He opened the door and turned on the light. I thanked him and he left me alone. I locked the door behind me and had a look inside the room. It was quite a large room and in the right corner there was a toilet and a shower. I smelled the smell of trees and I saw it was a room spray left next to the toilet. The light was so strong that I could see clearly in every corner of the room. On the sink, I found what I was looking for. It was a leather toiletry bag. I opened it quickly and inside where a line of razor blades, a comb and a brush. With a quick look on y watch I saw that I was almost five minutes in here. I needed to act quickly, I flushed the toilet and hoped Soldier Stone heard that I was busy emptying my bladder. Quickly I put on a pair of gloves and opened a small plastic evidence bag. I took the brush and held it against the light; I saw some hair on the brush and took them carefully placing them in the evidence bag. I wrote the name on Colonel Silk on the bag put everything back in my pocket. I had a quick look at the blades but couldn't see any beard hair to take with me. I turned on the faucet and washed my face, to have an explanation what I did in the toilet all this time, and went outside. I saluted the secretary and thanked him for his help. Only if he knew, how helpful he had been for me.

CHAPTER 15

He sat behind his desk and tried to work, but he couldn't concentrate or have a clear thought. He was too nervous to do his job and couldn't calm himself. He replayed constantly the detective's interrogation in his head. Who did the bastard think he was? How could he ask such questions? Did he have no respect? From the beginning he lied, about who he was and about the questions he wanted to ask. He almost gave himself away when he heard the real name of the detective, but luckily he held it back. The hell with the detective! From now on he needed to be careful, not to give himself away and get caught. When and how could this investigator get on base anyway without him knowing? How did anyone get to the point that these women were murdered? It was better to play nice now and work closely with the detective. So he would find out what he knew and could protect himself. When he asked him questions about the murder, he was sure his expression gave him away, but he quickly changed that. He was really smart about these murders making the look like suicides, so nobody would find out. Maybe they only had a hint and no evidence at all, that's why they send out the detective to ask these stupid questions. So many months had passed since the last murder and they had stopped investigating about them. What the hell happened, so that they would send this detective asking questions about the murders? He had to find out, what was going on here and this guy turned up, but first, he needed to do something even more serious. He had killed the wrong woman. How could he do that? Not that he was sorry for it, but a mistake like this hasn't happened to him before. Really soon the time of this other slut will come and she would feel his hands on her throat. With these thoughts he immediately felt better. With a smile on his lips he started working and also started making a new plan that could not go wrong.

CHAPTER 16

The sun had gone down giving its place to the round moon that shined down on earth in full glow. The sky was clear, not one cloud was visible, and you could count thousands of stars. The moon and stars were so strong you didn't need to turn any light on to find your way. I had planned to go to the shooting range and hoped that the weather conditions were the same as yesterday. Maybe I would notice something that I missed before. I drove passed the mess hall, lost in my thoughts. When I arrived at the shooting range that was flooded in light, I could see busses standing there. This meant that the forensic squad was not yet finished and that they were still at it in order to give me the answers I need. The first bus was surrounded by neon light; you could hear hardly anything coming from there and I noticed that the guy in there was focused on his work. I parked my car next to the first bus and started looking for Thomas and found his after a few minutes. I took the two evidence bags out of my pockets and handed them to him. He didn't waste any time and passed them on to a technician, ordering him to give them to the guy responsible for the DNA testing. I went with Thomas to the back of the bus and he showed me pictures just taken from the crime scene. He had pinned every picture on a black board next to the map of the base and the blue print of the toilet building where the victim was found. Next to the black board was a desk on which reports were piling up, and as it seemed the pile was growing fast. A file, with pictures of the victim, was lying open and next to it a few bags with evidence or objects taken from the crime scene. Every bag was marked with black marker so that nothing got mixed up. I looked outside the bus and saw another bus that was turned into a food truck. There were about ten men outside of it drinking coffee or eating something. I must admit, in that moment I had total respect for these guys. Nothing was too expensive for them; just so that they can work overtime and finish the job they were given. They, probably, hadn't any more important cases to solve, than the one we are solving here. The military had send all the best men to solve this case as soon as possible. Sometimes, I was speechless, how soon so many men in the military can come together by just one phone call of a superior. I turned to a coffee machine that was standing next to the desk and filled up a paper cup with freshly brewed coffee, of course, I filled up one for Thomas too. Thomas took the cup; not even looking at me, because he was reading tests results. Two hours had passed that I was with Thomas and I didn't even notice how time went by. My feet hurt and so I took a chair and sat next to Thomas, slowly drinking my coffee.

„ It can be that you got lucky with these hairs you brought earlier. I don't want to sound nosy but who do they belong to?"

„ Definitely not from you!" I answered him pointing to his bald head.

A technician working at a table beside us couldn't help it and started giggling. When Thomas looked at him with a red face, he stopped and went back to work.

„ Come on, you funny guy, I want to show you something on the microscope."

The technician stood up and gave me his seat to look into the microscope. He tried to explain what I was looking at, to understand it better.

„ The hairs on the right side were found on the sink, on the victim and in the toilet. This hair here was also found on the victim. This hair is, without a doubt, identical to the hair you brought us earlier. When I examined the two hair samples, I came to the conclusion that they are from two different persons. I am absolutely certain. When I was examining them, I saw that one was dark blond and the other a lighter blond. I didn't have any sample with the root on it to make a proper DNA test, for better results. You must know, that our hair has something unique, from which we could find different features, from which we could determine who they belong to. The problem is that the hairs found on the victim are identical but in order to be a hundred per cent sure, we needed to have some with roots. I want to say that we could then determine gender and certain characteristics of the person."

„ I think Detective John already knows that!", Thomas said.

„ Yes, Sir. I want to say something else. I found out that one hair sample blood type O negative and the other blood type O positive."

„ Now, that I look at them in the microscope they seem to look the same."

„ In my opinion, they belong to two different persons. Since they are short samples I have difficulties running other tests without possibly destroying them. That's why I can not give you more information."

„ I absolutely understand. Write everything in a report. I will study it later once more."

„ Yes, Sir."

„ Thank you for that."

„ You know, John, This is not enough for an arrest, do you?"

„ You are right, Thomas, it's not. But it is enough to examine a person closely and have an eye on him!"

„ Who is it?"

I took Thomas aside, away from the technician's desk, so no one would hear.

„ The samples belong to Colonel Silk. I took them without his knowledge. His office is in the School of psychology. He was Sonny Smith's boss, she was his secretary. He also knew Jane Olson. I would love to know where he was yesterday night, without him finding out I am looking into him."

Thomas was silent for a while, thinking. Then he looked at me and said:

„ You must bring me a couple of fingerprints from him, to compare to the ones we found on the crime scene. I can imagine it would be hard, to pull some of his hair out and bring them to me with a root!"

I started laughing and said:

„ If you want to pull each other's hair out like little girls, I would be happy to do that. If it would help you to give mw the answers I am looking for."

Thomas nodded, with a serious look on his face.

„ You are the detective here. I would say that he is our guy, but it is not my job. You are the one that needs to compare all the evidence and find he guilty guy. It could also be that, when you show him everything you have collected, he would confess his actions. But where is such luck!"

„ Don't forget that we still have the other hair sample! I believe that they belong to the date the victim had that night, the date we have found no information about!"

„ Did it come to your mind that there could be a couple doing all this shit together?"

„ No, I don't think so! I rule that out completely. The case does look like there is a couple behind that at all. The facts don't add up."

„ Yes, I think you are right."

CHAPTER 17

S arah Connors had just finished her shift and was packing up her things to go home. It was a long day and she was exhausted. She was constantly thinking about the death of her friends and the investigation. She wanted to help with the investigations because she wanted to get this guy caught as soon as possible. Last afternoon she sat down with her boss and asked for some time off. Her boss asked her what was wrong and she explained that she needed some time to collect her thoughts after all these deaths. She had no intention of telling him about the investigation, John told her not to let anyone know. Her boss was not convinced easily to give her the time off, but in the end he agreed with her. The only thing he asked for was for her to come to work until he found her replacement. She had to promise to be back in seven days, so she gave in and promised to be back in a week. With the thought of Detective Man, she smiled. She liked the fact that she would be working with him for a whole week. She found him very attractive and liked him as a man. She suddenly felt lighter as she was thinking of him. She grabbed her purse, through her jacket on and said goodbye to her colleagues. A cool evening breeze came on to her as she went outside and she stood there for a while. The whole day in the hospital the only smell she had was antiseptic and other medication. Suddenly she got an ice cold chill and felt her hair on the neck rising. She had this feeling that she was being watched and she slowly looked right and left of the entrance, but she could see no one there. She wanted to go straight home to rest, so that she was fit the next day. But now she was afraid to walk home alone and was thinking what she could do. She walked to work this morning and regretted this decision now. She didn't want to admit it but she was shaking in fear. That was normal with all of that she heard and saw today. Her house was located on the opposite side of the base and she did not need more than twenty minutes to walk, but now she did not want to walk especially not alone. She looked around, maybe she would see a friend or a colleague, but she couldn't see anyone. Always when you need someone, no one is there! If she saw someone she knew, she would ask for a ride home. She decided to go to the mess hall on the corner to have a quick drink. Surely she would be lucky to find someone there too drive her home. She held tight on her bag and walked quickly towards the mess hall. The street was not well illuminated and whenever she saw a shadow she made a big bow around it and walked even quicker. She couldn't shake the feeling that she was being followed, but she didn't want to turn around to see if she really was being followed. With small, quick steps she tried to walk even faster, because she thought this would be her end. She had just speeded up a little bit, when she heard steps behind her. Fear and panic came over her again. With massive speed her adrenalin pumped through her veins. She tried to control her body to calm down and relax a little. This whole situation was a lot for her. But she tried to calm down in vain. Did she have to scream to get noticed? In this exact moment she thought about the victims. She was frightened and stood still for a second. Pure fear paralyzed her and a few seconds she couldn't breathe. There was no time to think about the victims now. The time had come to run. She needed to run for her life as fast as she could. It took all of her courage, but she started running as fast as she could, so that you would think the devil got inside of her. The steps behind her speeded up as well and followed her without mercy. Now she was sure that somebody was after her and again panicked. It was not far to mess hall, maybe eighty meters, and then she saw the building already. Her heart felt lighter and she instantly felt more secure, when she suddenly bumped into a soldier, who she didn't see coming, and she fell down. Out of fear and panic she started screaming, because she thought it was the murderer wanting to attack her. Only when the soldier tried to help her get back on her feet she understood what was going on and stopped screaming. She apologized to the soldier in shame and explained that she was lost in her thoughts and hadn't seen him coming. This is why they bumped into each other and why she screamed so loud. What else should she say? She was so embarrassed. She apologized again and he apologized to her for scaring her. But it was not his fault that she was scared to death. While they were talking she constantly looked around, but there was no one there. Or she couldn't see any one. Whoever was following her must have hid so he wouldn't be seen. If she was lucky she scared him away with her screaming and got away with her life tonight. She said goodbye to the soldier and made it clear that she was fine and with quick steps she entered mess hall. While she was entering she looked over her shoulder and with all the strength left she pulled the door open to get in. At that moment, when she entered mess hall she was sure she was safe. She took a deep breath so that no one would notice what happened. She had no intention of telling anyone.

CHAPTER 18

The telephone rang and rang. I slowly opened my eyes and looked at my watch. It was eight in the morning. Who the hell could it be, who needed to talk to me now? I picked up the phone to answer.

„ Good morning. I hope you where not sleeping, were you?"

How I hated this question! Did Jack dream of me, to call me that early. Lunatic. What the hell did he want now? It was only eight o'clock.

„ Good morning to you too. It is an honor to talk to you now, but can you tell me what the hell you want from me so early?"

A little sarcasm was appropriate at this time and I was sure that Jack wouldn't take it the wrong way.

„ Leave the sarcasm so early in the morning and tell me, what is happening there. Did you find out anything new? Give me something, I must report progress to my superior later and I need to tell him something."

„ if you had waited until ten o'clock you would get a full report of what we have found out so far and you didn't need to call me now. When you read the report you will be thrilled!"

„ You want to tell me that we caught our guy?

„ No, nut I am right behind him and it is a matter of time to arrest him!"

I informed Jack about the findings of the investigation and the forensic tests and what we had so far. I informed him also on my suspicion of Colonel Silk and that I took hair samples to the lab.

„ It seems like you are quite sure that this Colonel Silk is the killer, if I get it right. Well, if this is not great news, what is? Did you mention him that he is under suspicion?"

„ Are you kidding? You never tell a suspect that. I didn't have any intention of telling him that, I will leave him in the dark for a while. I will watch him and when the time is right he will get caught. He will make one mistake. And remember, I cannot arrest someone out of a feeling, I need evidence. You taught me that, remember."

„ Ok, my friend. I want you to promise me you will handle this professionally. Don't make a single mistake. If anything goes wrong, I dint want to be the one firing you. Be careful and when you are absolutely certain, do your move."

„ You can be sure about that. You are talking to a pro here, or is this <you are the best man for the job> talk a lie! I will give my best! You know me."

„ I only say this because I know you! Do you understand? Be careful, we are talking about a Colonel. We will speak again."

After finishing this call I had a cold shower and shaved. I took a clean uniform out of my bag, got dressed and made my way to the mess hall, to get some breakfast. As my mother used to say: '' Without breakfast the brain cannot work!". And I must say that she was right. So I ordered a portion of eggs on toast with bacon and a can of hot coffee. The coffee smelled great and I drank him in big sips. The day could only get good when you drank good coffee. I had already had two cups, when my eggs were brought and I started eating. I just had a few bites, when the waitress came back to my table.

'' Sorry to disturb you, but you are Mister Man, is that right?"

„ Yes, correct. What can I do for you?"

„ You have a call waiting at the bar. Could you follow me?"

„ Could you tell me who it is?"

„ The call is from the Generals office. It must be important!"

„ Yes, sugar. You could be right."

I walked around the table and followed the waitress to the bar. The phone was laying on the bar and I picked it up.

„ Here is Detective Man. Who is this please?"

„ Good morning, Sir. Here is Secretary Fuller from the Generals office."

„ Oh yes. Good morning. How are you?"

„ Good, how are you? I am calling to inform you, that they found the soldier that met the girl before she died. You know, the one found dead yesterday morning in the toilets."

„ Is this true? These are great news. Really good! Where is our lovebird now?"

„ They locked him up in a cell. They are waiting for you there. The General apologized for not calling you himself, but he has an important meeting he could not reschedule. He ordered me to call you because, as I understood, it is a secret investigation."

„ You are absolutely right about that, my boy. I would be really thankful, if this stayed between us."

„ No worries, I won't say anything. You can rely on me!"

„ Thank you. We will hear each other."

I hung up the phone and went back to my table, to finish my breakfast and drive to the prison. My coffee was cold by now and I ordered a fresh can. I finished my breakfast in peace.

After finishing my breakfast, I took the car and headed to the military police's building. As I got closer, I could see that reporters had started to gather around the entrance. Some reporters I knew pretty well. I parked my car in a no parking zone, so that they would not recognize me. I had promised Jack to proceed quietly so I wanted to do just that. I parked my car and didn't bother locking it, I didn't want them to recognize me in any case. As I walked to the entrance of the building, I noticed that even two busses of TV stations had parked here. As careful as I was, I didn't see the reporters sitting just at the door and as soon as they realized who I was, they started coming towards me. Damn it, they had seen me! Suddenly they started shouting out questions and I had a hard time walking through them to the entrance. The reporter in the front, who saw me first, had a small dictating machine and held it right under my nose. Others were holding a pen and a notebook. Some of them were holding cell phones and were probably talking directly to their editors, to get the story quicker.

„ Are you Detective Man?"

This was what the first reporter asked, holding his machine closer to my nose.

„ No, mister!" I answered him.

„ I am an electrician, and came to get the air conditioner working again!"

They started throwing one question at me after the other, without hesitation. They probably didn't buy the electrician story. I tried to get up the steps to the entrance, but these reporters were very persistent and didn't let me go. An armed soldier was guarding the entrance and I nodded at him to open the door so I could escape them. I saluted him quickly before entering the building and I turned around to look down the stairs. A pack of reporters, around twenty of them, looked at me and waited for an answer. Some of them, who were sure I had an answer to give, held their pens ready; others were taking photos of me entering the building. I looked closely to them and said:

„ The investigations in the case of Pamela Simpson are running. We have a lot of evidence but, at the time, now suspect. I can assure you that every unit of Ford Creek and a brought in unit, work in full speed in order to catch the person responsible. We will inform you about any further findings in the next press conference in the future. I wish you a good day."

I had just finished talking as they started throwing questions at me again. They smelled something was wrong and wanted to know more then what I served them. Some questions I heard were, <Was she raped?>, <Was she found naked and strangled?>,<Who do you think strangled her?>. From every corner I could hear the same questions. i told them, once again, that every question would be answered in the press conference. We would make an appointment as soon as possible. At last I was in the building and bumped into the General.

„ I can't shake them off. They are like flies!"

„ Yes, General Sir, you are right. You really cannot get rid of them. They are like vultures, as soon as they smell rotten meat; they cannot wait to tear it apart and eat it up!"

„ These stupid reporters, sneaking around the base asking questions to anyone that is willing to give them anything. I had to put guard everywhere, in order to keep them off, letting everyone do their jobs. I don't even know how they managed to get on base. They come from everywhere. If it was up to me, I would lock the base down and wouldn't let anyone in or out of it. But then again is the freedom of speech. They know exactly that I cannot throw them out and are using the situation."

We stood there a few minutes in silence. Then he turned to me and said:

„ Do you have anything new to report?"

„ I talked to several witnesses and with Colonel Silk. General, I need to ask you something but I am not sure if you will agree with me. Anyway, I wanted some guards in front of his building so that they could keep an eye in him, if you know what I mean. I don't want him to realize that he is being watched and destroys any important evidence or files or takes them home with him. I just want him to know that he is not unimportant for the case."

„ Do you have anything more to report, that is important?"

„ At this moment only that, General Sir."

I informed the general about my suspicion and asked him to keep all of this to himself for now. We would reveal everything when the time is right. I asked him for patience for a day or two. I also told him that I am looking into the Colonel through a friend in the pentagon; I wanted to find out more about him. His file had too little information about him and I wanted to know more. I wanted to wrap the Colonel around my finger, but I needed more information about him.

„ Alright, John. You are the detective, and I demand that you work thoroughly, to catch this freak and get him in front of the military court. I will leave you alone now, to question the soldier in peace. His name is Bing. I read his file already and saw that he is a clean one. I don't think he had anything to do with her death."

„ We will see that, General. Never say never."

„ You are right. You are the investigator; you have the most experience in crimes. Don't forget. The military is counting on you. Good luck."

We saluted and the General turned to leave the building. As soon as he opened the door, the reporters started the questions again. I secretly laughed, thinking about the General trying to walk through all these reporters. Could he walk through them without saying a word?

CHAPTER 19

T here was a small room prepared for me to talk to the soldier without being heard. A soldier was waiting in the room for me.

„ Good morning, Soldier. What is your name?"

„ Good morning, Sir. My name is Moore and I was sent to help you with the interrogation."

„ Good. Thank you."

I pulled the chair and sat down at the table. In front of me was a thick file marked <confidential>. I took it and opened it. before I started the interrogation, I needed to read the file first, to know some things about his person.

„ Do you need anything else from me?", Soldier Moore asked.

„ Yes, Soldier. Could you, please, get me some fresh coffee."

„ Yes, Sir!"

He exited the room. A few minutes later, he came back with a tray. He left it on the table and then left me alone. I poured coffee out of the jug and drank greedy from the cup. Then I opened the file and read it. The soldier under suspicion had the name Roger Bing. He was born in Oregon in 16.02.1973. He came from an average family. By the age of ten he was put in a military school. They did not put him there because they had problems with it, but because from a young age he wanted to join the military. By the age of eighteen he started studying at West Point, one of the finest military schools in the country and graduated top of his class. So far, he had three different postings on three bases. It said here, that he had built a great carrier and was going to get very far in the military. I didn't find anything negative about Soldier Bing in this file. I found one new report about him, that was not even twenty four hours old, the report of his arrest. Soldier Bing had two days off and returned back on duty this morning. When he came on base, he went straight to the hospital asking about Pamela Simpson. I wanted to keep her death a secret, so I asked the military police to arrest anyone that asked about her. So they arrested him right away. Another reason for his arrest was that he was the last person to see her alive. The conclusion was made, when he was asked why he was looking for her, he said she is his girlfriend. So he was informed about his girlfriend's death and was thrown in prison. I closed the file and asked Soldier Moore in the office.

„ Soldier Moore. Could you bring in the incarcerated suspect, so that I can interrogate him."

„ Yes, Sir."

He turned and went outside the office to go to the cells to get the suspect. A few minutes later he came back holding the suspect by his arm. I looked at the suspect with a serious look, so that he knew he couldn't play with me. He was in handcuffs and he was wearing a prison uniform. I inspected him for head to toe. He had a good figure and muscles at the right places on his body. I must admit, if I had been only 1,70m high I would be a little bit intimidated by him. I must say that, with my 1,85m, I am quite tall myself and I am well build, to defend myself against a two meter high opponent, but still I felt insecure being left alone with this guy in a room. I asked him to sit across the table from me. Soldier Moore wanted to take the cuffs off him but I wanted to keep them on. I wanted to make sure, he would not attack me during our talk.

„ No, no. He can keep the cuffs on!"

Soldier Moore took a step back and put the keys back in his pocket.

„Thank you Soldier, that's all. You can leave us alone now, I don't need anything else."

The Soldier left the room and we were alone. I tried to intimidate the prisoner as much as I could so he would think I am a bad ass, so I just ignored him. It was supposed to look like I didn't care what would happen to him. If he was our guy or not. I placed the file in front of me again and started studying it, pretending to be thinking about something. With the corner of my eye I noticed that he was starting to get nervous, because he was jiggling in his seat. Without any warning I closed the file and threw it on the table, making a loud noise, I was sure you could hear outside.

Soldier Bing shook up and almost fell off his chair. Good. Now he was intimidated enough and I could do my job.

„ Alright. Let's begin!", I said and looked him straight in the eyes.

I stared into his eyes for a few seconds, I wanted to see, if he would lower his eyes or not. But I misjudged his strong character; he didn't blink once or lowered his eyes. He looked me straight in the eyes and didn't let go of me. Out of my shirt pocket I got a packet of cigarettes and took one out.

„ You don't mind me smoking, do you?"

„ No, absolutely not. If you would be so kind to offer me one as well, if you don't mind?". He answered.

It seemed like he needed some nicotine in his system and I smiled. I lit my cigarette inhaled the smoke deeply. The Soldier licked his lips and swallowed. Yes, he really missed this blue smoke that was filling the room. I held the packet in front of his nose and offered him one. As he was an addicted man, he thankfully accepted. He lit his cigarette and inhaled the smoke, closing his eyes. I let him smoke for a few minutes and we talked about unimportant things. We talked about God and the world and I noticed him getting more and more nervous. This was the point. I wanted him to feel safe and strike at the right moment. He was telling him about his position here, when he suddenly broke and said:

„ Listen, Sir. I know, I was the last person seeing Pamela alive and I also know how this looks like. But if you think this means I killed her, you are on the wrong path. Do you really think that if I killed her I would go to the hospital looking for her? If I was her killer, I would have packed my things and disappeared. What do you think?"

All this sounded right so I answered him:

„ The last person seeing Pamela alive was also the person who killed her! You must know that. This is how it goes in every murder case!"

„ Yes. No. Of course, Sir. You are right, Sir."

„ Soldier. Would you be so kind as to give me clear answers I can understand. That would be nice."

„ Sorry, Sir. You are right."

„ So, let's start at the beginning. And this time, step by step. Soldier, you must know, I am not a monster and I am sure that you must go through hell after you found out about your girlfriend's death. It is not always easy to find out about the death of someone near you from a stranger. Even more, if it is a gruesome death like this one. I am sure; I will be a hard time for you because you were arrested for her murder as a suspect. Isn't that so?"

„ Yes, Sir!"

„ Then explain to me, how can it be that two days passed since your girlfriends death and you only came today to look for her. I cannot wrap that around my brain. ''

„ The day before yesterday was my last evening on duty, because I had taken two days off. For about two weeks, I and some friends are planning a fishing trip to a lake. The lake is not far from here and is perfect for fishing and camping. There we spend these two days. One of the friends, I was there with, came back with me today morning, because we both needed to start our shift this morning. The third guy must return to base tomorrow. So, I had just arrived on the base when I went to the hospital to tell Pamela about my catch. But no one answered my questions about where she was, the only thing that happened was that the military police came and arrested me. They didn't tell me what happened to Pamela until later and now I am sitting here. But, to be honest, I still have not understood what really happened and why I was arrested!"

„ You were arrested as a potential suspect, but, you must know, that you are not yet considered one. You may have noticed that I haven't read you your rights, which means that you don't have to have an attorney present. Let us talk a little and I need you to answer every question by telling the truth, so we can finish this thing as soon as possible. I want to quickly close this case, and I can use harder methods to do so. Do you understand me?"

The Soldier looked at me and nodded so I started the interrogation.

„ When did your last shift begin that day?"

„ At six in the afternoon and finished at two o'clock at night."

„ What did you do after that?"

„ I waited to get a quarter past two, then I took my Jeep and drove to the toilette next to the shooting range. Pamela and I had arranged to meet there."

„ When did you arrange that meeting?"

„ We had arranged it early that morning."

„ That means, that you knew when her shift was ending?"

„ Of course, I knew."

„ How long did it take her to get to the toilettes?"

„ It must have been about ten to fifteen minutes."

„ Did you stop at any other observation tower on the way there?"

„ Yes, I did. I stopped at the second and the forth."

„ Why?"

„ In these two towers were the friends on duty. The ones I took the trip with."

„ And then you drove to the toilette rooms and met with your girlfriend. You said you had arranged that meeting in the morning. So, it was not a spontaneous meeting?"

„ This is what I said. We had arranged earlier that we would meet there after our shifts."

„ Tell me. What did you do there in the toilette room exactly? I need every detail, if that's ok with you, even if it means to talk about really personal moments. You must know, it is crucial to the investigation."

„ What do you mean?"

„ Come on. You know what I mean; I need answers to all of my questions to get the things in order. So, tell me."

„ We kisses, we hugged and then we did it."

„ Where did you do it?"

„ Does it matter?"

„ I am asking you, so yes, it matters."

„ In front and on the first sink when you come into the toilettes."

„ How did you do it?"

„ I think this is not of your business!"

„ And I am telling you, it is. This will justify the evidence we found on the scene and sort out some important facts."

„ Ok then. We did it <normal>, if it is what you mean."

„ While you were having sex, did something feel strange or did you notice something else?"

„ What do you mean?"

„ For example, that someone was watching you. Or maybe did you hear a sound. Or anything unusual! Did you see a car drive by or someone walking up and down in front of he toilettes. Something."

„ Believe me. In those minutes I spend there I didn't notice anything. I had eyes and ears just for Pamela."

While I was making notes he seemed to be a bit macho. But now as he was talking about his dead girlfriend, I noticed he was getting sad and his expression changed. I took a cigarette and offered him one as well. He took it. This time he smoked slowly and I could see he was lost in his thoughts. For a few minutes we said nothing and I started thinking too. Anyway I wanted to give him some time before my next questions. I looked at my watch and saw that it was getting late, so I started the interrogation again.

„ Could you tell me how she was that night? I mean was she nervous or did something bother her?"

He tried to remember and shook his head.

„ No. Pamela was as always. Of course she was tired from her shift but she was in a good mood, always laughing. No, I cannot say I noticed anything strange about her."

„ I nodded. If he hadn't notice anything there is nothing I could do. He told me here exactly that same things he said in his first interrogation and everything matched.

„ Tell me, how much time passed since the moment you entered the toilettes until you left again?"

„ About twenty to thirty minutes, not longer. You must know, I left the toilette room first and left Pamela in there alone."

„ How is it, you didn't leave the toilettes together?"

„ Because I had arranged with my friends to meet at three o'clock at the entrance of the base to start our fishing trip. Pamela had no problem going home alone. She did that every day, except of the days we finished our shift at the same time. Then we drove off the base together."

„ There is something else I need to ask you, maybe you know. What did your girlfriend do after you had sex?"

„ I think I know what you mean. Pamela had an obsession about cleanness. When we finished she went straight to the sink and started washing herself. She did the same thing at home. As soon as we finished she went into the shower to wash herself. We talked for a few minutes and then I left."

„ Now some things are getting clearer. I think this was it. I thank you for your collaboration."

I called Soldier Moore in.

,, What will happen with me now?"

,, Don't you like it here? I think you will find here just what you need. Peace and quiet, a lot of sleep and warm meals."

,, But I didn't kill her!", he cried out like a puppy.

,, I know!"

In this moment the door opened and Soldier Moore entered the room.

,, You called, Sir?"

,, Yes, I did. Please take the soldiers cuffs off and let him go. I will make sure the paperwork is done for his release."

,, I thank you, Sir!" Soldier Bing sight in relief.

,, But, believe me. This does not mean you can disappear from the base. I will have you followed and every step of you will be reported back to me. What do you say?"

He nodded and looked relieved. I told Soldier Moore the papers that needed to be done so that he could sign them.

,, If somebody asks for me, tell them I will be visiting observation towers two and four!"

I grabbed my bag and left the room. As I exited the building I looked at my watch. It was already late; to be exact it was one o'clock at noon. Damn it. Sarah and I had arranged to meet at two for lunch at the mess hall. I needed to call her and inform her that I couldn't make it. I needed to check on Soldier Bings story to see if everything he said lines up.

CHAPTER 20

Around noon he drove home, because he wanted to have his lunch in peace. He unlocked the door, went in the house and threw the keys on the kitchen table. He took off his jacket and opened the door to the wardrobe in his hallway, took out a hanger and hanged the jacket in the wardrobe. He took off his shoes and put them in the wardrobe next to the other shoes. He closed the door and went on to the kitchen. He opened the freezer that was fully packed with frozen ready cooked meals. He chose a portion of <spaghetti Napolitano> and took it out. The microwave was next to the refrigerator, so he closed the door of the freezer and opened the door of the microwave. He took the lid off his meal and set the microwave for fifteen minutes. While the meal was heating up in the microwave he wanted to have a shower. He needed to clear his head. After a few minutes he came back into the kitchen with his morning gown on. As he walked into the kitchen the microwave made a familiar sound, he took out his meal and sat at the table to enjoy it. In his head he was still playing different weird scenarios and he was constantly thinking about his discussion with the Detective. One scenario was crazier that the next. At this moment, he had the wish to find some slut and tie her up on the ping pong table and torture her to death. The ping pong table was in the basement and waited for his next victim. He wished for a slut that he could tie to her arms and legs and wildly torture her. On his face was a smile that turned into a big grin. The past few days he was only thinking about sadistic scenes that caused fear and pain. He loved feeding on their pain. His mother was to blame for his confused feelings. She was the biggest whore he had met in his life and he brought him on this path. He knew it was wrong, what he did, but he couldn't help himself. What he felt for women was pure hate.

He suddenly felt the urge to see his mother. He had lost his appetite and left his lunch on the table. He went to the door that led to the basement; he unsealed the door and opened it. He turned on the light and started walking down the stairs quickly. His heart was beating so hard he thought his chest would burst. The basement was separated into three different areas. Down here there were, on the one side, two regular rooms, where the heating boiler, the washing machine and the dryer were located. On the other side was the area where the workbench was, with all sorts of tools that he had all lined up in order. Next to the bench he had hung up a huge poster which showed a group of soldiers that were building a tank. He stood directly in front of the poster and pulled it to one side. The big poster was hiding a sliding door that led to a small room. The room was dark and his right hand pushed the switch automatically. The room instantly filled with bright light. He called the room his <darling>. The walls consisted of pure cement and he saw no reason to make them look prettier. Not one picture was hanging on the walls, nothing. On the left side he had put a couch and an old table in front of that. On another small table he had a black and white TV and a video cassette recorder. He liked it, to see the videos of the torture that he recorded. They were his memories of his happiest moments of his life. He started filming them, when he realized that he could do more and tried out more sadistic tortures. In the back right corner was a vault. It was one of these really old ones nobody was building anymore. He stopped in front of the vault and before he could turn the wheel to open it he put in the number combination. It was the date of his mother's death. He pulled the door open. In the vault were a lot of videotapes, which he had numbered, but he didn't even look at them now. His eyes went straight to a small photo album with family photos that he took out. With the album in his hands, he sat down on the couch and looked at the pictures. Every time he saw a picture of his father he got homesick and nostalgic. As the nostalgia for his father was rising, so was the hate for his mother. The woman that destroyed and killed his father. He took an old picture of their wedding in his hands. The picture was yellowed and creased, because he had held it like this in his hands many times. How elegant his father looked on his tux. He had a harsh face but friendly eyes and he was well build. He loving stroked over his father's face. He looked at his mother and tried to remember the expression on her face, but he couldn't. He had cut out his mother's face from every picture she was in. Hate was rising in him again and he got angry. Filled with anger he stood up, went to the vault and took a small aluminum box out. Carefully he was holding it in his hands and he sat back down on the couch. With shaking hand he slowly opened the box to look, for the thousandth time, at what was inside. He took two old pictures out of the box, from him and his father. On the one was father and son fishing, he must have been about five years old. On the other was his first day at school holding his father's hand, never wanting to let him go. With tears in his eyes he put the pictures back in the box and took out an even smaller box. The box was not bigger than five centimeters and he carefully held it in his hand. His hand started shaking as he took the lid of, because he didn't want the content to fall out. In this small box were some halfway rotten teeth and a finger. The finger had shrunk after all this years and had even lost his smell he had in the beginning from the rotting flesh. While he was looking at this keepsake, he got lost in his thoughts found himself in the year nineteen eighty five.

The sun was shining and there was not one cloud in the sky. It was an unusually hot day for this time of year, in November. He was seven years old and in the second grade of primary school. He was just out of school and he had planned to walk home because his father couldn't pick him up, because he was working. His was a sales representative for household articles and on the road a lot, sometimes even for weeks until he could make the sale he needed, so he was hardly ever home. He had his own key so that he could always get inside the house when he was alone, so he unlocked the door and entered. He called his mum but got no answer. He quickly took his bag of his shoulders, left it on one of the kitchen chairs and had a look around. Maybe she had cooked something and he was lucky to find something edible. He looked in the empty pots on the stove and, as always, he wouldn't get a warm meal. As he was walking up the stairs, he took off his jacket and called his mother again, but again, no answer. When he passed his parents closed bedroom door he could hear sounds coming out of it that he thought sounded strange. He stood in front of the closed door and put his ear on the door, tying to hear clearer. He could not imagine what these sounds could be that he could hear in the hall. He could hear gasping and mumbling that was loud and then lower. He could not understand where the sounds were coming from. Like every kid his age he wanted to find out what it was and quietly opened the bedroom door. They say that curiosity could kill you, but what happened to him was that his little heart broke into a million pieces with what he saw. Shocked he looked on to his parent's bed. He saw how his mother, his bellowed mother, had fun with two unfamiliar men. He was in shock so he couldn't take his eyes off the spectacle. Maybe it was out of shame that he could not look away. It was not that he didn't want to turn his head away but he couldn't. They hadn't seen him, so they continued what they were doing. The men's clothes where all over the room, his mother still wore some pieces of her uniform. In her hand she held a riding crop commanding the men how slow or how hard they should take her. She was laughing loud and telling them, with obscene words, how to take her. He could see in her face that she enjoyed what these men did with her. Suddenly he felt sick, he couldn't see this any longer and was about to slowly get out of the room, when his mother looked at him. For a few seconds they just looked each other in the eyes. These seconds felt like hours. He turned his head and wanted to go out of the room, when his mother spoke to him:

„ Stay, enjoy the play!"

He was not sure what he should do. Should he run out or spit her in the face? When the men saw the small boy and that his mother talked to him, they took her even harder. He finally managed to turn his head and ran out of the bedroom into his room. He slammed his bedroom door behind him and sat on the floor behind the door and started crying. He could still hear his mothers screaming that would follow him for the rest of his life. He was sure about that. He locked his door and hid under his bed. E was not sure how many hours he was crying under the bed, when his mother knocked at the door.

„ Open the door at once!", she screamed, but he was too afraid to open. He had no intention of answering her and stayed there under the bed in silence.

„ Open the door now. I know that you are in there!", she was still screaming.

„ If you don't open the door now, I will slam it and hit you so hard you'd wish you had opened it the first time!"

He didn't know what to do. Deep inside he wished that his father would come home now to rescue him, but he knew he would come home in a few days. He was still under his bed listening to his mother pounding on the door swearing. She couldn't find a way to open the door so she got wilder and wilder. She was swearing like a street whore. She was swearing so much until the boy could handle it any longer and came out of under the bed. He walked to the door, still not knowing what he should do. After a few minutes he decided to unlock the door so she would stop screaming and let him be. Maybe he was lucky and she wouldn't hit him. Shaking in fear he turned the key, opened the door and stood opposite his mother. She was red with anger and had such a bad face expression, that didn't mean anything good. As soon as she saw the boy she grabbed him by his collar and slammed him against the wall. The boy didn't even have the courage to breath, out of fear he would drop dead. Sweat was dripping down his face. His mother stared wildly at him at foam was coming out of her mouth, like she had rabies.

„ When I command you to do something, you do exactly what I told you to do! You will do it without wasting any more thoughts on it, or else the devil will come and get you all. Is this clear? Otherwise the devil will come get you and the sissy father of yours."

He couldn't make a sound and only nodded. He could say a word and thought it was wise not to talk at all.

She pulled him towards her and she started tearing his clothes off him. He tried to defend himself but had not that much strength left.

„ Take off your underwear, so I can punish you how boys get punished when they don't listen to their mother!"

With shaking hands he took off his underwear, and begged his mother not to hurt him. He had so much fear but all this begging was for nothing. She didn't hear a word. With the riding crop in her hand she waited for him to take of his clothes. Then, with no mercy she started hitting on his small buttocks. Her own flesh and blood, she hit him so hard that his skin turned red and then blue. All this time he begged her to stop, but every time she hit harder. Only when he was close to fainting she stopped.

„ Look at this piece of shit. And you want to be a man one day. You are a pussy. Exactly like your father. A sissy, like your father. I don't believe that!"

The boy laid on the floor in shame and couldn't stop crying. His whole body was shaking and tears were running down his face.

„ Put your clothes on immediately and hide this thing you call a dick. This is not a dick, it is a worm! Ha, ha, ha. I can se the woman that will marry you in front of me. The poor thing. You will never be able to please a woman. Like I said, a pussy just like your father!"

With these words she left him alone and went into the bathroom next to her bedroom. The boy did not know that on this day his life would change forever and his martyrdom had began. From this day on, the hate he had on his mother would grow every day and he could not stop it.

With these thoughts he felt that he got sick and jumped off the couch to go to the toilette and throw up. The only thing he could think about was, that whore.

CHAPTER 21

I stopped at observation tower two, to interrogate Soldier Bing's colleagues to see if his story checks out. And it did. What his colleagues told me was exactly what he had told me in his questioning. I was on my way to tower number four, where at this moment the third man, of the fishing party, was on duty. When I arrived there I parked my car in front of the tower and didn't even bother closing the windows or locking up. It wouldn't take long to finish this questioning. As I was entering the tower, a cold breeze from the air-conditioning reached me and I immediately felt better. It was still very hot, and from the rain that was supposed to come you could not see anything at the moment. I took a tissue out of my pocket and dried my wet forehead. The Officer on duty had just seen me enter, when he stood up and saluted me. From the name tag on his shirt I could see his name.

„ Good evening, Officer Sommer. I am here to ask Soldier Saint Mikels a few questions. Where can I find him?"

„ Good evening, Sir. Soldier Saint Mikels stepped outside; he will be back in about five minutes. What is it about, if I may ask?"

„ No, you may not! If it is ok with you I will wait for him here. Thank you."

I didn't want to be so harsh to Officer Sommer, but I was sick of answering these questions. Who I am, what do I need, why do I need to talk to someone. I was in the middle of a murder investigation, I didn't need to let everyone know what I was looking for. He sat back down and didn't bother me again, working on his paperwork. As I was waiting for Soldier Saint Mikels I opened my notebook and had a look at my notes. A few minutes past and a Soldier walked in holding a tray in his arms and having a lit cigarette hanging between his lips. Because he was holding the tray he pushed the door to close with his foot.. he wanted to say something when Officer Sommer nodded in my direction so he would notice me. But the Soldier didn't see the sign and still hadn't seen me. Watching this scene made me think of my years in training. Soldier Saint Mikels had still not seen me so I told his name. He was a little bit surprised but soon got over it. He saw my rank from my decoration and saluted me.

,, Yes, Sir! What can I do for you?"

,, I would like to speak to you, if you don't mind."

,, No, absolutely not."

,, Good. Is there a room we could use to be alone?"

,, Yes, Sir. Please follow me."

I followed him and we entered an office that was not used. I sat down on the chair behind the desk and asked Soldier Saint Mikels to sit on the opposite chair.

,, Relax Soldier. It will only take a minute."

The Soldier sat on the chair and looked at me. I could see that he had no idea what I wanted to talk to him about. He didn't sit long in his chair and he asked me what he did wrong. I explained:

,, You clearly want to know what this is all about."

,,Yes, Sir."

,, Before I start asking the questions I must inform you that you are not a suspect in any case and I have no intention of arresting you. I don't want to read you your rights and you will not need an attorney. The only thing I need from you is o answer some simple questions. Nothing else. Do you understand?"

,, My rights? Suspect? What are you talking about?"

,, I will inform you, but before I do you must assure me that our conversation will remain confidential, and you will talk about no details until the case is closed."

So I informed him about the murder of Soldier Bing's girlfriend and that I needed some answers to verify his alibi on the night of the murder.

,, So, let us start then Soldier. Are you ready?"

,, Yes, Sir. But I am not sure I can help you at all. I didn't hear or see anything."

I started the questioning with some simple questions about his rank, how long was on the base and so on. While I was questioning him I could have a better look at him. He must be about thirty years old with short cut blond hair. His appearance was clean and I couldn't see one stain on his uniform. His eyes were constantly in search for mine, this was a good sign, It meant he had nothing to hide. His eyes had that look that he was expressing himself with caution so I only got some answers to my questions. Hearing his accent I could understand that he was coming from the south. I asked him the first question about the girl's death.

„ So, tell me, when you were on duty the day before yesterday. From what time until what time?"

„ From six a o'clock in the evening until two o'clock at night."

„ Did you see a certain Soldier Bing that night?"

„ Yes, he came passed the tower and came inside."

„ When was that?"

„ It must have been around two o'clock. He stayed a few minutes and we talked."

„ Did somebody else see you talk to him?"

„ The Officer on duty, Logan."

„ After Soldier Bing left the tower did you see him again that night?"

„ Yes, Sir. It was about three o'clock. About one hour later. We had planned to go on a fishing trip. The lake is not far from the base and we camped there for two nights."

„ Well, so around three you met again, then you left for our trip?"

„ Yes."

„ Did Soldier Bing, when he left the tower, tell you where he would be until three o'clock?"

„ Yes. He wanted to meet his girlfriend near the shooting range. In the toilette building that is located there."

„ Why there?"

„ Why there? Because he didn't have time to drive home and so they met there. They did that a lot, meeting in toilette rooms. I mean not only there, but on different spots on the base."

„ Why? Did they not have a home?"

„ Of course they both had a home. You must know how it is to be on duty on the base. One is on duty this day the other on other days. When your shift ends the shift of the other begins. There is not a lot of time for a private life and you do what you can."

„ I do know what you mean. When you met Soldier Bing at three was he somehow weird? Did hid behavior change in the past hour, since he left the tower?"

„ What do you mean?"

„ I mean, if he was nervous or wanted to hide something. Or if he did something he wanted to hide. Somehow changed. Did he want to leave the base as soon as possible as if someone would come after him."

„ We all couldn't wait to leave the base as soon as possible to go on our trip. We waited for this for weeks."

„ Answer the question, if you don't mind."

„ Of course, Sir. No, he was as always. I could not detect any strange behavior."

I stood up of my chair and walked around the office. Everything the Soldier said, matched the story Soldier Bing told me. Lost in my thoughts, I walked up and down the office, then in stopped in front of the window and looked outside on to the base. As I was looking outside, I realized that I could get a good look on the shooting range from here. There was no building blocking the view and however held watch in this office could see anything and anyone moving on the other side. Nothing could pass by undetected. I turned to the Soldier.

„ Tell me, Soldier. From the time you started your shift until it ended did you see anyone pass by on this side or the opposite side?"

„ No, Sir."

We are not getting any further, I thought. The answers I was getting were not enough for me and I had to think of something else, in order to solve this case quickly.

„ Where you the whole time here in the tower or did you go on patrol?"

„ I was here most of the time. Why?"

„ In the evening, did you maybe see headlights from a car on the side of the shooting range? In the dark you can see headlights better, it would not be difficult to see them going to the range, or not?"

„ The only headlights I saw that night were Soldier Bing's driving to the shooting range."

„ How are you sure it was him and no one else?"

„ Because I saw him drive off here and five minutes later I saw him arrive at the shooting range."

„ Maybe you saw another car and confused it with the car of your friend. Could that be?"

„ No, absolutely not. One of his stop signals was not working and he wanted to repair it when we came back from our trip. I recognized him from this light."

„ That sounds reasonable. Are you absolutely certain that there was no other vehicle on that side besides your friends? Did you maybe hear the motor of another vehicle without seeing any lights?"

„ No, Sir."

I sat down on the chair again ad made some notes. The questioning was over, so I told the Soldier:

„ Thank you, Soldier. We are done here. If I need anything I will contact you. Thank you for your help."

„ I don't think I have helped you, Sir."

I closed my notebook and out t back in my pocket. Then I stood up and walked to the door, I turned to him and said:

„ I am certain, that you helped me a lot!"

CHAPTER 22

I sat in my car and had a quick look at my notes again. While I was reading them, I came to the conclusion that Soldier Bing was innocent and that the time of death must have been between two fifteen and three o'clock. I believed that the murderer was following the victim on foot or by car but had turned off the headlights. So he was sure that no one would see and recognize him. I ruled out the possibility of him waiting in the toilette room. I was quite sure he followed by car but had the headlights turned off. He must have followed her on a safe distance to make sure that none would see him. Maybe he left the car earlier and followed on foot so he would not be heard and seen. But how could he know that they were meeting in the toilettes? If you would have a secret meeting you would not tell everyone, especially if your superior could find out and you could get kicked out for it. You keep it to yourself. You would tell your best friend maybe, like in this case. But they must finish their shift. My head started spinning and I was starting to feel a headache. In about an hour it would get dark. Time was passing really quickly today and I felt exhausted. Suddenly I remembered my appointment with Sarah for dinner and my stomach started complaining. I started my car and drove off. I didn't want to let Sarah wait longer than necessary, so I drove to the hotel to have a quick shower and change my clothes. I didn't have time to get my uniform from the laundry so I put on a pair of jeans and a white short sleeved shirt. I stood in front of the mirror and I liked what I saw. To make everything perfect, I sprayed my favorite cologne all over me. When I parked in front of the mess hall I looked in the mirror one more time. All good. Now it was time, because I was already half an hour late. Quickly I got off my car, locked the door and went into the mess hall. At this time of the day it was really packed and you couldn't find an empty table easily. I looked across the hall and couldn't see her at first. The table was in a quiet corner where we could talk in peace. While I was walking towards the table I was observing her. She had her hair down today and they laid on her shoulders. She had the face of a blond angel. As I could see from a far she was wearing a pink top and I'd bet she has on hat perfect pair of jeans. She had not seen my jet and I could see she was absorbed in reading the menu. On a table close to her, I saw a vase with a red carnation, I looked at her to make sure she would not see me and took the flower hiding it behind my back. I stopped in front of our table and wanted to hold the flower under her nose, but, as soon as I did that she stood up like she was stung by a bee making a short shriek. She looked at me startled and astonished and she was not sure what to do or to say.

I could see that after she recognized me she relaxed and found herself again and the color came back to her cheeks, a little bit redder than before. She must be ashamed of this incident.

„ Good evening", she said.,, I am sorry to react like this but I was lost in my thoughts and didn't see or hear you come closer."

„ It's alright. I got used to scaring women when I get to close to them." I was fiddling around my scar on my chin and ran my hand over it.

„ No. No. I was completely lost in my thought. Please sit, Detective."

„ Are we back to formalities again?"

„ Oh, I forgot. Please sit, John."

She did not need to say this twice. I sat on the chair opposite of her in a way that I could admire her. From the first time, I saw her; I knew she was the woman of my dreams. The waitress that came to take our order, pulled me out of my dreams.

„ I want an ice cold beer."

„ And I want a glass of red wine."

To eat I ordered a grilled steak and Sarah a Pizza Margarita. The waitress wrote everything down and left us alone. For a few minutes, we did not say a word and I watched Sarah play with the flower in her hand. She smelled the flower and I was pretty sure, she liked it.

„ Do you like the carnation?"

„ Yes, I like it a lot. Thanks again."

Again silence. What was the matter with her today? Why didn't she speak? I was certain that something was wrong, so I asked her.

„ You are really quiet today and you seem pale. Did something happen?"

„ No. I am fine. I am just a little bit tired from work, that's all."

„ Are you sure?"

„ Yes."

„ Alright."

I was sure that something was going on, but I wanted for her to tell me herself without me pushing her. Maybe she was not sure if she could trust me. The waitress brought us our drinks. A few minutes later the food came. We talked about unimportant things while we ate.

„ Do you know that I took a week vacation to help you solve the case and catch the killer?"

„ Us? Are you really serious that you want to help me catch a murderer?"

„ Yes, this is exactly what I want! I want to find this bastard and bring him in front of military court to get his punishment."

„ This could get dangerous. I don't want you to get hurt, only to help me to catch the killer. I want you to understand that."

„ That is very sweet of you, to want to take care of me. Thank you."

She smiled even sweeter this time and it took a lot of effort not to go over there, grab and kiss her and everything that may follow from there.

He sat on a chair in the kitchen in the dark; he loved sitting in the dark. He could think better without getting any of these migraine attacks. He did not make anything for dinner, he had absolutely no appetite. He did not even have a drink to relax and clear his head. He was angry, at himself and this slut. How could he be so stupid? How could she slip through his hands? He was not very careful. Almost someone recognized him. What an idiot he was! He could not think straight, because he had this urge to kill this woman and almost someone would have seen him. Damn it, if this Soldier hadn't turned up. But he got lucky and got off lightly. This cannot happen again. He was sure it will not happen again. Mister John Man. The Detective. It was his entire fault. After his conversation with him he could not think clearly. This Detective challenged him and he almost gave himself away. How did he dare to talk to him like this and treat him this way? Who gave him the right to do so? But he would show him how it works. The detective could count on that. He would not let this slide. Suddenly he got up, walked to the bedroom and opened his closet. He wanted to get dressed and look for this investigator. After he dressed, he looked at his watch and noticed that it was half passed eight. He was certain he would find that damn investigator at the mess hall. About twenty minutes later he drove past the mess hall looking for the investigators car. After a minute of looking he saw his scrap car and parked his in an empty parking lot. He entered the mess hall and as always no one would greet him. He looked around to find him. There was no empty table in here and this was good for him. Suddenly he saw them sitting at a table in the back. My lovebirds! He walked towards their table and a wide smile was on his lips.

We had a lively conversation and we laughed a lot. She was good company and she made me laugh easily. I don't know how, but she got me to open my heart and tell her things without noticing. While we were talking to each other and, you can be sure about that, laughed a great deal, her face expression changed suddenly. And she became very serious. She sat stiff in her chair and her face got pale.

„ What happened to you?" I asked?

„ Nothing. I just got goose bumps and I have the feeling that I am being watched. I had the same feeling…!"

She didn't have time to finish the sentence and before our eyes Colonel Silk appeared and stopped at our table. I didn't see that coming. What did this idiot want with us? This couldn't get any worse than that.

„ This is a surprise, to find you to here! ", the Colonel said to us.

„ Good evening, Colonel. How are you?"

„ Very good. I came here to have my dinner, but as it seems this place is packed. I can see no free table in here. It will be better if I sit at the bar, waiting for a table to clear up!"

Secretly he wished that we would let him sot at our table. I didn't want to ruin his fun so I

„ If you want you can sit with us. Its fine!"

I hoped he would turn down my offer, I didn't want him around I didn't like him at all.

„ That is very nice of you, thank you."

He pulled a chair and sat with us. For a few minutes we were all silent. I noticed Sarah sitting stiff in her chair and didn't say a word anymore. She must have felt awful, from one second to the other she got really pale. Maybe she didn't like him and now I feel like a complete idiot for inviting him to sit with us.

„ Anything new, Mister Man? Did you catch the man responsible?"

„ No. Not jet, but I am close. I have my suspicions, but it is still early to talk about, I must complete the investigation first. Then I will strike."

„ These are great news I hear from you. To have a murderer between us, not knowing who he is in order to catch him, that's unbelievable. What do you say about that, Mrs....?"

The Colonel talked to Sarah, but she seems to exclude herself from the conversation. She looked at him and I had the feeling that she didn't even know what our conversation was about. The Colonel pretended not to know her. He did not want, to put all his cards on the table.

„ Miss Connors, please!" she answered and gave him a cold look.

„ What do you say about this, Miss Connors, about the murders, of course?"

„ I find it horrifying and I hope, that the killer will be caught soon. As soon as possible."

„ You can be sure about that. I believe that Detective Man will give his best in order to solve this case as soon as possible, so that we can go back to normal. Isn't that right, Detective?"

While he was talking to her, he gave me an ironic look and if I could I would land my fist exactly on his nose. On his face a wide smile appeared. The smile looked fake, because his eyes still had this ice cold look I could not understand. Again I had this feeling in my stomach. I was one hundred percent sure that this was our guy. I just needed to prove it. if he was not the one, the devil could take me.

„ You are absolutely right, Colonel. I will give my best to catch this bastard and drag him in front of the military court. While we are talking about the case now, I wanted to inform you that I have the intention of visiting you again!"

„ Why? I think, no, I am sure that I have told you everything I know."

„ I wanted to look at the files of the dead women, if you don't mind.

I also want you to make me a psychological profile of them. What do you think about that? I am very interested in making sure that these women were not mistaken to be unfit to serve in the military but served anyway. I was informed that people that are suicidal are not allowed to join the military. Is that not correct?"

„ I am glad that I can be helpful to you. And yes, you are right; those people with psychological problems are not allowed to join the military. Call my Secretary, he knows my work schedule better than me and he can make you an appointment. I will give my best to help you anyway I can!"

„ I really appreciate that you want to help solving the case. Thank you."

Suddenly, he jump off his chair and excused himself saying there was a table free and he wanted to let us finish our dinner in peace.

„ Thank you for your hospitality, but as I can see, I table is free and I will let you finish your dinner. I wish you a good evening and a good night."

He left our table and sat on the table next to us, without looking at us one more time. It looked as he build a wall around him and saw no one else but himself. Finally he had left our table. This detestable moron. I looked over to Sarah and she looked pale like a ghost. This transformation was unbelievable. Before the Colonel sat at our table she was the joy of life, now she looked like the death himself. Carefully I put my hand on hers and asked her:

„ Are you ok?", I asked and stroked her hand holding her gently.

„ Now that this man left our table, I am feeling better. Believe me. I cannot stand him at all and I get goose bumps only from looking at him. Don't ask me why, I have never felt like this in my life. Only with him, and I don't even know him personally, I talked to him today for the first time!"

I looked into her eyes and tried to figure out what she meant by these words.

„ What do you mean?"

„ I am not quite sure. The exact same feeling I had last night and I am really ashamed. You cannot imagine what happened to me last night."

„ What happened that you are so ashamed about? It could not have been that bad, could it?"

I realized that she was searching for the right words and did not really know where to begin.

„ So, last night after work, I wanted to walk home. I am not sure how to explain it but I had the feeling that I was watched the whole time!", while she was talking she got goose bumps and started shaking.

Then she told me the whole story and I looked at her astonished. I was not sure, what to think about all this. I could not believe my ears with what she told me and I was speechless.

„ Why didn't you call me immediately? I would come to the mess hall and would have driven you home. Don't you know what this means? This was for sure the killer that already has an eye on you."

With her pale face she looked at me and answered with a trembling voice:

„ Are you sure? Oh my God. Fortunately I fell in the arms of this Soldier. Who knows what would have happened to me if I hadn't bumped into me."

Unbelieving she shook her head and wrapped her arms around her, she started shaking again.

„ Who knows where you would have been today if you hadn't bumped into him."

„ I am an idiot. I should have called you and informed you about this from the first minute!"

For a few minutes we sat there not talking, both lost in our own thoughts. My brain was working on full speed, because I was sure, that Sarah was in the eye of the killer and I could leave her out of my sight for a second. I must protect her, before we had another victim in the base.

„ I must know where the Colonel was last night! He is our guy. I am a hundred percent sure!"

„ Can I tell you something? The same goose bumps and the same feeling that I had tonight here with him, I had last night. It was exactly like yesterday. This feeling to be watched as soon as he stood at our table, it made my hair stand. I can't stand this man. He has something evil, I cannot explain. Is that weird?"

„ That is not weird at all, this is what you call instinct!", I answered.

CHAPTER 23

Feeling happy he ate his dinner. He was watching them, without them noticing. If Detective Man wanted to use the psychological profiles to link him to the murders of these whores he was more than welcome. He didn't care. If he would work closely with him together, he could disappear if they would get to close to him with the investigation. He just needed to be very smart, so that Detective Man did not realize that he was the guy they are looking for. For the stupid cow he had already thought about a plan, how to kill her. This time there was no turning back. Last night, she slipped out of his hands, this will not happen again. Deep inside he was screaming out of happiness, he needed to contain himself, so nobody on the outside would notice. The time would soon come when he could get his hands in her throat.

He paid for his dinner and gave these two not one more look. He went out of mess hall and drove home whistling a happy tune.

Out of the corner of my eye I watched him and realized that he was paying his dinner. I didn't bother and made it look like I couldn't see him. After he paid his bill, we waited for him to leave. We paid our bill as well and went out to the parking lot. We stood there for a few minutes. Sarah had her arms wrapped around her and looked up to the sky. It was a beautiful night. The moon was almost full and was glowing on earth throwing light everywhere. There was a cool breeze and a smell of flowers was going around. I stood next to Sarah and could see that she had goose bumps; I put my arm on her shoulder and pulled her close to me. She smiled at me thanking me for the hug with the look in her eyes. I held her with one hand and with the other I pulled out a package of cigarettes. As I took a cigarette in my mouth and wanted to light it, Sarah grabbed the cigarette from my mouth.

„ Hey, this was my cigarette!", I said. I pretended to be offended and began tickling her, so he would give me back my cigarette and Sarah shook with laughter. But she didn't manage to get out of my arms, because I held her tight. In that perfect moment, our faces where so near and we looked each other in the eyes. We staid like this not saying a word. Slowly I lowered my head, so I could kiss her. The hole atmosphere was electric and I had the impression lightning would strike us. We had just touched each other's lips, when the door of the mess hall opened and we separated. I felt like a small boy who had done something wrong. I didn't want for her to be seen with me like that. Not everyone needed to know what was going on between us.

„ What should we do now?", Sarah asked and looked at me.

„ I don't know. To tell the truth, I wanted to walk through the shooting range, to have a closer look."

„ Why?"

„ I wanted to have a look around in peace, now that nobody is there to bother us."

„ Alright, let's go."

„ Are you coming with me?"

„ Of course I am coming with you! What did you expect?"

„ Then let us drive to the hotel first to get some jackets and my notebook, so I can make my notes."

We drove back to the hotel. When we arrived we walked up the stairs to the second floor where my room was, to put on something warmer and to put on some trainers.

„ You are staying in this room?", Sarah asked.

„ Yes, it is not exactly the Hilton but it is enough. I have my office also and I need the room only for sleeping." I answered her.

„ Couldn't you find anything larger? You get claustrophobic in here."

„ unfortunately not. The whole place was completely booked. A group of reservists came here to have some training for six weeks."

While we were talking I searched in my traveling bag to find a sweater, I handed it to Sarah and she put it right on and thanked me. I quickly put on a pair of trainers and a jacket. We left the room and locked the door. A few minutes later we were already in the car.

„ To the shooting range?", Sarah asked.

„ Exactly! Do you have a gun with you?"

„ No, why? Do you expect any trouble?"

„ The killer always comes back to the scene of the crime. You never know when, but it is certain."

I bend over and opened the looked in the compartment in front of her and started digging in there. I had a lot of crap in there, which every day I want to throw out. Finally I found my nine millimeter Glock and handed it to her. After I gave her the gun, I took out a flash light and put it on her lap. The sun had gone down for a few hours now gave its place to the moon. The good thing was that the moonlight was strong and we wouldn't need the flash light all the time. I hoped for the circumstance to be similar to the night of the murder so maybe I would get some clues to come closer to solve the murder. We passed the cinema and a group of people were waiting at the entrance. I looked at the board and the movie that was on tonight was <Die hard 3>. As it seemed the movie might be old but it was popular to young people as well. Then we passed some other buildings that were not that important to us. We had driven a few kilometers from the centre of the base, when I found the street to the shooting range. The moon was hidden behind some huge trees, so everything was wrapped in darkness and you could barely see where you were besides the spots my headlights were shining on. It was so quiet here on the shooting range. Because no one was here you could hear everything. We heard owls, frogs and other animals making strange noises. You could even smell the smell of the trees, it was very distinct.

„ How did you find Colonel Silk?"

„ I am sure, that I think of him exactly as you think of him. In my opinion he is a close, lonely person but at the same time very clever, too clever for my taste."

„ Do you think, he is the key in this case?"

„ I am quite sure. In my eyes he is a suspect who we cannot let out of sight."

„ Really?"

„ Officially, I don't want to say anything yet. But, unofficially I can say that I think of him as the killer. I need to find a way to make him sweat, so that he makes a mistake and gives himself away. Then, sooner or later he will tell us everything."

„ I find this impossible!"

„ Why do you say that?"

„ If he really is the killer it will be really hard to get him, because he is very clever. If he wouldn't be clever, he would have been caught long ago, don't you think?"

„ Between us, I am a hundred percent sure that he is the guy we are looking for. And I swear to you, I will catch him!"

„ What do you think is his motive for the murders?"

„ Well, it is not a clear case of jealousy. This all has a much deeper reason."

„ Yes, you are right about that, for sure."

„ Do you know, what that means?"

„ What does it mean?"

„ That the Colonel is a really dangerous man that would do anything to get away with all this. He is a sick man that is haunted by something so evil; he tries to escape from it with these murders. As we said, he is a very clever guy and I need to be very careful not to make any mistake if I want to catch him."

„ From what I hear now, I cannot think of anything that could be his motive. What could it be, in your opinion?"

„ I believe that it has nothing to do with sex. But I am sure that it gives his great pleasure to strangle his victims and this is the most dangerous thing about this. Why would he want to kill them this way, when there are so many easier ways to do it? Can you tell me?"

„ How would I know? We are dealing with a psychiatrist. With a sick, very clever psychiatrist!"

„ You are right."

The last few kilometers we didn't say a word and we were both lost in our thoughts about this conversation. When we arrived at the shooting range, I turned off the motor and the headlights. I looked up to the sky and noticed that it had a dark blue color now and as the humidity was increasing and the temperature was falling, it was getting cold. I opened the door, Turned to Sarah and said:

„ It is time to get to work now. Come on, let's go."

I grabbed my flash light and got out the car. Sarah did exactly the same and followed me.

CHAPTER 24

We had about a meter of distance between us, in front of the shooting range. We were trying to get familiar with the sounds of the night and the darkness around us. I was thinking about the last murder case and said to Sarah:

„ So. The headlights Soldier Saint Mikels saw were from Officer Bing's car. I believe that the Officer arrived here on the shooting range. He knew where the observation tower was and had nothing to hide. The reason he came here was to meet with his girlfriend in the toilettes just after he left his friend in the observation tower. It was about two o'clock at night. Nobody else saw him…"

„ If we assume he went to an arranged meeting, you are right."

„ It was really an arranged meeting. So, we assume he arrived here around two to two fifteen."

„ Possibly."

„ Alright. His girlfriend arrived first."

„ Why?"

„ They had arranged it like that. This is what he said I his questioning and he had no reason to lie about who arrived here first."

„ Good."

„ I believe, that whoever killed Simpson, ether followed her by car with the headlights turned off so he would not be noticed, or he walked here and hid near the toilettes when he noticed that her boyfriend came to meet her."

We left the path in front of the toilette building and walked around it to the back. We found ourselves on a parking space with gravel.

„ On this parking the big trucks and busses park that bring troops from

115

out of town, to do their exercises on the shooting range. The killer knew exactly how to move on the gravel, not to leave any clues behind him."

„ If he followed her by car!"

„ That he did. I am pretty sure. Follow me please."

We walked through the parking space. As we came closer to the toilette building the gravel became less dense and I could see tire marks with my flash light, on a place the huge busses had nothing to do. The marks led to a big bush and suddenly stopped. I walk behind that bush and searched the floor for clues. I came back in front of the bush and walked behind it one more time.

„ Whatever car stopped here could not be seen from the street, but it did leave some marks."

„ Really? Then we can have the tire marks checked out!", she answered to my surprise.

„ Whoever parked here didn't want his car to be found or seen. I don't think he was here before the couple met; this would have been too dangerous for him. How could he know that they would meet here anyway? I am sure that he arrived here the same time as his victim did and parked his car behind the bushes. He followed her, as she entered the toilette room, from a small path that goes around the building and watched her from a small window that is on the one side. He must have been watching her and was ready to kill her, when he heard her boyfriend arriving with his car, and went into hiding again. I am quite sure how it played out then. He observed them the whole time through this window, while they were having sex and waited until they finished and Officer Bing left the building and drove off in his car. Then he had the perfect opportunity to go in and kill her and leave on the same way he came here. Right?"

„ So far, it sounds right."

„ Let's go then."

We followed the path around the building. We could barely see it. We could see that years ago it was marked with wooden pegs, but now most of the pegs where taken out or were half rotten after all these years. As it seemed they didn't bother renewing the pegs because nobody really used this path anymore, it was almost fully covered in weeds. I turned around to the bush and measured the distance to here. It must be around twenty five meters from the bush to behind the toilettes.

„ Alright. So this guy waits patiently behind the building by this window. First, he saw Simpson in the toilettes. When he decided to strike, he saw the Officer coming in. he waited again, until they had finished what they started. When he saw, that the Officer left the toilette building, he sneaked in and killed her. He would not have any problems with the victim, she probably thought that her boyfriend had forgotten something or wanted to tell her something. So far, is everything understandable?"

„ So far, yes. But, to tell you the truth, I cannot understand, why he wanted to kill her here. So many people come past here. Day and night. There are patrols, and guards and even troupes doing night exercises. Every one of them could have stopped here to notice what was going on. Why didn't he follow her home, he had more chances to be undetected there? It was impossible for him be sure that her boyfriend wouldn't come back. Unless, he heard from the window that he had arrange with his friends to meet at the entrance and that he was in a hurry. This is the only way he could be sure about him not coming back."

„ You are absolutely right. I am also not quite sure why he killed her here. May it was just the right opportunity. Maybe he thought we would hold the boyfriend responsible for the murder. The more I look at this place here, the more I think it was all planned. It was not a coincidence to find her here. No, no. He must have planned it. Why he killed her here opens the door to many more questions I have. First, he must have known about the victim's relationship to the Officer and didn't want to risk following her home to kill her, where he could be taken by surprise by the Officer. Second, as the victim had planned the meeting in the toilettes, he must have been following her for a while before that night and knew what was going on in her life. Or maybe, he had asked around learning information about her. If he was following her, he somehow found out about the meeting here and thought it would be the best opportunity. He had the chance to kill her; she was alone, in the dark in the toilette room. The moment was perfect because the last person to see her alive, except him, was her boyfriend and they could pin her death on boyfriend and he would get away with it. What do you think?"

„ This all sounds real but I am a little bit confused. Don't mind my though. You are the Detective here, not me."

„ Come, let's go into the building!", I said and turned around.

We walked all around the building and stopped by the entrance.

The whole building and the surrounding area was marked with a yellow tape by the military police. You know what tape I mean. The yellow tape, which you see in all the movies, they use to mark crime scenes with so that no one enters. I pulled the yellow tape aside and we walked into the toilette building. After we turned on the light, we saw that the whole room was full of a gay dust, which was used by the forensic team to collect fingerprints. We stopped in the middle of the room and I went to the sink on the left side of the room.

„ Well, she was standing here washing herself. With her head bend over, she could not see him come in. He snuck in here and stood behind her. As she was busy washing herself, she only realized he was here when he attacked her and started strangling her. The element of surprise was on his side and he quickly grabbed her and did what he did. When he finished, he sat her on the toilette as we found her."

„ A little bit confusing but it sounds correct."

I couldn't hold myself from all the excitement, because I was sure I am on the right path on how this played out, I walked out of the building and shouted to Sarah:

„ Let's have a look on the track the killer used to get away from the scene, without getting noticed."

When I got out of the building I walked again across the path behind the building. But instead of going to the window I went straight to the big bush and stopped there.

„ Exactly from this bush he walked back. He didn't want to be seen by any chance. By any patrol and most of all by any…"

I hadn't finished my sentence, when we suddenly saw headlights and heard a motor breaking the silence. The motor was put out. We came out of the bush and saw the car that was standing there. It was a green Jeep of the military police. Both doors opened and I could see the silhouette of the men that came out of the car. Automatically my hand went to my back and I held my gun, Sarah did the same. The men looked in our direction but had trouble recognizing us because I flashed my flash light in their direction to blind them. One of them shouted:

„ Who is there and what are you doing here at this time? Don't you know this is a crime scene? You are not allowed to snoop around here!"

„ Detective Man and Connors!" I answered him.

I shouted at them who I was, because I didn't want this to turn into a disaster. You should not mess with an armed patrol, especially next to a crime scene. Although I had shouted at them, we stayed put in our place and waited for them to answer.

„ Stay where you are. We will come to you!"

„ Alright. Come over here. We are waiting for you."

They were about twenty meters away from us and we waited for them to get closer. As they approached us, I could see, they still had their weapons in their hand pointing at us. About two meters in front of us they stopped and looked at us closely. One of them asked:

„ What are you two doing here? Don't you know this is a crime scene and is no place for you to sneak around."

„ Yes, we know. This is the reason, we are here. I am investigating this murder case and wanted to have another look at the crime scene. What are you two doing here?"

„ We were ordered not to leave the scene undetected and to report anyone sneaking around here. We were not informed that anyone would be here tonight to have another look!"

„ Normally you should have put two guards in front of the entrance!"

„ I don't know anything about this, Sir."

„ Alright. In a few minutes we will be gone. There is no need for you to wait for us. Thank you!"

They were not sure what they should do. After another short conversation, I assured them that everything was fine and they could continue with their patrol. We saluted each other and they went back to the car continuing their patrol around the area. Because of this incident, I had now confused my thoughts and we decided to call it a night. We got back in my car. I started it and Sarah asked what we should do now.

„ What will we do now?"

„ I will bring you home now. We have a lot to do tomorrow. Now its time to rest."

„ Well, then. Let's go home."

Sarah's house was located outside the base. She was living in an old part of town that belonged to the military, on the George Washington hill. Even before the war the military had the best houses on the hill. The houses were given to high ranking officers after they were build. They were large houses where you could easily raise three or four children, as it used to be those years. The common soldiers were living on the base or in small apartments around it. The houses were build around 1910 to 1920. At the time, the Officers were still gentlemen. They came mostly from wealthy families and there were not many officers back then. There must be about forty houses as I could see when we were driving closer. Every house was build out of red bricks and had white windows installed. In front of every house was lawn and the driveway to the entrance was made of flagstone. The George Washington hill had roughly the size of three hundred hectares. It had both, woods and fields. Behind the houses were the forest and on the other side, in front of the houses were the fields. The forest consisted of fir trees, spruces and all sorts of trees that had an eye on the houses. One of the negatives about that hill is that it was about fifty kilometers far from the base. We drove up the hill, when Sarah said:

„ I live in house number eight. You need to take a left here.”

„ Alright.”

She started yawning and I started as well. I looked at my watch and couldn't believe my eyes, it was already half past two. How quick the time had passed. I easily found house number eight and drove up the driveway. I parked my car and turned off the engine. Sarah looked out of the car to the garage.

„ What's wrong?”

„ Strange. I am sure I left the light on in the garage, before I left.”

„ Maybe it burned out. It is nothing uncommon.”

„ You think? And if I tell you that I changed the light bulb about a week ago, what then? This is uncommon.”

„ Come on, get out of the car. We will go and have a look what is going on with the lamp. Can it be that you are a little bit more nervous tonight?”

„ Well, let us check.”, she answered slightly irritated.

We got out the car at the same time and closed the doors. We stopped in front of her garage doors. I looked at the light bulb and could not see if it was burned out. I stretched and tried to unscrew the light bulb, but as soon as I touched it began glowing again.

„ Look at that. It wasn't screwed on tightly. When you change the light bulb, you need to screw it back on correctly!”

„ Ok, smart pants. Now I know! Thank you for your advice."

„ Now, seriously. Why do you keep your garage door open and not locked, like a normal person?"

„ Because I am in no mood opening and closing the door every time. Like this, I can come in and out whenever I want without wasting any time."

„ You know that this is dangerous, right?"

„ Why?"

„ Because someone could hide in your garage and attack you. That's why! Have you ever thought about it?"

„, Oh, come on. You only want to scare me. Who should attack me? Have you seen these houses here? Everyone can look at each other's houses. Stop being hysterical and let us go inside. I am freezing."

She pulled her key out of her pocket and unlocked the door. She made an inviting gesture with her hand that I should go inside and said:

„ Come in!"

I entered the hall and on the left side was a small dresser. On the dresser she had put a tablecloth and s vase with dried flowers. Over the dresser she had hang a mirror and I looked at my reflection. Next to the dresser was a coat stand on which some light jackets were hanging.

„ Come on in, put the keys on the dresser!", Sarah said and I did as I was told.

„ I will pour us a couple of drinks now, to warm up. What do you think?"

„ Sounds enticing."

She laughed and showed me into the living room. I was very impressed with what I saw. The whole living room was white. The furniture was white, the carpets the lamps. Everything, really everything was white. On the walls she had different paintings. One of them was the Mona Lisa. Seeing the Mona Lisa made me smile.

„ What would you like to drink?"

„ I would like a Jonny on the rocks, if you have any, of course."

„ Today is your lucky day. I have both at home."

She poured us both a drink and we sat on the couch.

„ You have a nice house and a really good taste in furniture."

„ I am glad you like it. is it ok with you, if I leave you alone for a bit. I need to go to the toilette. I am dying to go to the toilette!"

I laughed and she stood up and left me alone. While I was waiting for her, enjoying my drink, I went through her music collection, suddenly something attacked me. As I hadn't seen or heard the attacker, I screamed. At once, I turned around and prepared for a fight. Sarah came into the living room and as she saw me she couldn't stop laughing.

I still hadn't realized what was going on, when I saw something big and hairy laying to my feet. This thing had also a long fury tail.

„ Oh bear, are you not ashamed, scaring our guest like that? Come here at once!"

She tried to sound serious but she couldn't, so she sat laughing on the couch and grabbed this big, fury something, holding it in her arms.

„ For God sakes! What is this thing?", I asked surprised.

„ This is bear!", Sarah answered and turned my way so I could see the face of this giant cat.

The cat was totally black and had such thick fur that looked amazing. I had never seen such a shiny fur. I looked the cat in and it took my breath away. One eye was blue and the other was gray with a touch of green. Sarah was still laughing and the cat looked at me baffled.

„ You don't need to feel bad, he does that to every guest I bring home. He loves scaring people."

„ To tell the truth, he didn't just frighten me, he scared me to death!"

After this small incident, we sat on the couch finishing our drinks. It was really late now and I felt bad to leave Sarah on her own. But it was time to go to bed. Sarah let the cat down on the floor and it ran into the kitchen and started hissing.

„ What a weird cat. What is wrong with you now?"

Sarah was walking towards the kitchen when the cat came out of it running and disappeared the other way.

„ I think he doesn't like me being here. What do you think?"

„ Don't be bothered by him. I am used to him by now. Maybe he is just pissed that I haven't fed him tonight. Come I'll bring you to the door."

We walked to the door and she opened it. I stood in the door and turned back to her. It was hard for me to leave her, but in a few hours, I would see her again.

„ Thank you for this great and exiting evening. It has been a while since I could really talk to someone like this."

„ It was an honor, young lady. And I must admit, I had a great time talking to you too.", I answered.

„ Well, then, I won't keep you up any longer and leave you now. Good night and will see each other in a few hours. I will pick you up tomorrow morning so we can drive together to the base."

I turned and wanted to go down the driveway to my car, when I suddenly turned around again, took her in my arms and kissed Sarah passionately on her ravishing lips. Her lips were burning in passion and had a fruity taste. I tried to open her mouth with my tongue and willingly she opened it herself. Sarah kissed me more and more passionate and it made it hard for me not to throw her on the floor here in her entranceway. Now, it was time to let go, otherwise I would not have the strength to say goodbye tonight.

„ I really must go now, otherwise we will get in trouble."

„ Well, ok. If you must go, you must go."

„ We have a lot of work ahead of us tomorrow. Did you forget?"

I kissed her one more time and then turned around to leave. While I was going to my car, I turned my head to throw a kiss at her. She grabbed the kiss with her hand and waved at me. We adults get like small children when we are in love. I opened the door and I waved at her one more time before she closed the door. After Sarah had closed the door I sat down on my seat and thought about her kisses. I got goose bumps and I could still feel her lips on mine. Still dreaming I grabbed a cigarette and put it in my mouth. I felt like a teenager who just had his first kiss. I didn't want leave so I sat a few minutes behind the wheel smoking my cigarette. Suddenly, like magic all the light went out in the house and it was quiet. Sighing I finished my cigarette and regretted turning down Sarah's invitation.

CHAPTER 25

After John had left her, she closed the door and locked. She left the light burning in the entrance and went into the living room.

„ Bear? Come on. Where are you? Pst, pst, pst. Come I have something to eat for you!"

At the same time she grabbed the used glasses from the living room table and wanted to bring them into the kitchen. Just before entering the kitchen her cat stood in her way hissing like crazy into the kitchen. His fur was standing up and he had arched his back letting his claws show.

„ Sometimes you are just too much. How could you behave like this? What is wrong with you?"

As if he understood her, he stopped and started meowing walking around her feet. She went into the kitchen and turned on the lights, holding the glasses in her hand. Her kitchen was not that big, but she liked it. The build in kitchen cabinets were old but still in good shape. Opposite the cabinets were the sink unit and some counter space. Directly over the sink was a window. She closed and locked the window and closed the curtains as well. In the right corner in the back of the kitchen was a door that was leading to the basement. Sarah did not realize that the basement door was slightly open. She went over to the sink and called for her cat. She put the glasses into the sink. She opened a cabinet door where she had her large stock of cat food. She chose a can and closed the door again.

„ Come here, you greedy cat. Where are you hiding again?", she shouted and opened the can with an electric can opener.

„ Come on! Pst, pst, pst! Don't get on my nerves tonight. In a few hours the night is gone and I want to sleep a little bit before that, if you don't mind. I have a lot of work to do tomorrow and I need to sleep."

She put her hand on her mouth and starts yawning. She could barely stand on her feet from all this exhaustion. She had just decided to let the cat go and just go to bed, when he appeared and was walking between her feet. She went to the refrigerator, because next to that was the feeding bowl from bear, and she emptied the can in there. Then she turned and walked to the sink again and opened the door under it to throw away the empty can. Suddenly her hair stood up and in that moment all the lights went out. It all went so quickly, that she did not have any chance to turn around and see what was going on in her kitchen. She felt someone putting one hand on her hip and the other he covered her mouth. That someone held her so tight, he tried to free herself but she couldn't. She could hear her cat hissing like crazy and this made her feel even more scared. Desperate she tried to get his hand off her mouth so that she could scream, hoping that someone would hear her. As she could not get the enemy's hand off, she bit in it and had the taste of leather in her mouth. She didn't seem to have hurt her attacker at all with this bite, because he made no sound. Quite the opposite, he pulled her really hard and they left the kitchen and he dragged her up to the bed room. She kicked around her like crazy, in hope she could get free. The only thing she managed to do is for the attacker to grab her even harder and he got really wild. No sound came out of his mouth. When he pulled her to him one more time, Sarah managed to set herself free and ran away from him. He ran after her and grabbed her by the hair, pulling as hard as he can. She screamed in pain. Again, the intruder had her in his hands and this time he pulled out a hunting knife holding it against her neck. She became goose bumps and stood completely still when she felt the metal against her skin.

„ He will kill me like the other girls.", she thought and tears ran down her face. The tears ran all the way down her neck. She tried to hold herself together, but she couldn't and started shaking all over. Fear took over her body and she couldn't think straight anymore. She didn't know what else she could do to escape the attacker. She tried to think of something but she did not have the slightest idea what to do. Here back in the kitchen, in the dark she had lost her orientation and did not know where they were standing. If she could only get hold of a piece of furniture so she could recognize where she was. Or maybe she had luck and could make it to the door. She couldn't stand her fear. Not knowing if she would live or die, she summed up all her strength and tried to break free of his arms. The intruder, on the other hand, didn't want to leave her so they fought with each other. They bumped into her furniture and knocked over the chairs, she was kicking around in hope to kick him even once. The stranger managed not to get kicked once. He managed to get her on the floor, jumped on her on and put his hands around her neck starting to strangle her. Sarah desperately tried to get his hands off her neck but the stranger didn't move at all. On the contrary, he closed his hands even harder around her neck and slowly Sarah's strength was leaving her. Pure panic took over her brain and again and again she tried to get this, in leather wrapped, hands off her neck. Before her eyes she could see stars shimmering on and off, and she could barely breathe, her only thought was that she was dying. She needed to act fast, she only had a few seconds then she would be dead. One last time, with all her strength, she pulled up her leg and kicked him in the genitals. She felt his hands get off her neck and that he fell down next to her. This was her chance. She stood up and wanted to run past him, when he grabbed her by the leg. She fell on the floor again. Her hands landed in her cat's food. She knew now she was next to the refrigerator, so the door was only three meters away from her.

She jumped up and tried to run out of the kitchen when the stranger grabbed her again, smashing her against the floor tiles. They fought wildly with each other, but again he was the stronger one. While she was fighting him, she had the feeling that she heard someone calling her. She thought she was crazy, who would be around her house at this time, calling her, that would save her from her death. In this moment, she realized that he smashed something over her head. Then, in a second, she was in a different dimension. She passed out and everything went black around her. Her last thought was that he did it, he killed her.

CHAPTER 26

I sat in my car, smoking my cigarette and dreaming of Sarah's kisses. I must admit I was pretty aroused and could get her off my mind. I put out my cigarette in the car's ash tray and searched for my keys in my back pocket. Unfortunately, I couldn't find them. I searched in every pocket, but nothing.,, Damn it", I thought,,,I left the stupid key on the dresser". Shit. What should I do know? I looked over to Sarah's house and everything was dark. The only light was this at the entrance. She must have gone to bed already. I am so sorry I needed to wake her up now, but there was no other way. I needed my car key. I looked at my watch and realized that not even 10 minutes had passed since they said goodbye. It could be possible that she is not in bed jet. I opened the driver's door, got out of my car and walked to the house. I pressed Sarah's doorbell, but it didn't work. So I knocked loudly on the door and waited a few minutes. I got no answer. I knocked on the door again, a little bit louder, still nothing. When I knocked a third time a heard something heavy falling and I tried to listen carefully. I put my ear on the door and tried to make out some noises, but again everything was totally quiet.,, Sarah?" I called trough the door and waited for an answer, nothing.,,, Are you ok, Sarah?", I shouted louder and started getting really worried. Again, no answer. I felt my stomach turn; this was not a good sign. With my right shoulder I smashed against the door, but she did not open. I tried another three times when I finally made it. The door opened and made a loud noise smashing against the wall.

He hammered a heavy object on her head. Since it was completely dark in the kitchen he could not see what he grabbed. Judging from the shape, it must be a fruit bowl. Finally she was lying still on the floor and was not moving, that bitch. It took a lot of strength to get her to sit up, and then he leaned over and put her over his shoulder. He walked to the stairs that led to the upstairs. Heavily breathing he got up the steps and she almost fall from his back, but in the last minute he grabbed her and put her on his shoulders again in the right position. He was already once in her house so he knew where the bedroom was and didn't have to search long. He threw her on the bed and took a moment to get his breathing back. While he tried to breathe he looked at her, she was still unconscious. This came in handy. In her right hand he was holding his knife and quickly cut the straps of her top. The he worked on her jeans. He cut it off her body and threw it excited on the floor. He had to control himself, not to cut her throat open right now and sweat was running down his face. Since he had cut down all her clothes she was lying practically naked in front of him. All she had on was a tiny slip, which was showing more than it was hiding. He looked at her from top to bottom and all he could say was;,, You pitiful person!''. He stood next to her and stroked her neck with his knife. He kneeled next to the bed and made a invisible line from her throat down to her belly button. When he reached her belly button he decided to wake her with small slaps. He loved it when his victims where awake and could see and feel what is been done to them. Begging for their lives, as he slams his hunting knife in their flesh, they open their eyes in pure fear. He had just slapped her a couple of times, when he heard noise from downstairs.

,, What the hell…?'', he asked himself and stayed kneeling next to the bed, trying to listen into the dark. He could hear someone calling the name of this slut from the downstairs. He immediately recognized the voice of this man. It was this fucking investigator, who was messing with his work again. He didn't need that right now. Damn it! What was he still doing here? Didn't he drive away in his car? He left the woman lying there, got out the room and silently walked down the stairs.

I had just broken in the door when I reached for my gun, only to realize I didn't have it on me. I had left it in my car.,, What an idiot I am.'', I thought to myself. I thought about going back to get it, but I didn't want to waste any time and moved on. I entered and called Sarah's name. I got no answer from her. I didn't like that. I walked further and the cat came towards me, walking around my feet. I almost fell because of the cat but I got my balance back at the last moment.,, Oh, bear!'' I said quietly,,, You almost killed me!'' . I bent over and stroked him.,, Where is your mistress?" I asked him. As if he understood me he turned and walked out of the entrance hall and I followed him as quickly as I could in the dark. I stumbled on to some piece of furniture and silently swear. I didn't want to make a noise. Like a blind man I tried to find the living room but I couldn't make out anything. I tried to find the switch and I did after a few minutes. I pushed the switch a few times but nothing happened.,, What the hell is going on here?" Maybe a fuse was burned out and Sarah went to the fuse box to check it out. Maybe Sarah went down the basement stairs and fell and injured herself? I decided to go into the kitchen, to find the door to the basement and look for Sarah. In the dark I tried to orient myself and find the kitchen. I pulled out my lighter from my pocket and felt stupid that I didn't do that earlier. With the small flame it was easier to find my way to the kitchen. I found the basement door, in the back right corner of the kitchen and started walking towards it. Again, the cat walked around my feet and he was hissing like crazy. I didn't like that hissing it sounded like a warning, so I slowly opened the already half opened basement door. I put my hand with the lighter in first and all I could see was a platform with stairs going down to the basement. On the left hand side was the fuse box and I could see that one fuse was pulled out. I didn't like how that looked. Something was completely wrong here. I had just turned around to go back into the kitchen when I could feel a blow on the back of my head and fell on the tile floor. I laid there unconscious and did not move anymore.

Slowly he came down the stairs and listened into the darkness. After every second step he stood still. He was holding his hunting knife steady in his hand ready for a battle at any time. He was constantly hearing someone walking around the down floor. Who the hell could it be, interrupting him in his work? Could it be this fucking Detective? It couldn't be. He saw him getting in his car wanting to drive off. Could it be another intruder? But he wouldn't call the doctors name, would he? When he got downstairs he could hear that someone snuck into the kitchen. As the kitchen had two entrances it was easy to get in undetected and hide in a dark corner. He had just hidden in a corner when he saw a shadow come into the room. He could not see clearly who it was so he remained hidden and waited patiently. The figure stood still for a moment, then walked to the basement door and opened it. he had lit a lighter to find his way to the basement. If he would find the fuse box and the fuse, he would turn on the lights and see him. He couldn't let that happen. Silently he stood up and sneaked up behind the person, not making a sound. He could see that this person was looking at the fuse box and so he hit him on the back of his head with the fruit bowl he had taken of the table. Immediately the other guy fell unconscious on the floor and laid there. He didn't move anymore. He made a step forward and screwed the fuse in correctly and the kitchen filled with light. Then he turned to look at the person on the ground and recognized the Detective. That bastard! How could he still be here? Didn't he go to hell? He collected all his strength and kicked the Detective in the ribs. He was still lying on the floor not making any move. He looked at him with such hate that his face took an ugly expression. He wanted to cut his throat so badly. He had already put his blade on the Detectives throat ready to do it, but then decided not to. He did not want any more trouble. It was different killing a Detective that killing these whores. He kicked him again and left him there. He walked through the living room exciting the house from the balcony door into the night. This was his way in, so it would be the way out. He didn't even bother to close the door behind him. He jumped over the fence to the other side, which led to the forest. He needed to walk back about one and a half kilometer to get his car. While he was running to his car, he constantly looked over his shoulder to see if anyone was seeing him. But there was no one there on the whole way there. Finally he had reached his car. He got in and quickly started the motor.

My head was aching so bad, like it got smashed by a train. Everything was dark around me. On the back of my head I could feel a burn and my head was pounding. I tried to open my eyes but I couldn't and everything was turning making me feel sick. My chest was hurting on one side. < What the hell happened?> I wondered. Did I hit my chest when I fell? Slowly I lifted my right arm to feel my head. It felt like three hundred kilos. I felt the back of my head and realized I had the biggest bump I had ever had. I was lucky because there was no open wound, but as soon as I touched it, it stung like hell. Finally I managed to open my eyes and saw that the kitchen light was burning. Slowly I managed to sit up. I definitely needed a few moments to clear my head a little. Luckily I have a strong head that can stand a few bumps. Suddenly I remembered Sarah and jumped up. At one everything began to turn around me and I felt dizzy, but I didn't care. The only thing that mattered was to find Sarah.

Nothing would get in my way. I couldn't find her on this floor so I decided to walk up the stairs, as dizzy as I felt I put one foot in front of the other. I practically jumped up the stairs to get there a quickly as possible. On the left side where two doors that were closed and on the other side there were three, two locked and one open. For a moment I stood there trying to find out what door I should choose, then I decided to take the open one. I walked to the open door and as I stood there I saw Sarah lying on the bed, not moving at all. My heart was jumping. My strength had left me and I could not enter the room. From where I was standing I could see blood that had run down her neck and dried. Oh my God. He killed her. That bastard killed her. I had to hold on to the door frame because my feet wouldn't hold me any longer. I had no strength left. So I just slid down and just sat there in the door burying my face in my hands. Tears were running down my face and I was wiping them with my hands, as I looked on to the bed. I could not believe that I got there too late. I just wanted to get my shit together to go in the bed room, as I noticed a small movement on her. What was that? Did she really move or did my head play tricks on me? I couldn't see clearly because of the tears and I wanted to make sure that she moved. With slow movements I made my way to the bed and looked down at her. I tried to see if she had a pulse. And thank God. She did. I slowly sat on the bed next to her and put her head on my lap. Carefully I felt her head and could find any more wounds besides the one behind her ear. The blow she got on her head was hard but not fatal. As I could see she didn't need any stitching it was not that deep. I could feel that she was waking up because she was groaning in pain. I held her in my hands and slowly stocked her head. I constantly whispered her name into her ear so that she could feel that someone is there, taking care of her. She had her eyes still closed but I could see her pupils going back and forth under her eyelids. As I was holding her I put a blanket on her and I was rocking her like a child so that she would get warm again. She was in a state of shock so she needed to be kept warm. Slowly she opened her eyes. She must have understood where she was and everything that happened to her because she wanted to break free of my hands and run away from me. I held her firmly in my arms and tried to calm her down.

„ Come here, my girl. Everything is ok. You are safe now!", I whispered in her ear. She looked at me at must have remembered everything that took place in here. She held on to me tightly and looked me in the eyes and I could see how tears were running down from hers. I hugged her and she grabbed me like I was a life saver, saving her from drowning. I could feel my shirt get wet from her tears but I didn't care, I just wanted her to cry everything out. At this moment she realized that she was lying there half naked and she held the blanket on her tightly so it would not fall down. For a while she couldn't stop crying. I was still whispering in her ear and I could feel her relaxing. I slowly lifted her chin to look at her. Forty five minutes must have passed since she woke up. I realized that she had fallen asleep in my arms. I tried to stand up so I could lay her in the bed, but as soon as she realized I wanted to leave her alone she grabbed me.

„ Don't go, please!" she begged me.,, I am afraid to be alone!"

„ Darling, I will not leave you. I wanted to go into the kitchen, to get some water to drink. You are safe now. Alright?"

„ Yes, but be quick and sit down next to me again!"

I smiled at her and promised to be back as soon as I could. I turned and left the room. I was still feeling sick from the hit to the head and I was really thirsty. In the kitchen I opened some cabinets until I found glasses. I took two glasses and a jug out of the cabinet and filled he jug with cold water. Holding the jug and the glasses I had a look around this floor to see if everything was as it was supposed to be. I realized that the balcony door was open and went there to close it. Before I did I had a look out in the garden and could not see anything extraordinary. Whoever broke into the house must have left the house through this door. For the rest of the night we were safe, he was gone. I walked up into the bedroom and saw Sarah tightly wrapped with the blanket fast asleep. I left the glasses and the jug on the night stand. I sat next to her on the bed and watched her sleep. I needed to sleep too; otherwise I wouldn't make it tomorrow. It was only a few hours until morning so I took my clothes off and laid on the bed next to her. Carefully I pulled her closer to me and fell asleep too.

CHAPTER 27

He was finally home and didn't even bother to put his car in the garage. He left the car in the driveway and walked up to the house. He was swearing like a mad man, to calm himself, but he couldn't. His body was shaking out of anger and he couldn't get it under control. He took his keys out of his pocket and due to his shaking it took him three attempts to put it in the keyhole. He opened the door and slammed to shut behind him with a loud bang. He didn't care if anyone would notice. He took of his coat and shoes, while he was headed to the kitchen, and just threw them in a corner. His hands he formed into fists and threw a punch on the fridge, to let off some steam. He kept pounding on the fridge screaming: Why? Why? Why? This idiot Detective ruined everything again. Again he got in his way. That bastard! This had to end. He would show him. This would not happen again, because he promised himself he would be more careful from today on. No more mistakes. In his head he made a plan, how he could shut this damn Detective up and if necessary he would kill him. He didn't care about the risk anymore. He just needed a few days time to think, but he needed to calm himself down first, so that he would not make any more mistakes. That was very important. Tonight the Detective had won. But next time he would be the winner. The devil should take you, Detective Man! How could he be so stupid and go to the slut's house tonight? He let his feelings guide him and not his brain. Why couldn't he wait until he found the perfect plan? This way he could have finished the job with no mistakes. He was certain that he would drive off. How the hell should he know that the idiot would come back? He could not believe, what happened there tonight. It is no good for him to get this agitated, he saw that in today's outcome. It is this slut's fault, what happened to him tonight. Yes, all her fault. She didn't care about him at all. She didn't speak a word to him all evening and just sat there at the table like a plant. By the way she looked at him; he could see that she was disgusted by him. She didn't like him. This would soon change. Soon she wouldn't stop talking to him. She would beg him to talk to her. Not only that, she would beg him not to kill her. She had no right to treat him like this. He would show her. She would, as well, get her punishment. He put out the lights on this floor and went upstairs to the bedroom. He needed to sleep a few hours. It was the only way to clear his thoughts and get rid of this nasty headache. While he was walking to his bed he took off his clothes and left them on the floor. He pulled back the blanket and sat on the edge of the bed. He opened the drawer of the night stand and took out a packet of pain pills. He took two tablets without a sip of water. He swallowed them and got in the bed pulling the blanket up to his chin he tried to sleep. He had just fallen asleep, when he started dreaming about his mother again.

CHAPTER 28

Slowly I opened my eyes and looked at my watch. It was quarter past six. I must have slept about two hours, but I didn't feel at all relaxed. My ribs hurt and the bump on the back of my head was hurting as well. My headache became stronger by the minute. If I only had pain killers with me! I turned around and looked over to Sarah. She was still sleeping. I slid over to her and held her in my arms. I put my head next to hers and immediately the smell of lavender surrounded me. Carefully I took a curl of hers in my hand, wrapping it around my finger to play with it. On the back of her head was dried blood from a wound she had, when she was hit on the head last night. I looked closer at the wound and I could see that it would heal quickly. For a while I played with her curl and inhaled her smell. I enjoyed every second of it. As she was lying so close to me in bed and smelling her smell, it didn't take long and I felt like I was in heaven. The damage was already done; I could feel my Hercules getting hard. As if Sarah realized in her sleep what was going on, she woke up and turned to me. We looked each other in the eyes and nobody said a word. It felt like the time stood still. There was so much electricity in the air that I didn't want to say a word, not to ruin this moment forever. The smallest movement would ruin this perfect moment. I am not that kind of guy to take advantage of a situation, because I didn't know if Sarah was ready. I would let her make the first move. She almost died last night and got away only with few scratches, it was out of question that she would think about sex right now. Sarah came closer to me, constantly locking me in the eye. She smiled at me and without saying a word she started kissing me. She kissed me on the forehead, then on either of my eyes, then on my nose and then neck. I got goose bumps all over my body. Then she kissed the one spot on my body I hate the most, the scar on my chin. She kissed me so soft I could barely feel her kiss. They felt like electroshocks going through my body and I couldn't hold myself any more. I grabbed her by the shoulders and put her on top of me. We were still looking at each other face to face. In her eyes I could see a pain I have never seen in another woman I've met. I pulled her closer and kissed her softly. At the same time I was ashamed, thinking of everything she went through last night and that I had almost lost her forever. Only one touch of her was enough to make me feel like I was losing my mind. One kiss of her and my whole body was aching. I was shaking all over and could hold it together any more. One kiss after the other and I could feel Sarah getting more and more willing, erotically moving her body on mine.

„ Make love to me!" she whispered in ear and bit me softly.

„ Are you sure?" I asked and enjoyed the biting on my ear.

„ Yes, I am absolutely sure. Love me, like it is the last time in our lives!" she answered and kept looking me in the eye.

Now nothing could hold me back and we kissed passionately. I never thought I could desire a woman so hard in my life. I pressed my lips on hers and immediately she opened her mouth and let my tongue in. Our tongues plaid with each other and it felt like she wanted to eat me up. Like wild we rolled around on the bed and the sheets wrapped around us. I pulled her under me kissing her passionately. I slowly went down to her breasts; I took them in my hand and massaged them gently. Her nipples stood hard in the air and I took them into my mouth licking on to them. She moaned in pleasure and held her body in a way I understood she wanted more. I went down with my tongue from her breasts to her belly button. Her abs twitched and I could see that she wanted to play a little more, because she opened her legs. From her belly button I went further down to her weak spot. She moaned full of lust. She was lying on her elbows and had left her head lean back. She put her hands on the back of my head stroking me while I was making love to her. She didn't need long to come and small screams of lust came out of her mouth. Her face became red and she was panting. Still panting she stood on her knees and pushed me under her. She took my Hercules in her hand and with her movements swelled him up again. She stroked him as gently as no other woman before. I was not sure how long I could hold myself not to come. I pulled her closer to my face and kissed her so hard, like an animal wanting to devour her. I wanted to get her under me but in one movement she was sitting on top of me moving her behind in rhythmical movements. Her long blond hair was moving with her and she kept riding me until we both came. Exhausted she laid on my stomach. I held her face gently in my hands and kissed her. She got off of me and laid down next to me. With a low voice I asked her-,, Did you enjoy it?" She kissed me and answered me:,, Yes, I enjoyed it a lot!" She put her head on my chest and why staid like this for a while. Sarah took my hands and stroked them gently. She looked at me and passed her hand over my scar.

,, How did you get this scar…?" She wanted to ask me but I didn't let her finish and kissed her. Of course I knew what she wanted to ask me but the issue with my scar was still very fresh and I didn't want to talk about it. I didn't want to hurt her feelings by not answering so I said:,, I will tell you the story another time, if that's ok with you!"

,, Why?"

,, Because if we don't get out of bed now, we would get on the base to late. Did you forget? Today at ten is the funeral of Pamela Simpson. Come on, we must get dressed."

,, You are right. I had totally forgotten about the funeral, with all of this here. I am sorry!" she answered.

,, I can totally understand why you forgot about the funeral, darling. With everything that went on here last night it's totally normal. We are both overwhelmed with different feeling that matters like this get lost in our head. You don't need to feel sorry about that. By the way, have you looked at your neck yet? I can see the fingers of your attacker."

,, Really?", she asked in shock.

Quickly she jumped out of the bed, went into the bathroom and stood in front of the mirror. She pulled her hair back and inspected her throat. She went over it with her hands and couldn't believe her eyes. I stood behind her and put her arms around her hips, kissing the back of her neck.

,, My hair is totally sticky from the dried blood. I must wash them. I don't know what to do about my neck, so that no one can see the marks. It is better if I wear a shirt and close the collar, what do you think?"

,, I will give you a piece of advice now. The best thing is to put a light scarf around it and don't tell a word to anyone about the attack last night. Ok?"

„ Why should nobody know about this?"

„ I have my reasons!"

„ Don't tell me that you want to hold Colonel Silk responsible for this. You cannot be serious, are you? When and how should he have the time to follow us here and to this to me? And how should he know where I live?"

„ I don't know, but I swear, I will find out. If it was him, I will rip him apart and make him pay for it. Believe me "

CHAPTER 29

For the funeral I wore my uniform and waited in my car. I had parked my car in front of the building of the military police. Sarah and I had arranged to meet here, because I didn't want anyone to find out about our affair seeing us together. So I had left her this morning and drove back to my hotel room to put on a clean uniform. I wanted to close this case first and then let everyone could know about us, but at the moment I didn't want to put her in more danger. I swore I would take better care of her and keep her safe. I got out of my car and entered the building. At the reception I asked if someone asked for me or left me any messages. The soldier at the reception checked my credentials and handed me a stack of messages. I thanked him and sat down at an empty desk to read them in peace. Just opposite the desk was a coffee machine with freshly brewed coffee and I stood up to get a cup. Holding the coffee I sat back down at the desk and went through the messages. A few minutes after I sat down, Sarah walked in the building. She saw me as soon as she walked in, came over smiling at me and pulled herself a chair to sit next to me. I stood up and poured her a cup of coffee bringing it to her. She thanked me and smiled. She was also wearing a uniform and had a scarf wrapped around her neck so that no one could see the marks. We talked silently about last night and what happened. We touched secretly so that no one would notice and that made me feel overjoyed. We were so caught up in our talk, that we didn't realize that Colonel Silk entered the building. At the last moment I saw him and give Sarah a small push under the table so she would notice him too. He looked a little bit tired and confused, as if he had a rough night. He was wearing a uniform too for the funeral. I inspected him from head to toe, gave Sarah a sign and she understood at once. She offered him a chair at our table and he accepted thankfully. He looked like a crazy professor and he was constantly messing around with his uniform. Without any hesitation I said:,, Colonel Sir, you don't look very good this morning. Are you not feeling well? You look like you had a rough night. You must have been partying too long last night! ''

I was hoping he would notice the irony in my voice and I was sure he would bite the bait.

,, No, Mister Man, I didn't party last night. I was in my office all night working; I had a lot to do. The past few days the work has gone up and I need to finish as soon as possible to show my results to my superiors. If you mean that by partying all night then yes, I did!"

,, Could someone verify that?" I asked with a sweet look.

,, What?", he asked surprised.

,, That you worked late last night!"

He seemed to think about it, although I was sure that he was prepared for this question from me. He had an alibi that was bullet proof.

,, Why would you ask about my alibi from last night? Is there a problem, maybe a new corpse I haven't heard about?" with these words he looked over to Sarah.

,, No, thank God. It is mainly out of curiosity. You know, it is a habit that comes with the job, always to ask about someone's alibi. Once a Detective, always a Detective!" I answered with a smile.

While I was talking to the Colonel, Sarah had left the table. As an excuse she said she wanted to find an ashtray to light a cigarette. She found one and put it next to the coffee machine opposite of us and watched us talk. She was nervously playing around with her scarf and had an expressionless look on her face, I wanted to know what she was thinking about.

My look went over to the Colonel again and I told him:

,, After the funeral I would like you to go back to your office and work on these profiles I asked you."

,, Of course. I don't know how long it will take to finish them."

,, I don't mind. The earlier you start, the sooner you will finish. Don't you think?"

He looked as if he wanted to contradict me, but he didn't. The Colonel stood up and exited the building. It seemed to me as if he was just a shadow of the man I met a few days ago. Something was bothering him and I needed to find out what it was.

I stood up, took the cups and walked to Sarah, who was still standing next to the coffee machine. After I poured two cups of coffee, I turned to her and started talking.

„ This case seemed difficult to crack, but from the beginning I had the answer under my nose. Just now everything becomes clearer and I understand what went on here."

I wanted to explain to her what I meant, but in this moment my boss, Jack Osborne, walked in and interrupted us. Out of respect for him and because he was my superior, I stood still and saluted him, while the strong build man was walking towards us. He stopped in front of me and nodded, he looked through the room and then we shook hands. I offered him a chair at the desk and we sat down, while Sarah was still standing next to us. I offered Sarah my chair and so I sat on the desk. Jack was wearing his official uniform as we all did. He took off his cap and threw it on the table. Jack was once an infantryman, as was I. we were on separate units in the Golf war almost at the same time. So, our uniforms had almost the same medals and orders.

„ Coffee, Sir?"

„ No, thank you. I have had three this morning. I must be careful otherwise I will have a caffeine shock."

We talked for a few minutes and then we got to the point. I smiled at him, because this was my boss: first a little small talk and then straight to business.

„ Tell me a little bit about the investigation. You didn't call me the past two days and that's why I made the effort to come here to see you."

„ Yes, Sir!"

I began to tell him about the findings so far, from the laboratory unit that had examined almost everyone around this case. I left the best bit for the end, the attack on Sarah. I told him every detail. Then I told him about my suspicion against Colonel Silk. The good thing was that he was hearing my report without interrupting me once. Only at the end of my report he asked me some questions that burned on his tongue. I saw in his expression that he was totally confused and looked at me and then at Sarah. He had a lot of information to process. He sat upright in his chair and crossed his arms, like an old man who is waiting for the answer to a rhetorical question. For a few minutes he remained still not saying a word. I knew he was thinking about it. I knew him all too well. Maybe he had his doubts about my statement, but in the end he believed me, because he knew he could trust me. I was not by chance the best man on the team. My boss looked at his watch.

„ Isn't it about time to go to church?"

He got up from his chair and we did the same thing. We grabbed our caps, put them on and left the building. We all got in my car and I offered Jack the front seat, next to me. Of course, I needed to hear his bleating about my car again. How often he had told me to get a new car. I just let him go on and didn't bother about what he said about my car. While we were driving to the church of the base he asked me:

„ You are absolutely sure that this guy killed her, right?"

„ I believe, yes. No, wrong answer. I am absolutely certain who killed her, but I need time, to collect more evidence. Only then I can nail the bastard."

„ Do you mind expressing yourself a little bit better and give me a clearer picture. Say it with easier words!"

„ Like I have told you, I have my suspicion, different hearings and some laboratory results. I just need a little bit more time to compare evidence and then, only then, I will get matters rolling, as I think it is right. I don't want to make any mistakes and then loose the whole thing."

„ This means that you are not yet ready to arrest the Colonel and charge him. Did I get this right?"

„ No. Not yet. I need two or three days more for a few more tests. The results must match absolutely."

I stopped the car in the parking space in front of the church. It was a big, old building that was build out of red brick stones in a Victorian style. The church was meant for military weddings, funerals and Sunday mass. We got off the car and stood under a large tree that was protecting us from the strong sun. The parking space was almost full and soon other cars had to park on the street in front of the church. While we were waiting for the ceremony to begin, Colonel Silk sneaked by. With sneaked I mean that he walked past us like an old man, not bothering about his surroundings. As he saw us he just nodded and continued walking his way. I turned to Jack.

„ This is Colonel Silk!"

Jack followed the man with his eyes as he was entering the church.

„ He does not look scared or nervous at all. He looks like an old man. Are you sure you mean him?" he asked surprised.

„ Believe me. He is fooling us. He really is scared and nervous but he has learned how to hide it very good."

My boss nodded understanding.

„ If you are right and if you can prove that he is our guy, then you have solved the case. But if you are after the wrong man, so help us God. We must find a good place where we can hide. You know that, right?"

„ Yes, Sir, absolutely. This is why I am working on this case 24/7, to make no mistakes."

„ You must get him to come out in the open and confess his actions."

„ Yes I know, if he would do that we would be done with the case in a moment."

„ You know that people would confess the strangest things if you give them the opportunity and listen to them. The killer is carrying a heavy burden inside of him and he needs to share it with someone. This does not come from the fact that he killed and he knows about it, it is because this burden is too heavy for him and he needs to get rid if it...."

He continued talking about this subject, and was only saying things I already know and I had no intention of hearing them again. The only thing I cared about was his permission to push Colonel Silk in a corner and finish him. I looked over to the church. The coffin had arrived and was already placed inside the church. Only a small group of reporters and TV crews were selected to be here. The only photographer that was here was from the military press release office. Jack gave me a sign that meant we should go inside the church, so we did. We walked up the stairs and entered the church. We all signed in the churches guest book and went further in the building. It was not cooler in here than under the tree we were standing under outside. We looked around and realized that all the seats were taken, so we had to stand during the funeral. The church organ was playing a sad song. I could see how many of the guests were wiping their eyes dry from the tears that ran down. I hadn't made a decision if I should go to the coffin or not, it was located next to the altar. After a few minutes I made the decision to go and Sarah and Jack followed me. A stood exactly in front of the coffin and looked down to the dead girl. She looked peaceful. Her head was placed on a pink satin cushion and her blond hair surrounded her face. She was wearing her official white uniform. This uniform was meant for ceremonies and festivities. I had a last look at her, made a cross and went on so that the other people behind me had their turn. While we were walking on the central path of the church, we found some free seats and sat down. The military priest, Officer Penn, stepped behind the altar. He was wearing a simple uniform. Priest Penn began his speech and everyone went silent, until you could hear no sound in church.

,, Dearly bellowed relatives and friends, we have gathered here today, before god and the church, to say fare well to our daughter Pamela Simpson…!"

The mass continued with hymns, songs and prayers. Some of her friends stepped up saying a few nice words, which I was certain were all true. Some of these words were quit touching and I could see a lot of the female guests drying their tears. The organ began playing again and Priest Penn began the last psalm. When he was ready he blessed the dead with the words:,, Rest in peace, my daughter!"

The guests stood up and made a cross. It was a simple but nice ceremony. The six companions of the coffin were also dressed in white uniforms; they stood up from their seats and placed themselves in front of the coffin. The four lifters of the coffin stood left and right of it. The four lifters lifted the coffin lid and closed it; on top of it they placed the American flag. Every one took their place and lifted the coffin in the air. Priest Penn led the way and the family followed, then the friends, soon every person in the room had stood up from their seats and had turned to the way the coffin was passing through, saluting it.

As the priest exited the church the six men following split up and let the four men with the coffin pass through. They saluted the dead as the coffin exited the church and the rest of the people in the church followed as well. The coffin was put on the loading space of a jeep, and then tied so that it would not fall of. On the street before the church stood cars ready to escort the jeep with the coffin. You must know that every soldier that is serving here on the base has the right to be buried on the base's cemetery with all honors. Pamela Simpson's body was to be send back to her home town, she was getting a place in her family's grave. Either way, if you were a general or just a simple soldier, you were saluted with twenty rifle shots. As on any funeral people were walking up and down until they found a place and stood still. Some were talking silently, others wanted to talk to the priest and others to give the family their condolences. I was watching the reporters that were thinking who to interview so that they could get one more story about the dead than their colleagues. So they ran up and down looking for people. You could spot the military photographer from miles away; he was the only one making pictures not bothering anyone and not saying a word. From what I read in the newspapers, they had mentioned the killing of Pamela Simpson without mentioning any suspects. But how could they know anyway what was going on here? They only said that the investigations are in full speed. Citizens were assured that they could soon sleep safely. Luckily they didn't know what was going on here on the base, otherwise the military would ruin its reputation. My eyes caught my boss, wildly chatting with General Pilot. They were talking silently but I could see that the General was not the same opinion as my boss. Or maybe he was? The General nodded his head. As I knew that I would soon hear about what my boss discussed with the General, I looked around and found Sarah chatting to some friends. They must be colleagues from the hospital and the talked silently. I must say I was proud of her, how she handled the whole situation. I always tried to avoid funerals and such sad occasions because I never knew quite what to say. She looked at me and left her colleagues to come to me.

„ We must go now, to be at the airport in a few minutes!"

„ Alright" I answered and said goodbye to some people I met here at the funeral.

I gave Jack a sign and we all walked together to the car. While we were walking we bumped into Colonel Silk. He excused himself for been so clumsy and by the chance I introduced him to Jack. The usual politeness followed. I am glad to meet you and such. Jack wanted to shake the Colonel's hand but he didn't bother about his hand. On the contrary, he didn't even look at Jack again. He turned to me and ignored Jack and Sarah completely.

„ I will be in my office around two. If you are so kind as to come by, I will have the profiles ready you wanted Mister Man."

„ Thank you for your interest and help. See you at two then."

We said goodbye and he left our small group. I watched him get into his car and drive off. He didn't seem to want to escort the coffin to the airport to say goodbye to the dead girl. We got into my car and, lucky for us, the air-conditioning worked just fine today so I put it on full power. We followed the line of cars that were heading to the north side of the base to the airport. Sarah sat in the back seat in the middle so that she could be between me and Jack and could talk to us.

„ The funeral was nice, wasn't it?"

We both nodded and continued sitting silently in our seats. Jack could not stay silent for long and so he started talking.

„ John, are you certain that the Colonel is our guy?"

„ Yes, Sir!"

„ Who else knows about this suspicion?"

„ Only you, her and the General."

„ Let it be this way."

Sarah interrupted our discussion and wanted to give her comment:

„ Do we have to talk about this subject? Don't we have time for that later?"

„ My boss has the right to get informed about the case any time he wants!"

Sarah looked at me surprised; she sat back in her seat and looked out the window. She didn't say another word to us. I watched Jack from the corner of my eye, who was also quite confused by my answer to her. He looked at me with a giant question mark on his forehead and raised one eyebrow. This was the sign that he knew something was up, he just didn't know what.

„ My friend, can I ask you something? I hope not, that…?"

I didn't let him finish his sentence.

„ Don't you dare say another word! You have no right to interfere with my personal life!"

„ But I haven't said anything. Yet! You know that you should never start a relationship with a suspect, a victim or anyone crucial to a case. This is perfectly clear to you, isn't it?" he said quietly and looked out the window.

He let it go and for a while we remained sitting next to each other, not saying a word. Sarah sat offended on the back seat and, I was sure, that he understood exactly what was going on and played dumb. Would we be alone he would chew me out. A hundred percent! This was the only thing missing, that my boss would mess with my personal life. I tried to avoid his look and looked out on the road. It was around noon and the sun was very hot. You could see the heat rising up from the asphalt. We were still following the cars to the airport. We passed several buildings and observation towers. I felt sorry for the poor guys that had to stand still in the heat saluting every car that drove by them. Finally we reached the airport; we held on a huge hangar and parked the car in front of the airport hall. We got off the car and stood with the rest of the people, to get through this part of the funeral as well. We lined up on a prearranged spot and everyone that was in the church was assembled here. It seemed as the military band and the shooters for the honorary rifle shots had arrived as well. As soon as the band saw the car line, it started playing a grieving song that was only interrupted by the humming from the Jumbo C-130. The four men escorting the coffin lifted it from the jeep and let it on the ground for a few seconds. Then they took position again and lifted it up again, walking into the open tail of the C-130. Again we all saluted and watched the coffin enter the plain. The men put it down in the plain and held the flag up on all four corners. Priest Penn spoke the last words:,, Lord let her shine in eternal light, amen!" The shooters held their rifles up and shot three times into the sky. Shortly the trumpet blew the last tune. The coffin companions folded the flag and handed it to Priest Penn. He gave the flag to a young woman, which I found out was the victim's sister. Suddenly, without any warning the plain started its engines making a very loud noise. The dead girl's sister walked up the ramp and it closed behind her. An air traffic controller with earmuffs on, so his ears will not get numb from the noise, was giving signs to the plain to start. The huge plain started rolling on the runway. As it was speeding up the sound it made was so loud it was just bearable to the ears. It gain on speed and then took off. After a few minutes it was only a dot in the sky after in vanished into the blue. Today was a great day for a funeral.

CHAPTER 30

,, I will give you two more days to close the case! If you do, perfect. If not, you hand all the files and everything you got over to the FBI and get it over with."

,, But…?" I wanted to ask.

,, No but. I just spoke with the Minister of Defense and he was not very friendly. In two days they cut of our heads if you haven't solved the case. Is this clear?"

And again he stated with his nagging and wining. This was typical, he had to play boss and kick me in the butt again. I know he was right; I wanted to close this case as soon as possible myself. But this was near impossible; I am not a miracle worker. I understand that he has a lot of pressure on himself but what did he want from me? If I was a fairy godmother I had already done my magic. He was still complaining but I didn't listen to him anymore and started looking at my papers and notes. He realized that I had stopped listening to him and so he stopped talking.

,, Are you ok?" he asked me with a strange tone in his voice and I looked at him.

,, To tell you the truth, so good as today I haven't felt in a while. Why are you asking?"

,, Just out of curiosity. Is that ok?"

,, No, it is not ok, I think, no, I am certain, that you don't need to know everything!"

,, What's going on with you and the cute one?"

,, Are you asking me as my boss or as a friend?"

,, Let us say as a good old friend that is worried about you. So, what is going on between you?"

„ Nothing is going on, and if it did, I would never tell you!"

„ Good. You know that I care about what is going on in your life. Besides your boss, I am also a good friend and I want to know if you are ok. I am on your side and always will be. Never forget that."

For a few minutes we looked at each other in silence, and then he grabbed his bag and his cap and stood up. We shook hands.

We will hear from each other in two days. I hope that you solve the case by then and we can all take a breather afterwards."

I nodded and escorted him out of the building where my office was located. I watched him go down the stairs and sit in his car. Before he closed his door he shouted:

„ Don't forget you have a two o'clock appointment. Go nail this son of a bitch!"

We saluted each other and smiled. I waited for him to drive off and then I headed to my meeting.

I looked at my watch and realized that I had only ten minutes to my appointment. Good thing that my small office was in the same building as his. So I didn't have to drive in this heat.

While I was walking to the Colonel's office I was lost in my thoughts. I thought about the case and I was sure that if I would hand this case over to someone, it wouldn't haunt me for the rest of my life. Jack threw a bone at me and I, the idiot, ran after it. I wanted to solve this case as soon as possible and be done with it do get of this base. I needed to clear my head and see what I wanted to do with my life. But Jack was always a step ahead and needed to push me. From the fucking moment I turned down this case, this case was mine. I needed to do some serious thinking. It was my life that was at stake and no one could talk into that. Deep inside I had already made my decision, without even realizing it. The only thing I wanted was a lot of luck so that everything went smoothly. Then Jack and his military could go to hell. I couldn't stand any of them anymore. Twenty five years in the service was a long time. I was so lost in my thoughts, that just at this moment I realized that I was already standing in front of the desk of Secretary Stone. I smiled and thought:„Now, I got you!"

As soon as the secretary saw and recognized me, he stood up and saluted me.

„ Good day, Soldier Stone. How are you today?"

„ Good, Sir, and you? What can I do for you?"

„ I have an appointment with Colonel Silk at two. Please inform him that I am here!"

„ I would like to do that, Sir, but Colonel Silk is not in his office!"

„ That's odd. Maybe I didn't get him right? I was under the impression that he is been here for a few hours. We saw each other at the funeral and I am pretty sure he said two o'clock."

„ Are you certain?"

„ Of course, I am!"

All that felt strange to me. I didn't know what it was, but I needed to think.

„ When did you start your shift today, Soldier?"

„ Today morning at eight, Sir?"

„ And the Colonel has not been into his office, yet?"

„ Something was wrong, I was sure, that this morning the Colonel told me he is going to his office and stay there to work on those profiles. Did he maybe want to disappear and wanted to trick me so that I wouldn't realize? Everything looked really suspicious.

„ Sir, if you want, have a seat and wait for him. If the Colonel said he is going to be here at two, he must be on his way.

At the same time he pulled a chair to the desk and offered it to me. Confused I sat down. He brought me coffee and now I was sitting here in his stupid chair, thinking and drinking coffee. If he wanted to flee they all would kick my ass. To hell with it. At least I would get rid of the case! But as a cop I couldn't allow myself to let my last case slip away like this. I had no choice and started asking questions.

„ Last night you must had a lot of work, this is why the Colonel was working so late, right?"

„ No, Sir, not really. I got of work at the same time as usual."

„ What time was that?"

„ My shift ended around ten. Why?"

„ Nothing, just curiosity. The Colonel left work with you, right?"

„ No, I don't think so. He stayed in his office when I left."

„ Aha. You left him here in his office. This means you don't know when he left?"

„ That's correct, Sir. I have no idea when he left."

„ Do you maybe know if he worked with someone?"

„ You must know, Sir, the Colonel is a very private man and works with no one. The past few months I work here I have never seen him working with anyone."

„ Aha."

Now we come to the good bit and I wanted to know more. I played innocent and wanted to get more information from the secretary. This was my chance. That meant that the Colonel had no alibi for last night. When his secretary left he could come and go how he wanted without telling anyone. The secretary pulled me out of my thoughts.

„ Around two o'clock at night I walked past the building and could see light still burning in the Colonel's office!" he said without lifting his eyes from the paperwork he was working on.

Damn it. This could have two explanations. One, the Colonel really worked all night in his office and was innocent, and two, he could have left the light burning to give himself an alibi. But, when he got of the base he must have passed the gate, and it was obligatory for everyone to report leaving the base and get noted in a book.

„ Are you sure it was two o'clock?"

„ It could even be two thirty. I had gone out with a couple of friends and drank a little bit more, if you understand what I mean."

„ Yes, I do understand."

While I was still sitting in this chair the door from the Colonel's office opened. The Soldier jumped of his chair and saluted Colonel Silk and stood still.

„ Good day, Sir. How are you? I didn't see you get in your office!"

When the Colonel realized who was sitting there in the chair he looked at both of us confused. He must have realized he made a mistake. After saluting the secretary he looked at me with an evil look. A look that I never wanted to see again, full of hate. He got his thoughts back together and tried to mask his embarrassment with a smile.

„ Good afternoon, Stone. Finally I find you behind your desk again. So, can you be so kind and bring me a cup of coffee, no two cups, I can see Mister Man is here. I must ask you for a few more minutes so I can finish some paperwork and then it is your turn. Then we can talk in my office in peace!"

He left a pail of documents on the desk and went back into his office without saying a word.

„ What the hell was that?" the Soldier asked himself, without taking his eyes of the door. Then he got up and prepared the Colonel's coffee. I was watching him and I could see that he was really upset and angry. He might be right about it and so I continued.

„ What are you saying, my boy?" I asked nicely, so he wouldn't understand that I was questioning him.

„ Didn't you hear what he said? That he finally finds me in my seat? I swear to you, I haven't moved from this office from eight o'clock this morning. I haven't left for a minute. How can he lie about that?"

„ Maybe he didn't see you here and thought you were off with some important business and left your desk."

„ No, Sir. I am sitting here since this morning. I have so much work finishing all this paperwork until my shift is over. I didn't even have time to go to the toilet!"

He put the cup on a tray and took it in his left hand. He walked to the door, knocked and disappeared from my eyes. While Soldier Stone was serving him the coffee I put my cup on the desk and jumped up off my chair. With quick steps I walked from one side of the room to the other inspecting it carefully. I needed to see if there was another entrance to this room that Soldier Stone didn't know about. In every corner I looked I couldn't find anything. My world fell apart, because I believed, no I was sure that there was still another entrance in this building that no one knew about. How was it possible for him, to get in his office without the secretary seeing him? Was the soldier a layer, taking every excuse to sneak of his post? But he didn't look like one. This didn't add up, because Secretary Stone was really pissed when the Colonel told him that he was not at his desk all day. Nobody could pretend that well, so I trusted the Soldier. The door to the office opened suddenly and Soldier Stone came out informing me that it was ok for me to go in, he was waiting for me. I grabbed my bag and went inside the office. Like the first time I entered this office I became depressed, I absolutely didn't feel right in here. I cannot explain what it is that gave me these feelings. Maybe the color of the walls or the Colonel himself that made me feel sick.

„ Sit down please. In about a minute I will be ready and then we can go on."

He didn't even look at me and kept on signing papers. As he was not looking at me at all, I took the chance to look around his office. As I was looking for a hidden door, I searched every centimeter of the walls with my eyes. Where could that door be?

The only entrance I could see besides the door were three windows, two of them where a normal window size and one was slightly larger than the others. In front of every window were hanging heavy curtains that were all closed. He did that probably to prevent the heat from outside to come in.

„ So, Mister Man. I am ready for you now. We can talk about these profiles now."

He talked really sweet but he couldn't fool me. This man was seriously clever. While he was talking, he opened a drawer, pulled out some files and put them on the desk. He pushed them to me and left them there. I didn't bother about them and continued looking at him, without letting him know what I was thinking about. He must have realized that I was thinking about something important so he cleared his throat, to make me notice him. I looked at the files. On every file he had written –confidential-. I counted the files and noticed that they were from all four victims. How did he manage, to get this done so quickly?

„ Thank you for your help on the profiles. I am sure that it was a lot of work for you but you found the time to do them to help me. You have no idea how helpful this is for me? I owe you one!"

„ Leave those formalities aside. I will stand next to you as good as I can and I am sure you will appreciate it, right?"

We looked each other in the eye. I couldn't really read him. He smiled, but his eyes remained ice cold. His eyes reminded me those of a rat that you had caught in a corner and knew it couldn't get out. The rats waited then for the right moment to strike back.

„ Yes, I am sure you want to help me as good as you can. As I can see you have a lot of work here, can you tell me what all these papers are about?"

„ I am sorry. I am not allowed to reveal anything. It is all strictly confidential! Not that I don't want to tell you, but you know what happens when confidential files get leaked, don't you?"

„ Yes, I understand! Then I will let you go back to work. I don't want to disturb you any longer. Ana again, thank you for your help."

We got up at the same time and the Colonel gave me his sticky hand to shake. I shook his hand. His hand was sweaty and so was his face. I left him in his office and closed the door behind me. Only as I was sure the door was closed I took out a tissue to wipe of my hand dry.

CHAPTER 31

B ack in my office, I sat at my desk with the profiles of these dead
women and started reading them carefully. The files did not include
their whole military carrier, only their psychological profile. This means
that in there was documented how they reacted to a certain experiment.
These experiments consisted of rhetoric questions and psychological tests
that were done to one person. There was also this experiment where the
doctor showed the person some figures and wanted to know what they saw.
The psychiatrist works close together with a person in order to create their
profile and then to decide if this person is fit for certain military actions
or trainings. In front of me I had the profile of Sonny Smith and I read it.
The report of her superior was surprisingly good. To tell the truth with an
Admiral as a father, I did not expect anything less. The military tests that
Sonny had to take were full of medals. Only in one test the girl had not
such a good result, the intelligence test. She was not so clever and so she
got an average note. The psychological report of the psychologist wrote:

Soldier Sonny Smith is very energetic, smart and committed person
that could handle any situation.

From the interview with Soldier Sonny and from the entire tests that
were taken, I could not see any psychological disorder, mood swings, and
disorders of the stress system or schizophrenia.

I conclude hereby that Soldier Smith has no psychological problems
that could be harmful for her carrier or be a danger to her colleagues. She
can absolutely proceed to her post.

Someone knocked at the door and I shouted <enter!>. I waited for the
door to open and Sarah came in my office. In her hand she held a tray

with two cups of hot coffee. The smell of the coffee hit me immediately and it felt really good.

„ I am sorry for coming so late, but I needed to go home and change.”

„ Its ok, thank you for the coffee.”

I smiled at her; she put the cups on the desk and pulled a chair to sit next to me. She looked curious to the files and asked me:

„ What are you looking at?”

„ These are the psychological profiles that Colonel Silk prepared for me.”

„ And? Did you find anything suspicious?”

„ Unfortunately not. All four women had similar background. None of them had psychological problems.”

„ This sounds good, or not?”

„ Yes, it really sounds good. So, we need to talk about the suicides. How could it be, that four healthy, physically and mentally committed suicide? Because if I should believe these profiles these women were perfectly fine and happy!”

„ You are right. That is odd! This can only mean that your suspicion that these women were murdered is true. Can we prove that? Do you have an idea how we could do that?”

„ Not yet. My boss gives me two more days to solve this fucking case!”

„ Only two days?”

„ Yes, only two days. He is under a lot of pressure from his superiors. Jack cannot do anything different.”

I read these profiles again and Sarah drank her coffee silently. But my thoughts were far away from these files now.

From the corner of my eye I watched Sarah who was busy with a pile of paperwork and didn't bother about me anymore. She tried to help as well as she could. People have become hard and unapproachable and I have become soft. I am not as hard as I used to be and I felt like an old man exhausted and rusty. Maybe the problem was that I was constantly traveling to work on different cases. I was not long enough in one place: Florida today, Washington tomorrow and the day after? Where would the day after find me? Where would my boss send me for the next days? The only thing I needed now is to be in one place for a little longer. Again, I was watching Sarah without her realizing it. I want to know her better;

I mean I don't want it to be only a one night thing. I wanted to be with her as long as it could possibly be. I want to know what she wants in life, if she wants to marry and have children or not. This was not about me, it was about her. Does she want to be with me or am I only a pastime? I closed the files and put them aside. I needed to sleep as much as I needed something to eat. Only now I realized how much hungry I was.

„ Sarah, I am hungry! Are you hungry maybe?"

„ To tell you the truth, I am. Do you want to us to go together or should we order something and eat it here?"

„ I think it is better if we order something; we still have a lot of work to do. We shouldn't postpone it."

Sarah took the phone in her hand and I heard that she ordered two pizzas and two cold beers. In less than twenty minutes our order had arrived and in less than five minutes we had eaten the pizzas and drank the beers. We lit a cigarette and tried to digest our food.

„ That pizza was really good, don't you think?"

„ Yes, really. And if I can fill you in on a little secret, if I hadn't eaten anything, I would have fainted."

We both laughed loudly and then got back t our files. I took my keys out of my pocket and opened the file cabinet to get Colonel Silk's file. I wanted to read it once more, to make sure I hadn't missed anything.

- The psychiatrist name is Thomas Silk.
- He was born 1963 in Baltimore and was an only child.
- At the age of fifteen he became an orphan.
- His parents died in a fire in their home.
- The fire started in the late afternoon and the Colonel was not at home, this was the reason he was spared from it and only the parents died.
- Some people saw them in front of the house and asked him about his parents but they couldn't get an answer from him. They said he was probably in a shock.
- After the fire, that destroyed the whole house, he had no other relatives except an aunt, the mother's sister. So the court decided to send him there give her the custody.
- Three months later the boy was brought to a military school.

- After military school he did his obligatory service.
- After his service he joined West Point Academy.
- He finished the academy with high scores and honors.
- He decided to transfer to another school and went to the school for information and officers.
- After that he went to a school in Georgetown to get his degree as a psychiatrist.
- Twenty years have passed from when he got his degree and he is in the military since that.
- He had some other postings before he landed here in Fort Creek.
- He lives in a house outside the base.
- He is not married and lives alone.
- He had not one report in his file; he had never caused trouble for a superior and got along with everyone.
- He was a loner that was committed to his work.

I closed the file and let it on the table; I had to think about the person Silk. No one could have such a clean file as Silk. Even I have a few dark spots in my file.

I picked up the telephone and dialed a secret number only a few people knew. The number was from a friend who was working at the Pentagon. He had his hands in espionage and all the information not everyone knew. I was certain he was working for the CIA. He had information about anyone and anything. To tell the truth I didn't even want to know more about his job. It is better not to know anything than to know something. I heard the phone ring a few times and then someone picked it up on the other end.

„ Yes, here is Mike Meyers speaking. Tell me what you want!"

„ Hello Mike old friend. How are you doing?"

„ Hello John. How long have I not heard from you? How are you?"

I met Mike around two years ago, when I arrested someone for espionage by mistake. It was a strange case and in a weird coincidence I could arrest this agent. This man had stolen information about a brand new secret weapon of the American military. They had produced a new kind of plain and everything was done in complete secrecy. When our enemies got wind of what was going on, they wanted to know more about that new project and get it for themselves. To make the long story short, this guy managed to steal a microchip with all the information and plans for building this new plain. He had even found a buyer for it and was ready to turn against the States. He would get millions of dollars for this chip. The spy and the buyer met to close the deal and I bumped into them by chance. I arrested them both and brought them behind bars. Thinking about the case makes me laugh, because it was too easy to be true.

„ Mike, I need to ask you for a favor. I need some information about a person in a case I am working on."

„ What is it about, my friend?"

I informed him about the case as much as I could and told him only what I was allowed to tell him.

„ If I am correct in this case you found your master, right?"

„ No, I don't think so. I cannot imagine that someone could have such a clean record and don't have even one negative point in his file. Something is up here, but I haven't figured out what it is yet. I am running in circles and I am not getting further. If I don't come up with something fast, this case will be ripped out of my hands and will be given to the FBI and I don't want this to happen. Do you understand what I am saying?"

„ Yes I understand. Give me the name of this guy and some more details so I can find him. Maybe we get lucky and you can nail this son of a bitch!"

„ Good. The name is Thomas Silk; he is Colonel and is posted on the base of Ford Creek, Florida as a psychiatrist. He was born in Baltimore 16.02.1963."

„ This is enough. In about an hour I will fax you the whole report on this guy. Give me your number and I will contact you, my friend."

I gave him my number and thanked him for his collaboration. I was feeling better knowing I had his help and I continued my work. While I was talking on the phone Sarah made a list of the information about the victims so that we can compare them and see if they have anything in common. Proudly she showed me the list and I must say I was amazed; this would definitely help with the investigation.

FIRST VICTIM

- Jane Olson
- 25 years old
- 1,75m tall
- Blond hair
- No trouble with any colleagues
- She was posted in Fort Creek as a Soldier about two year sago
- She died on the 20.03.2005 in a deadly car crash.

SECOND VICTIM

- Michele Johnson
- 24 years old
- 1,69 m tall
- Blond hair
- Some problems with colleagues due to her intense love life
- Was posted in Fort Creek as a nurse about two years ago
- She died on the 01.05.2005, suicide (she had cut her wrists)

THIRD VICTIM

- Sonny Smith
- 26 years old
- 1,75 m tall
- Blond hair
- No problems with colleagues
- She was posted in Fort Creek as psychiatrist's secretary about a year ago
- She died on the 01.07.2005, suicide (she hung herself in the shower)

FOURTH VICTIM

- Pamela Simpson
- 25 years old
- 1,70 m tall
- Blond hair

  — No problems with colleagues
  — She was posted on Fort Creek as a nurse three years ago
  — She died a week ago, cause of death, unknown

I looked at the list one more time and congratulated Sarah on her good work. She would make an excellent Detective if she was given the chance. When I looked at the list closer, I saw that the victims had a lot on common after all. I didn't realize at first but now seeing the characteristics like this it was easy to see the similarities. My face became serious. Sarah noticed that and asked me:
„ Did you notice anything?"
„ Yes. Didn't you?"
„ No!"
„ Look at the list closely. All the victims have the same hair color, are approximately the same height, age and they are all women. What does this tell us?"
„ What? I have no idea!"
„ That we are dealing with a serial killer! Can you imagine what this means for us?"
„ Oh my God! Now I get it! How can this be? How can it be that no one noticed that before and got him arrested?"
„ I told you already, we are dealing with a very clever criminal. But our guy here must belong to a different group of criminals."
„ Why do you say that?"
„ He doesn't act like a typical serial killer. This is why I didn't notice it in the beginning. He belongs to a group, that only a few serial killers belong, that are very difficult to catch and put behind bars. This type of serial killer kills his victims but does not take any trophies or a souvenir of the victim, as others do. Also, our guy does not take part in our investigation. You must know, serial killers always take part in the investigations and try to help the police to find the killer. Instinctively he needs to prove himself that he is smarter than the police and can get away with anything. He wants to fool everyone. He wants to prove that he is above everyone but deep inside he wants to get caught and brought to justice. It is very difficult to explain this killers psyche."
Sarah listened to me silently. She nodded sometimes but said no word

and did not interrupt me. I wanted to tell her more about this subject, but someone knocked at the door. We looked at each other and Sarah asked:

,, Are you expecting anyone?"

,, No!"

I looked at the door and said <Enter!>. A Soldier opened the door and came in with a big envelope in his hand. He saluted and turned to me.

,, Are you Detective Man?" he asked.

,, Yes, this is me!"

,, I have an envelope that I need to deliver to you!"

,, Who is it from?"

,, I don't know, Sir! I just got the order to deliver it to you."

The Soldier gave me the envelope, saluted and left. Only when he closed the door behind him, I looked at the envelope. I looked at him and realized that it was from my friend and colleague Thomas. I sat down on the chair in front of my desk and opened the envelope. In the envelope was an autopsy report. The body of her was completely examined now I had the results in my hand. Sarah stood beside me and asked me what this report was about and who it was from.

,, It is the autopsy report of Pamela Simpson."

I looked at the report and told Sarah what they found out.

,, Cause of death was suffocation due to strangulation. On the inside of her mouth small wounds were found that were caused by the strangulation. There was also a big wound on the neck and the biggest wound of all is that she bit her tongue. Everything was caused from the strangulation."

,, What else was found?"

,, It was proved, by the rigidness of the body, that it was not moved. The girl died on the spot where she was found. Except the blue marks on her neck, no other wounds were found."

,, What else?"

I told her a few more details from the report, like the content of her stomach, intestine and kidney. Sarah was getting paler by the second and held her hand before her mouth. I was sure that if I would say some more things she would throw up on my feet, so I stopped. While she turned her head from me she said:

,, If you do not stop with this report right now I will show you what happened to the pizza I ate in my stomach. Please!"

I continued reading the report but could not find anything important that would help us with the investigation. As there was no other report in the envelope I assumed that they have not finished with the micro examination of the bones and the toxicology tests either. There was however a full microbiological report in there. There was no trace of drugs in her blood. The coroner found some saliva on her lip that was running down her chin. This is totally matches the position that the dead girl was found in. Also some dried tears were found under her eyes and on her cheeks. The coroner that tested the fluids found that they were hers.

„ Tears?" Sarah asked surprised.

„ Yes, tears, a lot of them."

„ Really? The poor girl. I am sincerely sorry for her."

„ Don't forget that if you get in the hands of a mad man how is trying to kill you, you lose self control. Some people start to cry, others try everything to get away from him. Some make it, some don't. You are a woman, right? We men don't cry as easily as women do."

„ Of course. What else was found?"

„ There was no trace from other sperm on her body except her boyfriend's, which was on her hand from washing up. No trace of any kind of lubricant was found in her genitals of in her anus, to indicate the penetration of another person."

„ This means that she was not raped, right? This is good news."

I nodded.

„ Hear some more good news. Do you remember the tire marks we found in the back of the building behind the big bush?"

„ Yes I can totally remember. What about them?"

„ I asked Thomas to make a mold of them and compare them to every vehicle on the base that day. And bingo, the marks belong to the car of Colonel Silk! What do you say about that?"

„ I say, we need to drag him in front of military court to get him his well earned sentence. That means the case is closed, right?"

„ We will see when I talk to him. All we have now are indications that show that the cases can be related to one another. We need evidence to get him behind bars and this will be the hard part. So far he has been smarter than us and slipped through our fingers. I need to think of something good, so that he cannot get out of it."

„ And what happens if he wants to get away with it and does not want to say anything?"

„ Then I will show the attorney the file with the findings. I am not quite sure about that yet; there are still some unsolved things that I am not clear about yet. One thing I need to find out is the motive. I cannot imagine why he hates women so much and desires so much to kill them. This must have a deeper reason I need to find out."

„ Can we arrest him?"

„ I shook my head; I didn't think it would be a good idea. I wanted to talk to him first and then make my decision. The telephone rang and I looked at my watch. Almost an hour had passed since I talked to my friend and I was sure it was his fax with the information I was looking for. So I turned the telephone on fax and waited that the paper gets spit out the machine. After the beep sound the machine started to print out one page after the other. In the end I held a stack of papers in my hand, a report of nineteen pages. Sarah pulled he chair close to mine and sat next to me so we can read the report together. Reading the first pages I could see the same information that were in the file the General had given me, when he was born, where he grew up and his carrier in the military. My interest began after page three. I pulled the pages closer and had to light a cigarette out of excitement. Up until the age of fifteen the Colonel lived in Baltimore. His mother was a sergeant on a base near Baltimore she must have been a very dominating and despotic person. If I could believe the report, she had the upper hand in the military as well as at home. His father was a representative for electrical devices who was constantly traveling and was hardly ever at home. From what I read he must have been an honest hardworking man. The whole misery in the family began with the mother's behavior. From the questioning of the neighbors, the night their house was on fire and burned to the ground, it turned out that the mother was not loyal to the family. Rumors were going around that she was cheating a lot and had a lot of different male company when her husband was out of town. Of course they were only rumors with no concrete evidence. I am sure that they didn't want to investigate on it even further because it was already hard enough for women in the military back then. Surely they wanted to avoid a scandal that could hurt the military. They only investigated the fire that burned the house down. The firemen came to the conclusion that it was caused by the stove that was not turned down properly. The stove that ran on gas filled the house with gas. The specialists were certain that the fire started with the lighting of a cigarette and closed the case in a matter of days. The burned body of the mother was found in the bedroom and that of the father was found on the floor of the living room. As the house was completely burned down, it was a miracle that the son got out and escaped a brutal death before the house blew up in the air. The police asked the young man why he was not in the house and he answered that he had gone for a walk and when he wanted to go home he saw the fire that had already started. The police could not verify his story because they could find no witnesses that saw the boy leave the house to go for a walk. The boy had no friends in the neighborhood and he was constantly seen alone. When they autopsied the body of the mother they found out that she had died by several stab wounds and one of her fingers was missing. She must have been dead before the burn. The finger was never found and the conclusion was made that it had turned to ashes. But the coroner was getting suspicious and examined the corpse of the father. He found a big hole in the back of his head and that he had died also before the fire. He informed the police and they interrogated the boy again. When they started questioning him, he broke down in tears and told the police that his parents had a big fight that evening. He couldn't stand their fighting and shouting and this was why he went out for a walk to leave them alone. He said he didn't know the reason why they had a fight. The police closed the case blaming the father for the mother's death and that he had turned on the stove and waited for the house to fill up with gas and then lit a cigarette. As for the hole in his head they concluded that he hit himself falling on the coffee table from the blast of the explosion and died. The boy was send to the mother's sister. After the advice of the pediatrician, the aunt brought the boy to a child psychologist for a few weeks. Nobody wanted the boy to suffer from any trauma caused by his parent's death. The psychologist could not see anything unusual in the boy's behavior; the only thing he noticed was that the boy was really quite for what he had been through. He told the aunt that children often close themselves up and stay that quite until they get over the shock. He explained that every child has his own way of dealing with such a tragedy. Some get really quite and break off any contact to the world and others get loud, aggressive and hard to handle while dealing with such an event. The psychiatrist told her that she needs to take care of the boy really good and let him take his time to heal. After their parents death the boy lived with his aunt for about two years. She had a lot of trouble with him, he was a difficult character. He himself asked to join the military school.

I read the rest of the file about his schools and carrier in the military. I had just finished reading the file when the telephone rang and I asked myself who it could be. Out of the fax machine came more pages and I took them in my hand. My friend had sent me one more report. Again I had a pile of papers in front of me. With this report I hit the bull's eye. We had sat down our chairs again and wanted to start reading the report, when suddenly someone knocked at the door.

CHAPTER 32

He sat in his office chair, in the dark again. He drank already his third scotch, to calm down, but he was boiling on the inside. His feelings were a mixture of fear, hate and anger. He hopped that the scotch would calm him down as it always did, but today even that couldn't calm him down. He raised his right hand automatically to get the last sip of scotch out of the glass. He was so nervous and he couldn't explain why, so he was close to despair. Had the time come when they would arrest him? Was this Detective cleverer than any other before him? So far he could always get away with it and cover his tracks. The military police never got suspicious and he tricked them successfully. He didn't like this Detective from the first time he saw him, he could see that he was smarter than his predecessor. This fucking investigator must have realized from the beginning that he was the guy he was after. But today he didn't say a word that he was close to catching him. This confused him. This Detective brought him bad luck from the day he set foot on this base. Since then everything goes wrong. The hell with him. He knew that he had a strong character, who else would stand against him. Not even his own father had something of his character. He was a pussy. Gullible and good-natured, but much too soft. Up until the day his father died he tolerated his behavior, but then he had enough. He felt sorry for his father, but he should also receive his punishment for behavior. He had a bitter taste in his mouth, as he thought of them. Before he realized it he thought about the old times and got lost in his memories. It felt, as if he would press a button and the whole scenery around him would change and he found himself back in his old house in Baltimore.

In that moment, he was fifteen years old, it was a beautiful day in the fall and he was standing outside the front door. He left school two hours ago and had wandered around in the woods near his house. He had build a small house in the middle of the woods, where he hid almost every day, to get out of his mothers way. Even as a small boy, he didn't have any friends and he grew up alone, without not even one friend in his life. He had tried to make friends with some of the kids in the neighborhood but that didn't work out. The whole neighborhood, and the kids, found out what his mother was doing. The grownups looked at him with pity and the kids called him a bastard. So he constantly played on his own and then he got used to it and didn't need their company anymore. If they didn't want to play with him, he didn't want to play with them anyway. He didn't need them; he could manage on his own. It was a beautiful day in the fall and he got in the tree house, that he had build with wood that he found in the woods. He sat on the floor. It was a warm day today so he took of his jacket, folded it neatly and put it on the floor next to him. In the height of his eyes he had made two holes so that he can look out in the woods and watch the animals that lived here without them noticing him. He looked out of his holes and observed the woods and its inhabitants. After a short while a herd of deer walked past the tree house and stopped a little further away to eat. He stood still watching them so that they didn't hear or smell him. They were wonderful animals. They had thick, reddish colored fur and big black eyes. The stag was really big and had a huge antler on his head. He must have weighed over tree hundred kilos. As much as the boy could see he must have been the only stag of the herd. Around him were five females and each had a little one next to them that were grazing nervously, constantly looking around for danger. One little deer must have been around forty kilos. The boy carefully stood up and moved around silently so that he would not scare the herd away. He sneaked on his toes to the back of the tree house and lifted a small green tarp. Under there was a small wooden box. Slowly he lifted the lid of the box and took a small air gun. He took the gun into his hand and opened the barrel. He put in two bullets and closed the barrel again. A small clicking sound was heard from closing the barrel. Bend down he went back to the small window and took position. He looked out of the window and saw that the herd was still in the same place and hadn't moved at all. The boy lifted the gun and aimed. With the right thumb and index finger he aimed so that he had the small deer in sight. He had the deer's head in sight and held his breath. The only sound you could hear was a hissing sound from when the gun was fired and the bullet was released. The deer was hit and it dropped dead on the ground. The herd was frightened when the deer dropped and started running as fast as they can, not giving the dead deer another look. The boy ran to the wooden box, put the gun back in it and put the tarp back on the box. Before he jumped out of the tree house he looked carefully outside to see if any hiker had seen the whole thing. He saw that no one was watching and that he was alone, so he exited the tree house to go to the dead deer. The ground under the deer was flooded with blood that came out of the deer's wound. The wound did not stop bleeding until the last drop of blood was out. Since it was a small deer almost half of the head was destroyed by the blow and he could see the inside of its head. He grabbed the deer from its legs, put it over his shoulders and walked back to the tree house. The blood was still running out of its wounds and the floor wood soaked up every drop that was landing on it. But the boy didn't care. He never cared about such things. He loved looking at the blood flowing and get soaked up into the wood, it gave him the feeling that he was still alive. It was the first time he killer a larger animal and he had mixed feelings about it. On one hand he felt guilt and on the other hand he felt like god. He was the hunter and the deer was the pray. There was no turning back. No, he couldn't go back now. He found his path and he was sure that he could beat anyone. When he started hunting he only killed smaller animals, for example squirrels, rabbits, cats and sometimes dogs from the neighborhood that walked through the woods. Every time he killed an animal he shot it in the head so that it would be dead immediately and then he dragged it to the tree house. The fun part for him began when he brought the animal back to the tree house. The real fun. It was not that important for him to kill the animals. After killing them and their body was still warm, he took out his hunting knife and started to skin the animal. When he skinned them he cut open the chest. With the open chest he could see all the vital organs of the animal, the lungs, the heart and the liver. He had to kill a lot of animals so that he could do all that like a surgeon, open the animals and removing all the organs. But this was not that important to him. Not like the thought he had every time he opened a dead animal's chest. When he skinned them and smudged the blood everywhere, he thought about how it would feel if he would do that to humans. He was really excited as he took out their heart and held it in his hand. It was the most important organ of the body. For him the heart was sacred, as he took it out if animals he imagined taking out his mother's heart and destroying it. When he finished with the deer's organs he just let it lay there and took a shovel in the hand that was stored in the other corner of the tree house. He looked at his watch and noticed that it was late and he had to go home. He didn't want his parents to come looking for him and find out where he is hiding all day. With the shovel he got outside and dug a big hole, where he buried the deer and its organs. After he did that he brought the shovel back into the tree house and looked at his watch. It was almost nine o'clock and it was getting pretty dark. Quickly he put on his jacket and made his way back home. Not far from his house he saw his father's car in the driveway. He was eager to see his dad; he was away for a week on a business trip. He started walking faster and when he arrived in front of the door, he door opened and an unfamiliar man walked out. He quickly hid behind a bush and watched the man walking down the driveway. At first e didn't recognize the man, but when he turned around to look at the house one more time he recognized him immediately. It was one of the soldiers that worked with his mum on the base. He was here a lot and he knew exactly what he was doing here. The boy watched the man get in his car and he was looking if he could find a rock. He found one and threw it in this man's windshield. With a loud noise the window broke into pieces. Instead of hiding he came out from behind the bush and stood there looking at the soldier. He showed the soldier the finger and waited for a reaction. The soldier became furious and the boy laughed. At first, the soldier wanted to get out of his car and grab the boy, but then he thought about it again. He started his car and drove off in full steam. The laughing face of the boy became suddenly very serious and he walked in the house. As soon as he closed the door behind him he could see his father sitting on the couch in the living room. It seemed as his father was crying, but he was not sure. He stood in front of his father and looked at him. The worst thing was that not a single tear came out of his father's eyes, he was crying from the inside. His mother sat on a chair at the dinner table and was filing her nails, as always. She left the nail file on the table and opened a package of cigarettes. She lit a cigarette and sucked in the smoke, keeping it in her lungs for a few seconds until she blew it back out. As soon as she saw the boy she said:

„ Here is our good for nothing son. Did you find your fucking way home? Finally we can order some food."

Like nothing happened she walked over to the telephone and called the pizza service to order dinner for the family. She put out her half smocked cigarette in an ashtray next to the phone and started laughing on the phone. Someone probably made her a compliment and that was why she laughed. When she finished with the telephone she sat back down at the table and lit another cigarette.

„ I will go up and shower before we eat; when the food comes be so kind and call me."

With these words she left them both there and walked upstairs. The boy watched him mother walk up and could not hold himself. He had to let his anger go, otherwise he would explode. He sat in front of his father and looked down at him. Damn. How could a man sit like this on the couch and cry his eyes out? In this moment he was discussed by his father and he became even angrier.

„ Are you completely insane?"

His father raised his head and his looked his son in the eyes.

„ I don't understand what you are saying, son?"

„ What I am saying? You must be a bigger fool that I thought you where!"

„ I forbid you to talk to me in this tone! No respect. What are you thinking…!"

„ What I am thinking? You want to teach me respect? You? You come home from your trip and find your wife in bed with another guy and don't say a thing! And now you want to teach me respect."

His father's eyes filled up with tears and began to shimmer in the light of the lamp. For a few minutes they continued looking at each other not saying a word. With the head looking down he answered his son:

„ You must think I am a great coward, right? Do you think I just found out that your mother is cheating on me? I know that for years now, but I cannot do anything about it. You where so young and I was not sure what the best thing was to do. Maybe I had to leave her years ago."

171

„ What you should do? I would have killed her, if I was in your place. This is what I would have done!"

„ She was the love of my life and I still love her, even though she does this to me for all these years."

The boy looked at his father with anger and hate. He was still sitting on the couch sobbing and tears running down from his eyes. How despicable!? He went over to the dinner table and for a moment he didn't know what to do. Then his eyes fell on the big glass ashtray. He didn't think long and took it in his hand. The ashtray was pretty heavy, so he went back to the couch. This time he stood at the back of the couch so that he had his father's back in front of him. Quick he raised his hand with the ashtray and hit his father's head with all the force he had. When the big ashtray came in contact with his father's head he could hear his head crack and became goose bumps. His father immediately fell dead to the side and laid there on the floor motionless. From the hole in his head blood was streaming out, forming a pond on the floor. The blood got soaked up the white living room carpet, but the boy didn't care at all. He let the ashtray fall on the couch and walked around and stood over his father's body looking at him.

„ Father, believe me. I am sorry that this had to happen. But it is your entire fault. You were not the man in the house."

He kneeled down and gave his father a kiss on the forehead. He quickly got back up and went into the kitchen. He opened all the cabinets and drawers and looked for something specific. In the last drawer he found what he was looking for. He found the big chef knife and held it in his right hand. It was like new. No wonder, his mother had hardly ever used it, she never cooked. In the light of the kitchen lamp, he liked the way it shined.

„ Mother, prepare yourself. You are going to die tonight!"

He sneaked up the stairs and when he reached the last step he stood still. He heard his mother I the tub singing. The door to the bedroom was open and he sneaked inside. He walked through the bedroom and entered the bathroom. He saw his mother in the bath tub; she was still singing. He was watching her how she was washing her legs with a sponge. He sneaked carefully in the bathroom. His mother had a towel wrapped around her head so her hair would not get wet. She had folded another towel and put it under her neck as a cushion. She was lying there with her eyes closed and was enjoying the warm water. He stood in front of her without her noticing him and looked at her with pure hate. His innocent look was gone and his face made an ugly expression, revealing the true feelings he was feeling inside. His eyes fell on the robe that was hanging from the bathroom door. Quickly he went over there and took the robe's belt into his hands wrapping both ends around his hands. Without wasting another thought he wrapped the belt around his mother's throat. His mother screamed in fear; at first she didn't realize what was going on and she opened her eyes. Before her wide open eyes she could see her son who had wrapped that belt around her neck and looked at her with hate. His face was just a few centimeters away from hers so she had to look him in the eyes. Nervous she started laughing and stared her son in the eyes.

„ Hey, boy. What the hell is going on here? Can you explain to me what you want to do here? I am under the impression that you are more of a man than your father is, or am I wrong?"

She was talking ironically to him and smiled at him, but did not take her eyes from his.

„ What do you think is going in here?" he asked her and was still hatefully staring at her. his mother immediately understood that his voice was cold and emotionless and became goose bumps.

„ Let me go at once, or else I will call your father and he will hit you for the first time in his life."

„ You think?" he answered.

She felt that something was wrong from the tone of his voice and started feeling scared. She didn't feel comfortable in her own skin right now. Her son had transformed in a matter of minutes from a boy into a monster and she couldn't recognize him. She couldn't estimate the position she was in and she had to do something now.

„ Let me go now and take this stupid knife out of my face, or else I will give you the beating of a life time. I swear by God. You would want to hide away like a small mouse in a tiny hole, and I will find you every time!"

Out of fear she didn't know what to do and raised her chest high up and the dropped it again, taking fast small breaths. Sweat was running down her forehead, but she didn't want to move to wipe it dry, in fear of her son's reaction. With his left hand he took one of her curls and put it behind her ears. She pulled her face back so that he could not touch her and exactly in this moment he knocked her out hitting her with the back of the knife on the back of her head. With her head under water he pulled her out before she could drown. He dragged her from the bathroom into the bedroom and threw her like a piece of meat onto the bed. His parent's bed was a wooden old rustic bed, really well build. It was made of oak and had big heavy legs that stood firmly on the floor. As long as she was still unconscious he tied her arms and legs separately on the four corners of the bed. He didn't even bother to throw something in her so she was lying there how God had created her. He was fascinated by her body and stood there admiring her figure. She had the body of an eighteen year old girl. It was a shame that she was such a whore. He sat next to her on the bed and drew invisible circles on her belly. She was still knocked out and didn't move. He knew that the blow to the head was not strong enough to kill her and he could see that she was still breathing. His mother was tough by nature and could stand a few blows to the head. As she was lying there he felt the urge to kill her right then and it took a lot of strength to hold back. He was waiting for her to wake up so that she could feel what he was doing to her. Exactly like she was torturing him all these years. Just thinking about what he wanted to do to her, made him smile. He wanted to torture her like she did his father all these years. He wanted to hurt her so bad like she hurt them booth all this time. While he was thinking about these things she became conscious and she was groaning in pain from the blow to the head. She had just opened her eyes when she realized that she was tied up. With all her strength she pulled at the strings but she couldn't set herself free and started swearing. At first she tried the soft way to convince her son to let her go and when she saw that this was not working she started threatening him with anything that came into her mind. All the time she was begging and cursing and imploring, to let her go, her son didn't say a word. He was just looking at her amusing himself with the sight. Suddenly without any warning he jumped on the bed, sat on her body and stood still.

„ What is wrong, mother? Don't you like me sitting on you? I was under the impression that this is how you liked it, or not?"

He started moving his body rhythmically on her and pressing his body on hers as much as he could. Her nipples got hard and he realized that she really liked that he was sitting on her.

„ You are so wretched!" he shouted at her and spit on her.,, With your own son. Your own flesh and blood and you like it?"

He stood up and walked out of the bedroom to go down into the kitchen. She screamed at him not to leave her alone, but he didn't hear anything and he didn't even turn to look at her.

In the kitchen he searched for tape that he had seen earlier in one of the drawers he looked into. After a few minutes he found it and held it in his hand. He quickly walked up the stairs and entered the bedroom again. She immediately saw the tape that he held in his hand and asked him scared what he wanted to do with it.

„ Why the hell do you hold the tape in your hand? What do you want to do with it? I want an answer immediately. Do you understand me?"

She continued talking to him, but got no answer back. He cut of a piece of tape and covered her mouth. Although she turned her head left and right so that he could not cover her mouth, he managed to hold her head still by sitting behind her head and putting his head between his thighs. She couldn't move anymore so he could tape her mouth easily. Furious she tried to set herself free and scream, but she couldn't move and no sound came out of her mouth. Finally he had enough of her and started to slap her and jell at her.

„ Even now, in this position, you still have to say the last word. You fucking slut!"

He got angrier and slapped her in hate. He was only hitting her in the face. One slap after the other. One slap harder than the other. Her face was red from all the hits and she tried to scream in pain, but nothing came out of her mouth. Like a maniac he was hitting her, boxing her in the stomach and didn't stop at any of her body parts. He was hitting her like wild and he never felt sorry for her. She was groaning in pain and she wanted to shout at him to leave her alone, but no words came out of her mouth. She tried to avoid his punches the best she could and estimate where he would hit her next so that she could move this body part a little bit, but she couldn't. She saw his face filled with hate and she felt nothing but pure panic. Again and again she wanted to scream but in the end she realized that she couldn't escape him. He enjoyed torturing her. He enjoyed beating her without her being able to fight back. In her eyes he could see the fear and he went on without feeling bad about it. For years she had tortured him and his father and now was his turn to torture her. Suddenly a perverted thought went through his head and he started laughing loud. When his mother heard his laughter her blood froze in her wanes and she laid there completely still. She didn't dare to move one centimeter from her spot. The only thing she knew was that she didn't recognize her son anymore and that she didn't trust him. Her son, who was still a boy, grew up sooner than she thought and turned into her worst nightmare. With hate written on his face, he unzipped his pants and put his penis in his mother's genitals with all his force. With all his strength he took her and she screamed without him understanding even one word of what she said. He took her breasts in his hands and started to pinch them so hard that they immediately turned red. With his lips he sucked and bit her nipples until he had ripped open large wounds and blood was running out. Seeing the blood and how it ran down on the bed sheets got him fully excited and he got even wilder. His mother lost consciousness due to the pain and laid there not moving at all. When he saw that she was unconscious he took the knife and freed her hands and legs cutting off the rope, he turned her around so that she was lying on her belly. He wet his lips with his tongue; they were dried out from the ecstasy he was in. The boy, who had never in his life loved a girl, was immediately hard when he felt his mother under him. He would never share the experience with a girl; how it feels to lose your virginity and make love for the first time. The feeling to fall in love and discover love day by day. He laid on his mother and laughed diabolical. With clumsy movements he rubbed his penis on her back up and down. Again he forced himself into her and took her from above and down, from the front and from behind. Her torture was never ending. His sperm was running down her neck and back. It was coming out of her vagina and her anus. In the meantime the mother had gained consciousness again and was wishing for it to be over soon; but the boy was young and inexperienced, he had no problem getting an erection very quickly. He just couldn't get enough and so she laid now again on her back in front of him. For the sixth time he was now ready to put his penis in her again, when she saw his penis and laughed. He had taped her mouth shut but he could still hear her laughing. He screamed in her face that she should shut her mouth but she didn't stop. He punched her in the face and broke her nose. Blood started running down her nose down her chin. As she had her hands free she could take off the tape and answer him laughing.

„ Maybe you will have a bigger boner when I help you with our sex and choose a better position!''

She was laughing so hard as she laid back down that she choked and started to cough. This was the last that his mother gave from her. With quick movements he took the kitchen knife that was on the dresser and held it firmly in his right hand. In a split second, without hesitating for a moment he pushed the knife in her stomach. One stab came after the other and constantly he was shouting at her – Shut your mouth-, - Shut your fucking mouth-. When his mother felt the first stab in the stomach she sat up on the bed and looked at him astonished, not believing what was happening and then... The only thing she saw was a red explosion in her eyes and then she fell back on the soft cushions and laid there. The only thing she heard was her son's screaming voice to shut her mouth. Then everything was over and she stopped moving. When he realized that she was dead he let the knife glide on the floor and stood up, zipping his pants back up. With the right hand he wiped his forehead from the sweat. He looked at his hands; full of blood. He stretched his hands out and looked at every single finger. He liked was he saw; it made him feel like God. It made him feel unbeatable. He turns around and went into the bathroom, opened the faucet and washed his hands. As hot water was running he took soap and washed his hands completely clean. After he was done washing his hands, he carefully dried them with a clean towel. The boy left the bathroom and walked in his bedroom. He was not quite sure what he should do now, he had not planned the whole thing, but he thought it would be a good idea to put on some clean clothes. Quickly he opened the closet and took out whatever clothes he found in front of him. He put them on and went down into the kitchen. He stood in front of the stove, turned it on and let the gas flow into the room. He looked at his father's body and walked to the dining table where his mother had left her cigarettes. He took out a cigarette and counted to fifty. When he was sure that the gas had almost filled the house he quickly lit the cigarette and left it in the ashtray so that it would not fall down. He quickly put on his jacket that he had thrown on the couch and walked to the kitchen door. Before he exited the house he opened the door a little bit to see if anyone was around that could see him. When he was sure that no one was there he got out. With quick movements he shut the door behind him and disappeared in the dark. He walked around the block and hadn't gone that far away from his parent's house when he heard the explosion and the ground shook under him. A wide smile was on his lips. It was time to turn around and go back. He didn't was to miss the spectacle. As he was walking towards his house he could see big flames raising to the sky and lighting up the whole neighborhood. The roof was gone from the explosion and he could see the flames eating up the house from the inside out destroying everything that came in their way. From the far he could hear the sirens of the fire department and the police that came closer and finally stopped in front of the house. He watched the firemen trying to put out the fire. The boy stood there not moving watching the house turn to ashes. It was the most beautiful sight he had ever seen.

He stopped dreaming and found himself back in the office, with the glass of scotch in his hand and he emptied what was still left in there. He made the decision that he needed to destroy this Detective Man if he still wanted to walk free. Tired he got up from his armchair, left his glass on the desk and walked to the door. Maybe it was a good idea to pay this Detective a visit. He exited his office and took a set of keys out of his pocket so that he could lock the door. While he was locking the door he talked to his secretary that was working at his desk.

„ Soldier, I have something to do outside the office that is very important. I don't know when I will be coming back. You can call it a day now, I don't need you anymore. Good night."

„ Thank you, Sir. See you tomorrow morning then. I wish you a good night too.

They saluted each other and Silk left the room and made his way to the office of the detective. In front of the investigator's door he stopped for a few seconds and put his ear on the door trying to hear what was going on in there. The only thing he could hear was that two voices where talking about something, but he could not understand what they were talking about. He pressed his ear more on the door and now he could hear something. They were talking about the autopsy report. Sweat appeared on his forehead, he couldn't stand standing here, doing nothing and lifted his hand to knock on the door. Suddenly the phone rang and he took his hand back and waited until the call was over. He thought it would be a good idea to knock now so that he would find out what the call was about. The moment he knocked, the conversation stopped in the office and for a moment there was only silence. Impatiently he waited to be called into the office and he finally did call him in he opened the door immediately. He saw the Detective and the doctor sitting at the desk staring at him as he entered the room. It seemed as they couldn't believe their eyes that he was standing in front of them.

„ I wish you both a good evening. I hope I am not disturbing you at your job, am I?"

He could see that the Detective gathered a stack of papers that were laying by the telephone and put them in front of him.

„ No, Colonel. You do not disturb us. How can I help you?"

„ I stopped by to see how you are doing with the case, actually. Did my profiles help?"

„ We are doing great with the case. Come, sit down."

Sarah stood up from her chair and offered it to him; he thanked her and sat down. He tried to have a look at the papers the Detective had in front of him and on one paper at the bottom of the pile he could see his name on one edge. He was confused but didn't show anything. He was still looking at his name, it was written in big red letters. He caught and his eyes went back to the investigator who was looking at him and tried to act calm and not show his anxiety.

„ So, how are coming along with the investigation?"

„ To tell you the truth, really well. You know, what I mean; there are a lot of files to examine and a lot of reports to read so we are making good time for now. It takes time and patience."

„ Yes, you are completely right. I am glad that you coming along great."

Silk smiled friendly at the investigator and played cool.

„ But you haven't answered my questions yet. Did the profiles help that I prepared for you?"

„ You have no idea how much they helped me."

„ Ah really? I am glad."

For a few minutes they didn't talk and stared at each other. They both tried to read each other's eyes. Nobody could know what was going on in their heads right now. Everyone was lost in their thoughts when Detective Man coughed and drank a sip from his coffee, to clear his throat. As he was leaving his cup on the desk he noticed that one edge of the fax his friend had send him was visible with the Colonel's name on it. He carefully stacked the papers together. His eye fell on Silk who was still lost in his thoughts and was hoping that Silk didn't see his name on the paper. Suddenly Silk jumped of his chair and said to them:

„ So, I will no longer keep you from your work and leave you alone so you can finish the case. I am glad I could help."

„ I thank you for your help and your interest on how the case is coming along. I wish you a good night."

„ No, I thank you for giving me a chance to contribute to solving the case. It was my pleasure. So, if you have anything new, inform me. Good night."

„ Of course I will inform you if I have any news. Good night."

We saluted each other and Silk left the office without looking back again. Sarah said that what I was thinking:

„ What was that for a quick goodbye? Like he was stung by a bee. Weird!"

„ I just thought that. I have no explanation for this man's behavior and I probably will never understand him."

„ I will agree to that."

„ Except he…!"

I didn't finish the sentence and looked on the stack of papers thinking. Did he maybe by accident see his name and became suspicious?

„ Except he what, John?" asked Sarah looking at me.

„ Nothing. I just had a strange thought. Nothing serious!" I answered.

He left the Detective's office thinking. He saw his name on a paper with big letters, by accident. He didn't like that. He didn't like that at all. Behind his back the investigator had searched for information about him. Of course he had the right to do it, but again he didn't feel good about this. He himself knew what was written in his file inside out. So far he did his best for the military and there was never a reason to write something bad about him in his file. He had a clean record. So far he didn't allow himself to make any mistakes. He always showed up on time and he did his job the best way he could. What he was doing in his free time was not the military's business. This was the reason he hasn't get caught all this time. Now suddenly, everything changed. He needed to be careful and not leave any trace behind. The Detective almost caught him killing this doctor bitch in her house. He was getting closer so he needed to run. They didn't see him that night. Lost in his thoughts he unlocked the door to his office, entered and locked it again behind him. He turned on the light and stood motionless behind that door looking in the direction of the hidden door that was located behind those heavy curtains. So far no one had seen this hidden door and he was sure that no one thought about it. When he was first posted on this base and started working in this office, he accidently found this door. He searched for the blue print if the building and was not sure where it led. He had these curtains made and hang them up himself, so that no one would see this door again. All this had the result that nobody knew of this secret passing. Everyone that came into his office; and there were not many people coming here; thought that behind the curtains was another window. With quick movements he walked to his office and packed some of the personal items in a bag. He turned off the light and walked to the secret door in the dark. He pulled the curtain aside and took out his keys to unlock the door. He didn't need light to find the key and unlock because he had used this in the dark to get in and out without his secretary noticing. Behind the building was a forested area and so he only had to walk a few meters on grass until he could get lost in the woods. This piece of forest they used to prepare troops for war and surviving, but tonight there were no sounds coming from there so he could easily disappear in the wood without anyone noticing. Quickly he locked the door behind him and ran to the forest. He stood there for a few seconds listening and letting his eyes adapt to the dark. It was quite, so he walked up to the north side of the forest. On the north side he arrived at a line of thick bushes which were hiding a hole in the fence. Since he had walked through here many times he didn't need a flash light to find his way around here. He could walk this way with his eyes closed; he knew where every little stone was laying. It was the best to escape. To fool everyone on the base that he was still there, he had left his old car parked in front of his office building. Until they would find out that he was not there he would be many kilometers away. Like a dancer he danced around the trees in the dark and moved forward silently. One could never be sure who would be in the woods, so he still needed to be careful and don't make a sound. Since he knew the woods he moved around every trap without any hesitation. Lost in his thoughts he stepped on a dried wooden stick and it broke making a loud noise. The noise was so loud in the night that could be heard meters away. Startled by his mistake he stopped moving and listened into the woods. He heard some birds that flew away frightened and he could also hear an owl from the far. He waited for every noise to stop until he was sure that no one followed him. When everything settled down he continued. After about fifteen kilometers he reached the bushes; he looked around nervously. He couldn't see anyone so he stopped to take a breather. With his bag in one hand he pushed himself through the bushes and scratched his hands o the way and they began to bleed. He did not bother about the wounds; he just kept going. Finally he had pushed himself through and exited the base from the hole in the fence. He had almost made it. He followed the dirt road along the base and kept walking for about a kilometer. This road was not used a lot so he didn't need to worry about getting caught. After walking one kilometer he reached another forested area with thick bushes. Behind the bushes he had hidden an old car. This car had no license plates and no papers where in the car. If it would have been found nobody could relate it back to him. He always made sure it had a full tank and he also had extra petrol in the back in bottles. The car was covered with a green tarp from the military so that it was not visible from above. It was parked I the bushes with the tarp on top so it was hard to see it from anywhere. He uncovered it and threw the tarp on the floor not even bothering to pick it up. He bent down to grab the keys he had hidden behind the right back wheel. After a few seconds he found it and opened the driver's door. He threw his bag in there and sat down. He closed the door and started the car. He pressed the gas pedal a few times put in the first gear, then the second and drove off into the dark.

CHAPTER 33

When Silk left our office I continued reading the papers that Mike had sent me. There was a detailed report with all the places Silk was posted during his time in the military. He had been in many bases around the States, like Baltimore, Nevada, Kansas and a lot more. With this report Mike had sent me some police reports. From these police reports I found out that some brutal murders took place in the areas where Silk was posted exactly around the time he was in every place. In every of these cases the murder was never found and they stopped when Silk left the area. I read carefully and noticed some of the details. Every girl that was murdered was blond, young and in approximately the same height and age, the day that they died. I got goose bumps. He must be playing his game for a long, long time now and I am sure he was really successful with it. But on the other hand, it must be a coincidence. I picked up the phone, called Silk's office and waited a few seconds for them to answer. I couldn't waste any more time, I wanted to interrogate him now on the other murders. Maybe I got lucky and he would testify. With all this evidence there is nothing left for him to do then testify to the murders. It rang five times until they picked up.

,, School of psychology, who is speaking?"

,, Here is Detective Man. Is the Colonel in his office?"

,, No, Sir. He hasn't come back yet. His office is still locked!"

My heard pounded in my chest.

,, Is it possible he went home?"

,, I don't think Sir, his car is still here outside the building. He said he had to take care of something important and then he would return to his office to work. He gave me the rest of the day off, he said he doesn't need me.'

„ Is that so?"

„ Yes, Sir. Can I help you with anything Sir?"

„ No, you can't. Thank you."

I put down the phone and picked it right up again. I dialed the number of the military police and asked for the officer on duty. After a few minutes I had him on the phone.

„ Yes, Detective Man speaking. I want you to put out a arrest warrant in the name of Thomas Silk, Colonel."

„ Excuse me?" he asked me unbelieving what he heard.

„ Exactly what I told you. I want you to issue an arrest warrant and don't waste any more time, for premeditated and planned murder resulting death. And the other thing I want from you is to send your men out to search for him. Inform the gate to stop him when they see him if he wants to leave the base. I will be there in ten minutes to help you with the warrant!"

„ Yes, Sir. I will wait for you here."

I put down the phone and looked into Sarah's face, he was pale as a ghost from the minute she read the police reports. Quickly I grabbed my car keys and said to her:„ Come on. Let's go!" She followed me and we made our way to the Colonel's office. As soon as his secretary saw us he jumped up and saluted us. Out of breath I asked him:

„ Is he here?"

„ No, Sir. He has not come back yet. What...?"

He didn't have time to finish the sentence we had already left the office. Quickly we walked down and went to my car. In the corner of my eye I saw Silk's car, it was parked next to mine. Seeing his car relieved me a bit because it looked as he hadn't left the base yet. We would find him quickly if he was still here. Quickly we got in my car, I started it and we hurried to the military police.

„ Watch out for Silk. Maybe we bump into him and don't need to chase him."

„ Ok, John."

My brain was running in full power and I had to keep a clear head, not to mess this up. Where could he be? Did he notice anything? Something he shouldn't hear or see? Did he leave the base on foot and left his car here so that we would think he is still around? Many more questions went through my head. Come on, John. Focus. You don't want this guy to slip through your fingers and get away with everything. Sarah talked to me but I didn't hear what she said and I asked her to say it again.

„ What did you say?"

„ I said, we will nail this son if a bitch. He cannot escape, right? He needs to pay for what he did to me and my colleagues."

„ Yes, it will happen. We have him in our hands now."

We stopped in front of the military police building, got off my car quickly and hurried up the stairs. The two guards that were standing in front off the door saw us coming and opened it for us. As we entered the building the cool breeze of the air-conditioning welcomed us. Immediately we felt refreshed. We searched for the officer on duty. He saw us come in and had stood up saluting us.

„ Did you issue the warrant as I requested?"

„ Yes, Sir. I have. Here it is."

With a quick move he gave me the warrant and I read it thoroughly so that there were no mistakes for Silk to move around it. Pleased, I nodded and padded the officer on the shoulder. I was pleased with his work. He didn't have to say where I should sign, my right hand went automatically to the end of the page to sign.

„ Have you send out your men to search for Silk?"

„ Yes, Sir. I send out three unit around ten minutes ago, but so far he hasn't been found."

I was swearing like a sailor and I didn't know what I should do. Like a tiger in a cage I walked up and down in front of the officer's office.

„ What do we do now?" Sarah asked me.

„ I have no idea!"

And that was the truth. I really did not know what we should do. Again I was walking up and down thinking what we could do next. Maybe I missed something important, and I just couldn't see what it was.

„ Did you inform the gate to stop him if he tries to leave?"

„ Yes, Sir!"

„ I need two more men send out to confiscate this man's car. I hope that he is still on the base. The car needs to be parked here in front of the building and watched around the clock. Do you understand?"

,, Yes, Sir."

The officer called two men and explained what they needed to do. I coulnt wait any longer so I said to Sarah:

,, Come on. Let's go!"

,, But where?" she asked.

,, We will help with the search and look for him ourselves."

Sarah followed me out of the building. Before I exited I told the officer that I want to be informed of every move they made. We stood in front of my car and I looked around.

,, Where do we start?" Sarah asked me.

,, I don't have the slightest idea, to tell you the truth. I just thought we could drive around and maybe see him somewhere. It could be that he has just gone for dinner and we think that he left the base. Everything is possible."

We got into my car and closed the doors behind us. I started the car and we left the parking space in reverse. I turned the car and from first to second gear we drove onto the central road of the base. We past the mess hall which was packed at this time of day, we could hear the chattering and laughter from inside, out here. We couldn't find Silk in the mess hall, so we left and drove to the cinema of the base that tonight showed the movie < Die Hard> with Bruce Willis. The movie was still very successful judging from the line of people waiting there to see it. We kept driving, we drove past three towers and we arrived at the shooting range, where Pamela Simpson's dead body was found. It was totally quiet around us. On the left side we could see the shooting range although it was dark. No more practice was done for today and so there was not a soul to be seen on the range. I stopped the car and grabbed the package of cigarettes and lit one for me and Sarah. I opened the windows completely and rested my head on the door so that I could enjoy my smoke. I looked at the sky and noticed that it was pitch dark tonight. From a far I could hear thunder and see lightning shoot into the sky, which prepared us that a storm was coming tonight. The rain would cool us down a lot. It was about time. After a loud thunder, lightning struck down on earth just near where we were. It threw light on the whole shooting range and made it seem like day all around. Due to the lightning we could see the fake figures standing all around the shooting range, which they used for practice. They looked like ghosts standing still. Some of them were positioned behind obstacles other stuck in the mud surrounded by sacks of sand. Suddenly we heard another loud thunder and shortly after that another blinding lightning struck down. Sarah shook up and a short scream came out of her lips. I looked at her at I had to laugh.

„ Why are you laughing? Has that never happened to you, that you got frightened by lightning?"

„ No, it has never happened to me."

Sarah's face turned red and if she could she would hide under the seat. I stopped laughing, I didn't want her to feel ashamed and so I started the car. We drove back to the building of the military police. They informed us that Silk hasn't been found or arrested yet.

„ How can it be that he hasn't been found yet? The base cannot be that big!"

„ We checked every centimeter of the base but it was impossible to find him. I am sorry, Sir."

„ Did you check the gate again? Maybe he was seen there?"

„ Yes, Sir. I call every few minutes to check, but he is nowhere to be seen."

„ If he hasn't passed the gate, how can it be that he hasn't been found anywhere?"

„ I don't know, Sir?"

I grabbed a chair and sat down. I was thinking about what mistakes we made so that he could disappear into thin air. About three hours had passed and we hadn't found him yet. Meanwhile I was sure that he had read something on the papers, maybe his name or something from the reports about him on my desk and so he felt the need to disappear. He tricked me with his behavior and I fell for it like a small boy. Silk played innocent and I believed like an idiot that he didn't notice anything. The Officer on duty called for a hundredth time Silk's secretary and again he got a negative answer. No, Silk didn't go back to his office. Sarah was so kind to bring us each a cup of freshly brewed hot coffee. She left the cups on the Officer's desk and pulled the other chair closer and sat down next to me. We were both lost in our thoughts and didn't say a word to each other. Every fifteen minutes a message came through the radio, that the search hadn't brought any result. Slowly I lost every hope I had left that we would find him. I had to admit that I made a huge mistake and Silk slipped through my fingers. The Officer on duty stopped right in front of me and asked me:

„ Mister Man. You gave us the order to confiscate the suspect's car, is that correct?"

„ And what don't you like about this order?"

„ I thought, why you don't give the order to do the same with his office!"

At first I didn't understand what he wanted to say, but when he said <office> a bell rang. There was something about this office I didn't like at all, but I couldn't think of what it was.

„ You are absolutely right. It totally slipped my mind. Gather some men and go immediately over there and confiscate everything there is in this fucking office. If anybody should stop you, inform me immediately and I will sort it out!"

„ Are you not coming with us?"

„ No. I have to take care of something else and I will meet you there. Tell me, where I can find the blue prints on the buildings of the base?"

„ In the General's office. They are kept there."

„ Thank you. Gather your men and make your way as quickly as possible to the office!"

The Officer left, I called the Generals and approximately half an hour later I had all the blue prints of the base laying in front of me on the desk. Of course, the only thing that really interested me was the blue print of the psychology school. We unfolded the print and I studied it. I checked every centimeter and found exactly what I was looking for.

„ Here it is, what I was looking for!" I pointed on one particular spot on the print.

„ What is it?"

„ It is sort of a hidden door. I had a look yesterday in his office but I couldn't find it. He must have hidden it so it will not be seen. Now that I have the plans of the building it is easy to find."

„ What do you mean? What hidden door?" Sarah asked.

„ Yesterday, as I was waiting in the Colonel's office, something weird happened."

„ What was that?"

„ It went like this. When I arrived there his secretary told me that he was not in the office yet and that I should wait for him. So I sat there waiting. After a few minutes the office door opened and the Colonel came out of it. I think that he didn't think we would be there and he was pretty surprised to see me and the secretary there. He tried to talk himself out of it by blaming the secretary for not being in his place when he himself was sitting in his office for a quite a while. I found this weird and so I asked the secretary and he swore that he hadn't left his desk since early in the morning. This is also the reason I have such a big interest for this office and as it turned out I was right."

„ And now he escaped from this secret door!, Sarah said frustrated.

„ Yes, unfortunately. I should have asked for the blue prints earlier. Then we would have caught him by now. Come, let's go to the office and check this door out. There is nothing else we can do now."

When we reached the building of the office, we saw the men of the military police leave the building carrying heavy boxes. Everything was sealed off and carried out of the office. When the Officer in charge saw us he informed us about everything that was going on.

„ Sir. We are almost done sealing off the Colonel's personal and official stuff. What should we do next?"

„ I want everything that is in his office to be packed, sealed and brought into my office. When you have everything there, post two guards at the door; they should wait for more orders from me."

„ Yes, Sir!"

While Sarah and I where inspecting Silk's office further, men of the military police where carrying out everything what was to be found in his office. They packed everything in cartons and sealed it up. The men took down the diplomas of the Colonel and wrapped them up in paper. As soon as they filled a box they closed it, sealed it with red tape and handed it to the next man standing next to them who carried the box out. Every file cabinet was opened and every last file and every piece of paper was taken out. The furniture that was in there was taken out and loaded onto a wan, to bring to storage. Meanwhile Sarah and me examined the windows, we pulled back one of the heavy curtains but behind them was only a window, behind the second window the same. When we pulled back the third curtain, we found what we were looking for. Behind the third curtain we found the treasure, the hidden door. It was a really old iron door with a round door knob. I took the door knob in my hand and turned it left and right but the door wouldn't open. I looked at Sarah and said to her:

„ Wait a moment here for me. I am back real soon."

„ Where are you going?"

I didn't answer her because I was already outside the office and opened the trunk of my car. After a few minutes I found what I was looking for in my tool box; a crowbar. I grabbed it and ran back into the office. Sarah looked at me surprised when I walked back in with the crowbar in my hand and stepped aside to give me some space. As much as I could I pushed one end in the gap between the door and the frame and with all my power I tried to break the door open, but it wouldn't. Sarah came next to me and grabbed the crowbar to join her force with mine and together we tried to open it. But the door would not move one centimeter. It was an old door but it was the most unbreakable door I have seen in my life. It wouldn't break open. I called a guy from the military police over, to help us. All three of us tried to break the door open with all the power we had left. At first it wouldn't move, but after a few seconds we heard a loud crack and we knew it wouldn't hold any longer. One last time we gathered all our strength and with a loud noise the lock broke and the door opened in front of us. We wiped the sweat of our foreheads and tried to catch our breath, as it took all our strength and we needed to cool down for a minute. I looked through the open door and all I could see was darkness and the last drops of the rain that fell on the floor. Luckily it had stopped raining and so we could follow the Colonel's track easily.

„ Do you think, Sir, that the Colonel sneaked out of this door?"

„ Yes, I am absolutely certain about that. But how could it be that no one knew about this door? I cannot understand that."

„ I don't want to be misunderstood, Sir, but the base is very old. Soldiers come and go and I am sure that if anyone knew about this door it would be heard around the base. Even more if we are talking about catching a killer. I will examine this matter with the door further and make sure that this entrance is closed down. We will build a wall here instead."

„ Alright, alright. I didn't want to offend you in any way. It is just that this whole situation got out of my hands and now this bastard has slipped through my fingers because I didn't deal with this door sooner. I am sure that he is laughing his ass off for tricking me."

Silent I stood in front of the open door and looked outside so I could clear my head on what I should do now, when suddenly a thunder was heard and lightning lit up the back area of the garden. This area led to the forest. Exactly in this moment I saw footsteps that could only belong to Silk, in the mud leading to the forest. I turned around looking for a light switch that would bring light to the back side of the building, but there was none.

„Bring me a flash light, at once!" I shouted to one of the soldiers.

Not even two minutes later I was holding a flash light in my hands and walked out the back side of the building following the trace that was clearly leading to the forest. They where fresh marks and luckily the storm had not destroy them. I turned around and walked back into the office. Quickly I opened the map of the base and laid it out on the remaining desk. Soon o found out where the forest ends and I was a hundred percent sure that Silk had taken this road to get away.

„ I need a troop that comes with me to walk through the forest and get to this point here."

I pointed at the spot on the map so that the officer could see it.

„ Yes, Sir. What else do you need?" he asked me.

„ I want every man to be fully armed, holding their guns. Another troop should wait on the outside of the fence for us to arrive. Two or three Jeeps should be enough. There is a great chance that we will need to chase after the Colonel and I don't want to lose any more time."

„ Yes, Sir."

In twenty minutes he had called together a group of twenty men. Ten men would join me in the woods and the other ten would wait on the outside of the fence on the other side. With our flash lights at hand, we walked through the woods without any problems. In some areas we heard birds fly away scared, other than that we heard nothing else. It was completely silent in the woods; we couldn't hear anything besides our steps. Nobody said a word and we focused on making our way through there. We moved as silently as we could, because we were not sure if Silk was still in this area. If he still was we didn't want to tip him of. With every brick that broke under our weight, our hands automatically reached for our guns. This showed how tense and nervous we were. After a few kilometers we reached the fence and stopped. I ordered the men to search the area for foot marks. It didn't take long for them to find some. The marks led to a thick bush that was exactly next to the fence. I was sure that we were getting closer to him and I ordered the men to examine the bush and pull it apart. We pulled the bush apart and found a big hole in the fence that was behind it. I started to swear, not minding about the other guys around me. Everyone walked through the hole and soon we were all standing on the dirt road on the other side of the fence. I tried to find foot marks on the dirt road and shined with my flash light on it in the dark. Unfortunately there was not even one lantern on this road to shed some light and so we could barely find some marks in the dirt. Not far away from where we were standing I found some marks of Silk's boots. I followed them and realized that they were moving north of the base. The men were following me without saying a word. I stopped walking and turned to them.

„ Two of you must stay here and wait for the other troop to arrive. When they arrive, follow us in the Jeeps."

We let two men stand there and walked for another kilometer, when suddenly it began to pour out of the sky. Due to the heavy rain we had trouble following the foot marks, because they were slowly getting washed away. Not far away we saw large bushes and a small group of trees and we hid under them to find shelter from the rain. I was hoping that the other troop with the jeeps would come soon so we could get dry, when suddenly one of the men said:

„ Sir, look at this!"

„ What is it Soldier?"

„ Come here and have a look at what I found. Behind the bush is a large tarp that was painted in camouflage colors."

That was weird, so I walked towards the soldier and he pointed at the tarp he found. Carefully I walk through the bush. At first I couldn't really see it but as I came closer I could see it. I walked over there and kneeled down to examine it. It could be that this tarp was left here a while ago and someone forgot it while exercising in the woods. As I examined it further I could see that it was almost new. I thought about it a little bit and drew the conclusion that someone was hiding a car under here so it would not be found. I thought so because the tarp was big enough and could cover a car completely so that it would not be visible from the road or the air. That's why it was here! A car was hidden here outside the base just in case he needed it to get away. I was absolutely certain it was Silk's car. I stood up and walked around the bush; I found a set of tire marks that came out under the tarp and were slowly washed away by the rain. After that we couldn't see any marks; they were all washed away by the rain already.

CHAPTER 34

H e started the pickup truck and drove, like the devil was chasing him, to his house. It started pouring again but this time the rain was heavier and he could barely see the road in front of him. His right hand went automatically to the radio and turned it on. He searched for a good radio station for a few minutes but couldn't find anything so he turned it off again. He was not so far from his house anyway. Approximately one kilometer away from his house he slowed down a bit and drove slowly into his street. He found a spot on the street where there was no light and parked the car there. Since it was still raining so much and he had parked in a darker spot, there was no way the neighbors would see him. He opened the door, got out and closed the door behind carefully not making loud noises. As soon as he stood outside he was wet to the bone, but he didn't bother. Carefully he walked to his house and hid behind a flower bush that was in the neighbor's garden to look around. He didn't see anyone around the house so he was sure that no one was looking for him yet. He didn't want to waste any more time and ran to his house, unlocked the door and entered it quickly. As soon as he was in he locked the door behind him. Now he could take a breath. He didn't need any light, he knew how to get around in his house without it and if a patrol would drive by, they should think the house is empty. Quickly he walked up the stairs and went into the bedroom. He stood in front of the closet and opened the doors. With the right hand he turned the lamp on that was hanging in the closet. It was just the light ball without any cover but it was so week that there was no way it could be seen from the outside. In the closet was a small stool and he took it in his hand. He put it in front of a shelf and stepped on it. On the top shelf of the closet he had an already packed suitcase, just in case he needed to disappear quickly. With both hands he grabbed the suitcase and threw it on the bed. He sat next to it and opened the locks. On top of his clothes was a small leather bag which he took in his hands. In there were passports, cash and a few different credit cards issued in different names. The cash came from his life insurance policy which he got paid out recently and also the inheritance of his father, so he would never have to worry about money. He had so much money saved in the bank that would easily be enough to start a new life. Of course, the account was in another name. He opened the account and had all the necessary paper work and ID in the same name. He knew that one day they would get close to him so he had everything planned. Now it was time to leave the country as soon as possible and start a new life somewhere, maybe Mexico. He wanted to continue his experiments someplace else. Somewhere where nobody knew him and nobody would disturb him. He left the suitcase on the bed and ran down to the basement, turned the light on and walked to the safe. He put in the code numbers and took the small box out of the safe and locked it again. With the box in his hands he went back upstairs in the bedroom. He stood there thinking with the box still in his hands. He put the box on top of his clothes in the suitcase and wanted to close it but then he opened it again. He took the box out of the suitcase again and opened the lid to look at the content. Every time he looked at what was inside the box his breath stopped and he starred at his treasure. Suddenly he had a really crazy idea. Quickly he closed the lid to the box and put it back in the suitcase. He closed the suitcase and put it on the floor next to him. He walked to the closet and got dry clothes. Quickly he changed his clothes and threw the wet ones in the back of the closet and left them there. He took the suitcase in his hand again and walked down to the hallway before the front door. He took a light jacket from the coat stand and put it on. In the jacket's pocket was a cap and he put it on his head. Next to the coat stand was a small closet, he opened it. From a shelf in the closet he took out a small green metal box and held it in his hand. He brought it in the kitchen and left it on the table. Out of the box he took a nine millimeter pistol and it was so well polished that it seemed to glow. It felt good in his hand and he held it up to his left eye to aim. Due to the moon light that was coming in the window, the gun was shining even brighter. In the dark he shouted so loud that if anyone could hear him they would freeze out of fear.,, Tonight you will die, slut!" He put the pistol in the waistband of his pants and put the box under the table. He took the suitcase, walked out the kitchen door and disappeared into the dark.

CHAPTER 35

Packed in warm wool blankets we tried to warm ourselves up, drinking hot coffee, back at the desk of the Officer in duty in the building of the military police. Like a cat that was thrown in the water I was sitting here now talking to my boss, with the tail between my legs. I informed Jack about what happened and he was not happy about how the Colonel managed to slip through my fingers. I held the speaker about a centimeter from my ear because I was in no mood to hear his speech and I didn't want to get deaf from listening to him yell in the phone. I let him yell and swear at me and sometimes I answered,, Yes, Sir" or,, You are right, Sir!"

He was right; how could I let him get away like that. He was a dangerous man and he needed to get caught right away, because if we wouldn't catch him, we would have so many more victims. After about half an hour of yelling and swearing from my boss, I could finally put down the telephone. Frustrated I raised my shoulders and let them drop again. I needed to think of something fast otherwise I would lose control over the case even more. Sarah looked at me realizing what I was thinking and asked me:

,, What do we do now? I mean what can we do to catch this bastard?"

I looked at her and raised my shoulders again. God, I really didn't know what we could do! I had another sip of the hot coffee and I got this blanket off of me; I was getting really hot now. I finished my coffee, put the cup on the desk and turned to Sarah.

,, Come on, I will drive you home now. It is late and you look really tired. You could need a few hours of sleep!"

The poor girl was yarning all the time and I felt sorry for her. I looked at my watch and noticed that it was three o'clock in the morning already.

„ Alright. Let's go home, I have the feeling I could fall asleep here on the spot."

She got up and said goodbye to the other men. Twenty minutes later we were outside her house.

„ So, I wish you a good night, the rest of it. Will you sleep too?" Sarah asked me while she was opening the door.

„ To tell you the truth I am too nervous to think about sleeping. I have so much energy right now, I cannot even explain it. Adrenalin is flowing through my veins and it is impossible for me right now even to lay down for half an hour. Do you want to have a drink and watch some TV?"

„ I don't believe you my friend! I need some sleep and I am in no mood for your games right now!"

„ You are absolutely right. I need to go back to the officer any way. Maybe he has some news for me. And I also need to write a report for my boss, otherwise he is going to tear my head off. He needs to see the report on his desk by today morning."

She gave me a quick kiss and turned around to walk up the drive way to her house. I watched her while she was unlocking the door and soon the closed the door behind her again. I started the car and drove towards the base again.

Sarah walked up the stairs to the first floor and while she was walking she took her jacket off and let it fall on the ground. She had no strength left to carry the jacket with her until the bedroom, only thinking about it made her yarn again and she stretched her arms in the air. She didn't even bother to turn on the light in the bedroom and started taking off the wet clothes, even before she got in the room, letting them fall on the floor. Now she had nothing on except her string tanga. He came out behind the open door of the bedroom and watched her get undressed. He sneaked up on her from behind, without making a sound. One step after the other he got closer to her and was now about twenty centimeters away from her back. He held the pistol in his right hand and was watching her how she got undressed without her knowing that he was right there behind her. When she put her hand on her string to pull it down he talked to her without warning.

„ Good evening, beautiful!"

When she heard his voice she froze and was afraid to move again. With slow movements she turned around and when she saw him in front of her she started screaming. The scream got cut short because in this moment he hit her with the back of the gun on her head and she passed out on the floor. Her body was laying not moving on the ground. He put the pistol back in his waistband and to get her up and put her over his shoulder. With her body hanging over his shoulder he walked back down the stairs into the living room. He threw her on the couch and left her there for now. From one of his pockets he got tape, that he had brought with him, cut of a piece and taped her mouth shut. The he took her hands and legs and taped them together so that she couldn't move. He turned around and moved the coffee table so that it would not be on the carpet. He pulled Sarah down on the edge of the carpet and started rolling it together with her in it. Finally he had a big roll laying in front of him, he bent down and threw the carpet with Sarah in it on his shoulder. With the carpet he went out the front door and walked to his truck, which he had parked down the street. He got there and threw the carpet in the back and quickly got in the car. The storm became wilder but he didn't care that he got wet. The girl? A little rain wouldn't hurt her. If she would get sick, he did care, in a few hours she would be dead anyway. With this thought in mind he started laughing and couldn't hold himself together anymore. He started the motor put in first gear and drove back to his house, without anyone seeing him.

CHAPTER 36

The drive back to the base seemed unending, I could barely keep my eyes open but now I was finally there. I went into my office to write a full report about what happened last night for my boss. I felt like a complete idiot and couldn't deal with the fact that Silk had played me like this. I should have nailed him from the beginning, but I could never have seen this case turn out like this. What the consequences of this case were I was not completely sure, but I would need to deal with some sort of punishment for sure. I looked at my watch again and saw that it was almost six in the morning. Finally I had finished my report and put it in the fax machine to send to my boss. As far as I knew him, he was already in his office waiting on this damn report. I was sure he would rip my head off, but to tell the truth, I didn't really care. I had made the decision that this would be the last case I would do for the military. I sat down at the desk and started writing my notice. When I finished writing it, I put it in an envelope and called a soldier in my office. I gave him the envelope and ordered him to send it Washington. When he left I sat back in my chair, put my feet up and my hands behind my head. Let the serial killer and the military go to hell. Determined I got up and started packing my personal items and clear my desk. The files I put in my bag, grabbed it and started walking towards the door. One more time I turned around and looked at my desk and turned off the light. When I got out the office the soldier that was on watch saluted me. I got out of the building and put on my sunglasses as I was walking to the car. I took the car and drove towards hotel. On my way there I passed the building of the military police and drove past it. Then I thought about it again, turned around and parked in front of the military police. I walked up the stairs of the building and this time no one opened the doors, because the soldiers were not at their places. I thought they would all be out looking for Silk and that's why there are so little men in the building. I opened the door and entered the building, finding the officer of duty talking on the phone to someone and making notes. When he saw me coming he put down the phone and saluted me.

,, Good morning, Sir. How are you?"

,, Not so good. And you? Do you have any news about the search of the Colonel?"

,, No, Sir. Unfortunately not. Still no sign of him. We informed all stations about his arrest warrant. I took the liberty and informed the state police and send them a picture, but so far they have nothing. It is as he has vanished from the face of the earth. I am sorry!"

,, You should not feel sorry, you have done everything in your power. It was my entire fault not yours."

,, Last night I send a patrol to his house and they searched it. They examined the house from top to bottom but could not find anything incriminating. The men searched every floor but couldn't find anything out of the ordinary. I was informed that the house does not look abandoned and as I understood everything was still in its place."

,, What do you mean;,,everything was in its place"?

,, I mean, that nothing unusual went down I this house. His closet was full of uniforms and track suits and there was no indication that anything was missing. Besides that there was a large suitcase found inside the closet. All the clothes where neatly placed on the shelves or on the hangers. The bed was made perfectly and nothing looked like someone was rushing to get away. The men said that they had the impression that the owner is away on vacation, not on the run, if you understand what I am saying."

,, Weird, very weird."

,, I absolutely agree, Sir." he answered me.

,, This bastard was definitely prepared for running, this is the only explanation that explains the hidden getaway car under the tarp we found. What orders did you give out for the house?"

,, We have tapes all the doors and exits of the house and every fifteen minutes a patrol drives by and checks the area. I ordered to question and write down name and address of anyone that is found near the house. By any suspicious move or person we will be informed immediately."

„ Alright. I will go back to the hotel, have a shower and pack all my stuff. At noon the FBI will arrive to take over the case. We will meet here again in an hour so you can update me."

CHAPTER 37

I threw the dirty and sweaty clothes on the floor and walked naked into the bathroom. I turned on the water and stood under the hot shower letting the water wash away all of what happened. I closed my eyes and relaxed with the hot water falling down on my head. With closed eyes I reached for the shower gel, I found it immediately and started washing my body. I washed everything of, turned the water of and came out of the shower. I grabbed a large towel and wrapped it around my waste. With the right hand I went over my chin and realized that I needed to shave. So, I stood in front of the bathroom mirror and wanted to take the razor blade and the gel out of my toilet bag, when I looked into the mirror and froze. Something was written with invisible ink on the mirror.

„ COME AND ARREST ME; IF YOU CAN! SILK"

For a moment I stood there staring at the mirror and I was not sure if I should move at all. My brain worked on full speed and I was thinking about the Colonel. When and how could he come in to my room without being seen? This man was an evil genius with an evil mind.

Slowly he really started to piss my off. Swearing I left the bathroom and went into the room to put on a clean uniform. While I was getting dressed I sat on the bed and called the military police to speak with the Officer again. I asked if he had any news, but again I got a negative answer. I thanked him and put down the phone. I picked it right up again and called Sarah's house number. It rang and rang but no one picked up at the other end of the line, somehow that made me really nervous. I threw the phone on the bed and rushed out of the room. I run the stairs down two or three at a time so I would be outside the hotel quicker. I didn't stop once to apologize for my behavior to the other guests because I didn't want to lose any more time. I opened the driver's door of my car and hadn't even closed the door when I started the car. With squeaking tires I drove of the parking area towards the exit of the base. I drove with a hundred miles an hour and was thinking constantly about Sarah. If this bastard had her, it will not end well for her if I cannot find her. Let her be in her bed sleeping tightly. This must be the reason she didn't pick up the phone. Last night she was exhausted and desperately needed a few hours of sleep. O drove so fast that I didn't realize that I was already driving up her driveway. I stepped on the break so hard that I left tire marks on the drive way. Quickly I opened the driver's door and didn't even bother to close the door behind me or turn off the car, I just ran to the house. When I arrived at the door, I wanted to knock on the door, when I realized that the door was open. My hand went straight to my gun and determined I entered the house. As it was still early in the morning, the house was wrapped in darkness but I didn't want to turn on any lights; I was not sure what or who was in the house. By now I knew my way around the house and made my way quickly without knocking over any of the furniture. I listened in the dark but couldn't hear a thing. Everything was quiet. With careful movements I searched every corner of the ground floor but couldn't find anything out of the ordinary. Now I wanted to check the upstairs and walked silently up the stairs. Here I had exactly the same result as downstairs, nothing. The bedroom was empty and I could see Sarah's dirty clothes laying on the floor. The bed was made and was waiting for someone to lay in it. But Sarah was nowhere to be seen. Spontaneously I called her name, but got no answer. With the gun in my hand I walked around, making sure that I was alone. The house was completely empty and Sarah was not here. Still holding my pistol I walked down the stairs and wanted to go into the living room. As I still hadn't turned on any light, I reached for the light switch and turned the lights on. My eyes needed a second to adapt to the light, and then I saw what went down. I found the coffee table pushed to the other side of the room. The big couch was knocked over. The two small side tables next to the couch were knocked over and I realized that the large, white carpet is missing. What the hell happened in here? Maybe a burglar came in and took the carpet with him? But why take the carpet; he would have taken the stereo or the TV? This was no burglar. It was Silk! I looked for the phone and called the base. In a few minutes, cars of the military police where outside the house. Everything in this house was examined top to bottom and every piece of furniture and every door where checked for fingerprints. Even I got questioned by the state police. They asked all those stupid questions, like, how I got in the house, why I am here and so on. I answered every question as good as I could. The men of the military police went from door to door to collect information from the neighbors, if they had seen anything suspicious last night. But, as always in such cases, no one of the neighbors heard or saw anything or anyone that should not be here. I looked at the crime scene again and figured it out by myself. Silk rolled Sarah in the carpet and carried her out this way.

CHAPTER 38

He threw her like a sack of potatoes on the back of the truck and drove back to his house. He parked in the same spot he had parked a few hours ago. He turned the car off and waited patiently in the dark. From this point, he had a clear view on the house, on the houses next to his and on the road. He wanted to wait a little while in the car and have an eye on the street. He was not sure yet but he could feel they were looking for him, especially since he wrote the note on the Detective's mirror. By now he must have the military police looking for the doctor. A smile was on his face as he imagined the Detective's face when he saw the message on his mirror. This was the cherry on the cake. He made himself comfortable on the seat and he didn't bother that it was till pouring outside. In fact, he liked it, because it was harder to be seen in the dark and in the rain. He wanted to wait in his car for a while because he had this feeling that something would happen in the next minutes. A few minutes after arriving he saw a patrol car driving down his street, stopping in front of the house for a few minutes and drive off again. He was right to park here in the dark. He watched the patrol driving all the way up the street and then back again until he lost sight of them. The same thing happened every few minutes and slowly he became restless and couldn't wait any longer. He decided to enter his house from the other side that looked to the forest. On this side was a hidden door, which he had build himself some years back. He thought he was a complete fool; why didn't he think of this door earlier? He waited for the patrol to drive off again and started the car. He left his parking space and drove down the street. It took him about twenty minutes until he reached the spot in the forest where the door to his secret tunnel to the house was. It took him a while to get there because he was driving with the lights off. He didn't want any of the neighbors to see him through the window. Finally he made it to the right spot. He had found the two trees he was looking for and abruptly stopped the car. Quickly he turned the motor of. He got of the car and searched in his pocket for his key chain. Hastily he looked for the key to open the hatch to the tunnel and he found it at once. He walked to the trees and kneeled next to them. With quick movements he cleared the leaves he had laid on top of the hatch and pushed them aside. Under the leaves was a green tarp and he took it off and just threw it next to him. Before unlocking he looked around again to see if anyone was looking. He couldn't see a soul, so he unlocked and left the lock on the floor. Maybe he would need it later on, so he decided not to throw it away. With shaking hands he pulled at the chain that was attached to the hatch. Finally he opened it. Again he stood still for a minutes and listened into the forest. Slowly the sun came out so he would be visible soon. He had to hurry; the neighbors would wake up soon. Quickly he walked to the truck, took the carpet and let it down on the floor. He took Sarah out of the carpet and threw it back on the truck. He picked Sarah up, threw her over his shoulder and walked to the hatch. He let her glide down into the hatch. She was still unconscious, so hard was the blow to the head. He squeezed himself into the tunnel with her and closed the hatch behind him. Now he could lock the door from the inside. He had build the door this way so that it was easy to lock from the inside as well. Suddenly he heard a groaning from Sarah which meant that she was gaining consciousness. He turned to her and slapped her gently to wake up sooner. He cut the tape which he used to tie the legs together. So he wouldn't have to carry her all the way to the secret room and she could walk there. The tunnel that reached all the way under his house was not longer than 120 meters. As he had build the tunnel himself it became narrower at some point and wider at other. The same thing happened with the ceiling. One moment they could stand up and walk and the next moment they had to bend over so that they wouldn't hit their heads. Sarah's mouth was still taped and her hands were too, he even covered her eyes, so she had to walk in the dark. She was only wearing her string and her feet were bare so it was even harder for her to walk down this tunnel. She realized that she was walking barefoot over dirt and sometimes tripped over roots that came in her way. As she had no idea where she was walking she tripped a lot and fell down on her knee and grazed it. Then she felt this disgusting creature grabbing her from the back and shouting at her to move quicker. Her head was hurting and she had a bitter iron taste in her mouth. It must be from the wound that she had on her head from when he hit her. She could barely move and wanted to rest for a moment but the Colonel hit her in the back and pushed her to keep moving. Suddenly she stepped on a stone and wanted to scream in pain, but no sound came out of her mouth. She could feel the wound on her foot and that blood was coming out of it. Some more silent moments passed and he said no word to her, when suddenly, he pulled at her arm and ordered her to stop. She felt that he squeezed past her and stood in front of her. She tried to listen and understand what he was doing and then she realized that he was looking for the right key on his keychain. After a few seconds she heard the lock open. He ordered her not to move or else he would shoot her right here and just leave her laying here. She begged him not do shoot her and she promised to behave and wait here. Although no real words came out of her mouth, he must have understood her. He laughed at her because he could see that she got goose pumps all over and started shaking when he threatened her. Then he turned around and walked in the small room that was behind the door. He tried to hear any noise in the room but there was nothing, slowly he pushed the poster aside that hang on the outside wall of the room and walked into his basement. Again he listened carefully but everywhere was complete silence. Pleased he got back into the little room and put the poster back into its place. He turned on the light and went to the door where Sarah was waiting and pulled her by the arm to get her in the room. She tripped and almost fell down again but in the last moment he grabbed her and kept her from falling. She didn't want her to break anything because she would only be crying out of pain. Then she would be useless and he would have to shoot her. He couldn't stand women crying. He wanted to be the one to cause her pain and when he would be done with her he would shoot her, and only then.

CHAPTER 39

S ara's house was filled with military police officers, people from the
forensic team I had never seen before in my life. I sat on the couch in
the living room and smoked the last cigarette that was in my packet. Her
black cat sat on my lap and I ruffled him behind the ears. He let me touch
him but he was hissing at everyone else he didn't know that came to close
to him. My friend Thomas from the laboratory of the forensic team sat
down next to me.

„ Well John. We checked the whole house for prints and I am sure that
we will have him in our results. Because he left you this message he must
be sure that you are on to him and looking for him. This is why I assume
that he wore no gloves to hide his identity. Don't worry. We will free this
girl from his hands."

„ How can you be so sure Thomas?" I asked him exhausted.„ I am also
sure that we will find her but that she will already be dead. And I cannot
help her anymore. I shouldn't have left her here, I should have insisted to
stay with her here. Now it's too late. It is much too late."

„ Now you listen to me, you stubborn blockhead" Thomas said and
made me look into his eyes.„ It is not too late and you know it." I wanted
to turn my head away from him but he was holding it in his hands.„ Even
if it is too late, what I absolutely don't believe, we will have his fingerprints
in her house and that will be his sentence. Do you understand me, John?
We can connect him to the murders and that was it for him."

„ No, you don't understand me, my friend. I will be his sentence and
you can bet on that. He messed with me and I will not let him get away
with it!"

I let the cat sit next to Thomas and just walked away from them. All this noise in the living room got too much for me and I couldn't stand it anymore. Where should I look for her? How did he manage to get her out of here without anyone seeing him? First of all, where did he take her? I wanted to light a cigarette but then I realized that my packet was empty. I remembered that I had a new packet in my car and so I went outside. As I was walking to my car, my phone rang. Great, Jack called me. What did he want now? Basically I didn't want to answer him and I let it ring, then I changed my mind.

„ Yes, Jack. What can I do for you? I asked him over tired; my legs wouldn't hold me much longer.

„ John, what is going on there? I just had a call from Thomas and I don't know what I should think of it!"

„ What do you want me to say Jack? That I am sorry he took her. That you should all go to hell and leave me alone. What do you want me to say, Jack?" I asked him.

I tried to sound hard but tears were running down my cheeks and my voice began to tremble. My legs lost their strength and I just fell on the lawn and just sat there. I heard Jack shouting out my name like wild, but I had no strength left to answer him. My cell phone fell out of my hand and I buried my face into my hands and started crying; I couldn't hold it any longer. I had found the woman of my dreams and lost her shortly after that forever in such a cruel way. She didn't deserve that. I don't know, how long I sat there on the lawn crying like a small boy, but suddenly I heard the voice of Jack again. I looked at my phone and saw that the line was still open and he could hear me. He heard me all this time crying and didn't interrupt my once. I picked the cell phone up again and talked to him.

„ Jack, are you still there?"

„ Yes, my friend, I am still here. Do you want me to come over there and we can all rip this guy apart together?", he asked me and wanted to calm me down this way.

„ Thank you for your offer, but I am feeling much better. Either way you always say, that I am the best man, or not?"

„ You are absolutely right. You are. You are my best man. Get yourself together and find him and the girl. Did you understand me?"

„ Yes, I understood you. We will hear from each other!"

With these words I ended this call and put my cell phone back in my pocket.

I needed to clear my head now and lit a cigarette from the new packet I had in my car. Lost in my thoughts I inhaled the smoke deep into my lungs and held it for a few seconds. When I felt almost dizzy I exhaled again and already I was feeling better. I looked up the street and noticed that at almost every door a soldier was standing talking to the neighbors. Maybe we had some luck and someone could say something that could help us move along. For the hundredth time I took out my cell phone and called the Officer at headquarters to see if they had any news about Silk. As on my previous calls I got the answer that there was still no sign of him. The search for him hadn't stopped a second and was running on full power, but still no success. I thanked the Officer for his information and put my phone back in the pocket. I threw the cigarette bud on the lawn and lit the next one. This case would turn me into a chain-smoker. I looked at the soldier that was talking to a home owner just across the street. It looked as he just came back home. The soldier asked him a few questions and the man answered with an intense tone and was constantly pointing to me and the house. Did we maybe found the witness we were looking for? I was very interested what he was saying so I walked over there. I stood there with them and showed the man my identification. He looked at it and saluted me at once when he read my rank.

„ Good morning, Soldier."

„ Good morning, Sir."

„ Do you have anything to report that would help us with our search for Officer Connors?"

„ I couldn't say, but as I told the Soldier, I saw something last night that felt strange especially in this weather."

I was getting suspicious but I had the feeling that this man would help us get closer to finding Sarah. I released the soldier that was questioning the man, thanked him and send him back to the house to inform his superior. Now I was standing with the witness on the street alone. I lit a cigarette and offered him one too. He thanked me but said that he was not smoking. Again these damn non smokers.

„ So, tell me what you saw last night."

„ Yes, Sir. Well it was like this. I got up last night around two o'clock because my shift started at four. You need to know, Sir that I own a dog and so after I had my coffee, I took him out on the street for a walk"

„ Around what time was that, can you say?"

„ It must have been around three, three fifteen. I cannot tell you exactly."

„ Alright, then what happened?"

„ As I told you all this felt strange especially in this stormy weather. Anyway, I was with my dog about two houses away from here when I saw a guy with a rolled up carpet on his shoulder coming out of Officer Connors house. I remember that because I found it weird."

„ Why? It could be that Officer Connors didn't have any other time available and found a man that could help her at that time carry the carpet out of the house and get it cleaned. What do you say?"

„ At first I thought that too. I must admit. Especially with the weird shifts we all have on the base. But as closer I got to the guy the stranger he appeared."

„ How close did you get to the guy? Did you, by any chance recognize him?"

„ I was about thirty meters from him. Maybe a few meters more or less. I am sorry, I saw him but I didn't know him."

„ Did he see you?"

„ No, I don't think so, in the moment I wanted to talk to him, my dog pulled me behind a bush to do his business."

„ What was it that made you feel strange and suspicious?"

„ This was it. I thought that if Officer Connors would order someone to clean her carpet he would put it in a car and take it to the cleaner's but he would never throw it on the back of a wet, dirty pickup truck in the heavy rain. Not a nice large white carpet, don't you think?"

„ And what if she wanted to throw it out?"

„ She could have let it outside the door at any time. The bulky refuse garbage pickup comes in a few days where she could throw out anything she didn't need."

„ How do you know that?" I asked him surprised, but I knew I had a great observer in front of me.

„ Two weeks ago they left a note on the garbage bins to have anything prepared when they come if we want to throw something out."

„ Alright. Can you describe the man that you saw last night?"

„ Not really well, as I said it was raining really heavy at the time."

He gave me a description of the man he saw and it sounded exactly as the Colonel. The soldier gave me a pretty good description of the truck as well, that was parked here on the street. Except the license plates, because there where none. He brought me to the exact spot the car was parked. We talked for a while and he wished me good luck on the search for Sarah. I stood there on the street looking from the spot where the car was parked up to Sarah's house. He had found a pretty easy hiding spot in the dark and as it was raining so much last night he was not seen. I could slap myself. Why didn't I see him last night? I blamed myself, but I must admit that we both were overtired and so exhausted. This is why we didn't pay attention. I went back inside the house and informed the leading investigator what I had found out and the description of the pickup truck. Again I lit a cigarette and looked around in the house. Because of the investigations so many unfamiliar people were walking around here that had no place here. Sarah's private life was completely out in the open and I hated it. I would like to throw them all out now. I looked at my watch and realized that it was almost eleven o'clock. In about one hour, the people from the FBI would be on the base to rip the case off my hands. I had to do something to find Sarah as soon as possible. I didn't trust the FBI with this sort of cases.

CHAPTER 40

I left Sarah's house and drove back to the base. In the hotel I quickly packed my suitcase and left the key at the reception. After that I drove back to the building of the military police and left the pile of files on the Officer's desk so that he could hand them to the people of the FBI and they could finish the case. I looked at my watch and it was twelve o'clock so the FBI could arrive any minute now on the base. As I had no interest in meeting them I left the building and went outside on the parking lot. Officially I was now off the case, but unofficially I still needed to find Sarah and the bastard, if it would be the last thing I would do. I just wanted to light a cigarette when I realized that I had none left. Great! Where would I get cigarettes now? I got in my car and drove on the base's main street. I was so lost in my thoughts that I didn't even know where I was driving to. Colonel Silk had everything well planed and had us all running in circles. That he still had the nerve to kidnap Sarah was the tip of the iceberg. The idea with the carpet was not bad; he could get her out of the house without anyone seeing her in his hands. As far as our witness told us he just saw Silk coming out of the house with a rolled up carpet over his shoulders. Would Sarah be found dead the only thing we can tie him to is the carpet; nobody saw him with her. He could easily walk away with this murder but I wouldn't let him. Why did he break into my room to write me this note? Did he want me to catch and arrest him? How was he so sure that I would take a shower before leaving my room? He was also sure that I was on to him and wanted to catch him. That is why he ran. He knew that I would find the hidden door and that I would follow him to the woods. As it was raining he knew that we would get so wet and dirty and that the first thing I would do when I got back is go to my room, have a shower and change clothes. That is why he wrote that note. Sure he also knew that something was going on between me and Sarah. He knew that from the time he attacked her in her house and suddenly I showed up and scared him away. He must only count one and one together. He challenged me and I accepted the challenge. I only had to think about it with a clear head. Ideas where spinning through my mind, when I suddenly realized that I was driving in the street Silk was living. As I was already here I thought I would look at the house a little closer. He was on the run anyway so I wouldn't disturb him in the shower or something. I parked my car in front of his house and turned the motor off. I had just opened the driver's door when I saw the patrol car coming closer. They must have seen me and drove slowly my way. The stopped next to me and one of them got off the car and came over to my side. He didn't even have time to ask me any questions when I showed him my badge. He saluted me at once.

„ Good day, Soldier", I said.

„ Good day, Sir."

„ How long are you on patrol on this street?"

„ Since ten o'clock this morning, Sir!"

„ Did you see or hear anything suspicious, Soldier?"

„ No, Sir!"

„ Did anyone come near the house? No one dressed as an electrician or a gas man? Nobody that looked suspicious?"

„ No, Sir. Not a soul came near the house."

„ Did you have a look inside the house, maybe he got in from the back door?"

„ No, Sir. We were only told to patrol on the street."

„ Is that so? Okay. Then I will personally have a look inside. Continue your patrol."

„ Yes, Sir!"

We saluted each other and he turned and went back to the Jeep. The Jeep drove off slowly away from me. I walked up the driveway and I was standing in front of his door. I didn't even think to ask the patrol if the door was unlocked. I reached for the door knob, turned it and I was surprised but the door opened up in front of me and I could see into the dark hallway. They didn't even bother to lock the door. My hand instinctively reached to my back and I held my gun firmly in my hand.

CHAPTER 41

He took her through the tunnel as fast as he could, to get to that basement fast. She was walking so slowly, like a snail, and if he hadn't boxed her in the ribs constantly, they would still be in this tunnel. He must admit, it was not easy for the girl to walk through there blindfolded and barefoot, but again, the needed to get there eventually. When they got in the basement and he was sure that they were on their own he drugged her using ether. She fought like a lion and kicked around but in the end, the drug was stronger than her. Unconscious she fell into his arms and he picked her up and laid her on a ping pong table and tied her up so that every arm and every leg where tied up at one corner of the table. He left her there on the table and walked into the other room; the room where the safe and the other furniture was. Exhausted he sat down on the couch and put his head in his hands. He was pretty tired because he got no sleep last night, but he didn't want to lay down. He didn't want to be caught while sleeping. He got up and walked across the room and bend down. On the bottom shelf of a bookcase there were some small bottles with different names on them. Valerian drops, caffeine tablets, morphine and some more, that were used as painkillers. With his right hand he opened the bottle with the label caffeine tablets. He took four of them in his left hand and swallowed them without water. Then he wanted to close the lid again, but then he thought it was not necessary, he would be out of the house in a few hours anyway. Forever. He felt that the tablets were kicking in and he felt the adrenalin pumping in his veins. At once the tiredness was gone and he felt awake. Now was his time. He went back into the room with the ping pong table and looked at the doctor. She was still unconscious. Perfect, now he had time to prepare her for the torture.

CHAPTER 42

With my gun in my hand I stepped inside the house with slow steps. After a few meters I stopped to listen if I would hear anything inside the house, but I could hear no sound. I decided to examine the ground floor first and walked to the closet that was next to me in the hallway. I turned the key, opened the door and had a closer look. The closet was packed with summer and winter jackets, some trainers and boots. Except the thick winter coat and a few hats nothing else was on the top shelf. The Colonel didn't seem like a person that cared much about fashion and has his closet full of stuff. I could see that because his jackets and shoes looked a little older. O closed the closet and walked into the living room. I didn't hold down my pistol, not even for a second, just in case. I could feel his presence in the house and it was killing me. I didn't have to turn on any lights in the living room because the sun was shining through the windows. I turned around and was surprised by how old all the furniture looked that was in this room. This furniture must be at least thirty years old, maybe even older. Despite their age they were in a pretty great condition. There was no CD player, Radio or TV in the room, not even a record player. How did this guy live here? He didn't have a single picture on the wall and no family photo on any of the furniture. I got goose bumps. Everything in here was so impersonal. I walked over to the living room closet and opened the drawers. I was amazed; everyone was completely empty. I couldn't believe that, if I thought about mine at home, how much small stuff was in there and I almost couldn't close them. I closed the drawers again and went into the next room. It turned out to be the kitchen. In the middle of the kitchen I stopped and looked around. I opened one cabinet after the other but there was hardly anything in there.

After that I opened the fridge. Except a few rotten pears and some black bananas, I found a piece of bacon on a plate and a few slices of bread in a plastic bag. The freezer was full of ready to serve dishes, that consisted more or less if pasta dishes. Enjoy your meal then. I just wanted to walk around the table when I stopped. I must have kicked something metal as I was walking. I looked down and saw a small green metal box; I picked it up at put it on the table. It was not hard to guess what kind of a box it was; I see boxes like that every day. It was the kind of metal boxes you get from the military to store your gun. You could see the outline of the gun in the fabric that was inside it, you could also see where the bullets were. Now I knew that this bastard had a gun. Of course he did. I was sure it would be not an easy game arresting this guy without him fighting back. I left the kitchen and walked upstairs, on the top floor where three bedrooms. As it turned out, two if the rooms were guest bedrooms that had their own little bathrooms. He hadn't even bothered to put some sheets on the bed, but anyway who would want to visit him or spend the night here. I made my way to the third bedroom that was the Colonel's bedroom. Looking around I noticed, just like in the living room, there was not one photo in the room. The large bed was covered with silk sheets and you could see not one wrinkle on them. I opened the nightstand's drawer and apart from a package of sleeping pills there was nothing in it. On the nightstand was a carafe of water with an empty glass standing next to it. Again nothing found. I left the nightstand and walked to the closet. I opened the closet with my left hand and held my gun steady in the right hand. I looked for the light switch in here and found it on the left side of the closet. A few seconds later the light was on and before me were all the Colonel's uniforms neatly hanging. I had a closer look and realized that all his uniforms were here and all his truck suits and his shoes. Nothing seems to be missing and I didn't know what to think of it. I still had the feeling that his getting away was well planned. He must have had a separate suitcase ready with false IDs, money and clothes. So that he would not even care if he would leave stuff behind in the house. My look went over to the back if the closet. Everything in his closet was perfectly organized so it confused me when I saw a pile of clothes in the back of the closet. I went back in the closet and walked to the pile of clothes. I picked them up one by one and noticed that they were wet. This was the proof for me that he did come back to the house. He needed to change into dry clothes and who knows what else he did. I got up again and left the closet. The only room I hadn't inspected was his bathroom. I walked in the bathroom. It was not a very large bathroom. On the right side, behind the door, was the bathtub. As I looked at the tub I could see that his bathrobes were hanging behind the door. I wanted to get a closer look at his mirror cabinet but again, a huge disappointment was waiting for me. Except shaving foam, after shave and a few razor blades nothing else was in here. On the sink was nothing except his toothbrush and toothpaste. And in the closet that was on the other side were only a few towels and a few toilet paper rolls. Disappointed I left the bathroom and went downstairs again. I hadn't seen a house like this in my life; so impersonal. This man had no personal life and no family member he had still contact with, nor any friends of some sort. He must be the loneliest man alive. On the one hand I felt sorry for him, but on the other I couldn't wait to get him in my hands. I decided to leave the house again and I was on my way to walk to the door, when I suddenly shook up. I heard a scream that went through my bones. At the same time somebody opened the door.

CHAPTER 43

Caffeine was running through his veins and he felt like he was flying. In front of him was a small surgery table that had wheels on every leg and he rolled it over to the ping pong table. He left it there and had a look at his tools. On the table were many kind of tongs which he used on his victims to pull out fingernails or teeth. Two scalpels, a few syringes, some bottles of different anesthetics, which allowed the victim to endure the pain a little bit longer, and many more little toys for him to play. As he was organizing his table he noticed that the doctor was slowly waking up. She tried to groan but because her mouth was taped, no real tone came out of it. At the same time she tried to break loose from her ties but it was impossible for her. A wide smile appeared on his face and he felt that his time had come. He walked up next to the ping pong table and just stood there. With one move he unfolded her eyes and smiled at her. With her eyes widely open from fear she looked at him and he enjoyed her fear so much. It was a great feeling to have her under his power and play God. He felt almighty and with this slut he would be at his best game.

She realized that she was slowly waking up. Her head was hurting so bad and she had the feeling that any minute it would explode. It was pounding in there and she tried to remember what happened but she had a black veil in front of her eyes. She tried to open her eyes but they felt so heavy and she didn't have the strength to open them. She got goose bumps and she felt that she was laying on something cold with her bare back. With her right hand she wanted to go over the eyes, but she couldn't move it. She tried again but again, she failed. Desperate she tried to move her whole body until she realized that she was tied from all four ends so she couldn't move at all. Panic rose inside of her, she tried to say something she realized that her mouth was taped as well. And then,,boom!". Suddenly she could remember everything. She was standing naked in front of her bed and just wanted to lay down, when she heard that cold voice behind her. Her blood froze in her veins and she slowly turned around to face the voice. She had just looked at him when he knocked her out. He must have dragged her here unconscious. Where were they? Her whole body was shaking and the feeling of not knowing where she was and what would happen to her didn't let her go. A familiar smell went up her nose. It must be disinfectant or something like that, she recognized the smell. She smelled that smell every day in the hospital and knew that it was used to clean scalpels and other surgical tools. Where the hell did he take her? What did he want to do to her? She felt that someone was close to her and she wanted to say something but no words came out of her mouth. She was panicking more and more, she couldn't stop shaking in fear, when suddenly the blind fold was taken from her eyes and she could look her enemy in the eye. With her eye wide open from fear she looked at him and recognized Colonel Silk.

He enjoyed her fear and his ugly smile got even wider and an evil laughter came out of his mouth. Hearing that she started shaking even more, and couldn't control herself anymore. This is how the other victims must have felt, when he was killing them. As far as she could remember he tortured his victims before killing them, but somehow she knew that he wanted to take everything out on her. She wanted to scream, maybe someone would hear her but there was no point. Nothing came out of her mouth.

,, Well my beautiful, how are you? Did you sleep well and rest from your journey?"

As if he was waiting on an answer from her, he looked down on her and stared at her.

,, Yes, as far as I can see you look pretty relaxed. What do you think, should we begin our little game?"

With these words he turned around to his tools and for a moment he couldn't decide which toy he should pick to begin the fun. He wanted to grab the tong to pull out her fingernails but the he decided to go for the scalpel. He held it in his right hand and turned it a few times. As he held the scalpel like a surgeon between his thumb and index finger he turned to Sarah again. When she saw the scalpel she tried to move and break her hands and feet free. With all her strength she pulled on the strings hoping that she was not tied right and the more she pulled the more they cut in her flesh. He stood next to her at the ping pong table and asked her with a sweet voice.

„ What should we begin with? What do you think of the idea to cut off all your fingers one by one and then preserve them in alcohol so that I can remember you forever?"

With these words he walked around the table and looked at her delicate fingers and wanted to take her hand in his. Sarah made her hands into fists and screamed as much as she could. He thought it was funny that she wanted to avoid him; she must have understood so far that she couldn't go anywhere. Slowly he went to the end of the table where her feet were and gently pushed the scalpel into her sole. The scalpel was so sharp that he had no trouble opening a wound. She winced with pain and blood started flowing out of the wound. He screamed in pain but her scream was muffled from the tape. Tears from pain and fear ran down her cheeks.

„ What is wrong with you? Pain is a part of our lives and we must live with him every day. We must learn how to deal with him. Do you understand, my love?"

He talked to her in a sweet tone and she didn't like it at all. Her foot hurt and she knew that this was not the only wound he would give her. Her naked breasts went up and down fast because she was panting through the nose. She needed to forget the pain from her wound so she could survive. Survive? Maybe she wouldn't even survive the next half hour, but she was sure that John was looking for her. It could be that he was close to her and would save her soon. This thought calmed her down a little, but fear was deep inside her soul and she could not get rid of it.

„ Don't be such a stubborn woman and answer me!" he ordered her with a harsh voice and quickly cut a wound in her other sole. Her sole that were really dirty from the walk through the tunnel formed an even bigger wound than the other and blood was starting to gather behind her heel.

Again she tried to scream in pain but nothing really came out her mouth. She felt like fainting but she didn't want to close her eyes. This could be her death. Seeing her like this turned his sweet voice into an evil laughter that filled the room. She shook up and was so frightened of this laughter. She didn't know what hurt the most, the wounds on her feet or this laughter. With the scalpel in his hand he walked around the table saying:,, Eeny, meeny, miny, moe…!" He could absolutely not decide which part of her body he wanted to play with next. He enjoyed keeping her in agony of what he was going to do next. He was done counting out and the hand with the scalpel appeared again and he moved to her right breast. She took a deep breath and held it in as if she could avoid his cut. She felt him cutting in her flesh under her breast and again she wanted to scream but she felt like fainting and her head dropped to the right side and she looked at the sadist that tortured her like a cannibal. Again an ugly smile was on his face and he stopped moving. He couldn't hold himself with from all the ecstasy, threw the scalpel on the ground and with one movement he was sitting on her. She tried to move and get him off of her but he was too heavy for her. He bent down and came so close to her that his face was only a few centimeters away from his and they were staring each other in the eyes. With one move he ripped the tape of her mouth and she screamed. When he ripped the tape of her lips small wounds opened and blood started running in her mouth and down her throat. Automatically her tongue came out her mouth and went over her lips. They were burning and they hurt her, with the iron taste in her mouth he she said to him:

,, If you think that you could break me with the things that you do here, you are mistaken!"

She didn't even know where she got the strength to tell him that but she wasn't afraid of him anymore. She knew that sooner or later she would die and that there was no chance that John would find her. He heard her cold voice and stopped moving. He was still sitting on top of her and stared at her. He liked that she stood against him. Most of his victims cries and begged to let them go and most of the times he lost his interest and killed them on the spot. With this one here he found his interest again and adrenaline was running through his veins. He would have a lot of fun with that one. He couldn't hold himself from all the ecstasy he felt and he realized that he was getting restless.

,, What's the matter? I am under the impression that you like it in this situation. I knew that you would put up some resistance, but this I couldn't even dream of that!" he replied and stepped down again from the table.

„ Fuck you, you asshole!" she answered in that cold tone in her voice. Oh yes. This woman had guts and he rubbed his hands.

„ My beautiful, you cannot imagine how much you much me with those words. We will have a lot of fun us two. I am sure you can't wait."

With these words he left her and walked back to his small table to find his next toy. He decided to go for the hunting knife and he took it in his hand. With the hunting knife in his hand he stood next to her and announced her with a crazy voice:

„ Now the fun can begin! Prepare yourself, because what I am going to do with you now you could not have imagined in your craziest nightmares."

It was more of a conclusion than a statement. When she saw the knife coming closer she opened her eyes wide, but she didn't want to show her fear so she tried to stay as calm as possible on the table. The knife was shining under the light of the lamp and he was holding it before her eyes so that she could see it up close. In the light she could see how sharp the knife really was. He wanted to intimidate her. With the knife he drew an invisible line from her throat to her belly button. It looked like he didn't know with which part of her body he should begin. Suddenly and unexpected he stuck the knife under the left breast and pulled a line with the knife to her right breast. Immediately blood was flowing out of the wound and ran down her body forming a small pond in her belly button. She could feel that he continued cutting that wound and the cut was burning like fire and she could feel the blood coming out the wound hot, running down her body. No, she would not scream. She didn't want to do him that favor, to amuse him even more with her pain. She didn't want that so she just laid there on the table, she clenched her teeth and no sound came out of her lips. The cut he made was more superficial than deep but he wanted to test her and he found out that she could endure a lot. It was not yet the time to give her any pain killers because she wouldn't open her mouth that quick. Again he drew an invisible line on her abdomen, this time he wanted to play with her intestines. And again he put the knife I her flesh and opened another wound. This time the wound was deeper and he could see that she was in pain. But she didn't say a word, even though she was close to fainting from all the pain. She didn't get hysterical and didn't start to scream, like all these other women before her. He liked that she didn't say a word or screamed in pain but he couldn't stand it any longer that she was so quite. She must say something to him. She had to let go of the pain somehow, scream or curse. Something. He was so aroused form anger and hate, so he sat on her again and yelled at her.

„ Why don't you say anything? Why don't you scream in pain? Some sound must come from your lips!"

She had trouble speaking and the only words that she said were:

„ Lick my but, you fucking sadist!"

When he heard these words he had to think about his mother and instead of Sarah face he saw this of her mother. How she yelled at him and despised him. His face got even uglier when he saw his mother's face. He let the knife down next to her and suddenly started hitting her in the face like a maniac. One slap after the other, one punch after the other he hit her in the face, which started to get red. She groaned in pain but she did not scream. She didn't beg, to stop hitting her. No word came out of her lips. She screamed inside of her, because she didn't want her fear and panic to show. Again and again he hit her in the face and didn't stop. Her face turned blue from red. He hit her with all of his hate he had for his mother. It made him even angrier that she didn't scream and beg him to stop.

„ Why don't you say a word? Why don't you say a word?" he shouted at her.,, Mother I am waiting on a word from you and I insist to hear something from you!"

With swollen lips, covered in blood and looking at him she said silently:

„ I am not your fucking mother, you son of a bitch!"

With these words she hit him in the heart. Full of anger and hate he grabbed the knife. With both of his hands he held the knife high in the air. For a few seconds he held his hands up high and then he stabbed it in her abdomen. The knife whistled from the air as it was coming down until it reached its destination. He felt how the knife was separating her flesh and found itself deep in her abdomen. Blood was streaming out of the wound and his hands got red. In the moment he stabbed her she screamed in fear and pain. He hadn't heard a louder scream in his life.

She could see the knife coming down to her and she could feel how the cold knife made his way through her inside. She could feel her flesh separating and the knife eating through her it. It was burning like fire and she couldn't hold it any longer. She could see stars around her and she knew her time had come. A scream came out of her lips and filled the room.

In this scream you could hear her feelings and her fear. A scream hat she didn't think she had in her. She let her feeling get hold of her, she started crying and tears of fear and frustration that she wouldn't be found ran down her neck. Slowly it was getting dark around her and her last image and thought was, John.

CHAPTER 44

I was already down in the hallway and wanted to open the door to leave the house, so I could continue with the search for Sarah. As I couldn't find a trace of him or Sarah in the house, to tip me off where they might be, I decided to leave again. It was clear now that the Colonel had planed his getaway well and that he only took with him what he thought was necessary. Sarah's kidnapping did not fit in the picture, and I was sure that he only did that to get me. I was praying to God that she would still be alive when I found her. As I was walking to the door I could see two dark figures coming closer outside the door. I pulled my gun out; I couldn't be sure who they where, when the door opened. This two figures where the men from the patrol who controlled the house. When they saw me in front of them with my gun pointing at them, they automatically reached for their guns. I gave them a sign and calmed them down.

„ Guys. Relax. It's me. The house is clear."

A few seconds later they relaxed and breathed calmly again.

„ What are you two doing here? Shouldn't you be patrolling the street?"

„ The other patrol changed shift with us five minutes ago. As we hadn't seen you in an hour and your car is still here, we thought we would come in. Maybe something happened to you and you cannot come back out. As it seems everything is ok with you. So we can go again."

„ That is really nice of you, to worry about me. As you can see I was just about to leave the house when you came in."

„ Did you find anything, Sir?"

„ No, unfortunately not. I didn't find anything that could point me to his direction."

„ I am sorry, Sir."

„ Let it be and let's get out of here. Maybe the other patrol is luckier and bumps into him."

With these words we turned around and wanted to leave the house, when we heard a terrifying scream and we froze. The scream filled the entire house and it seemed as the echo bounced off the walls. We shook together and tried to figure out where this is coming from.

„ Where did this scream come from?" one of the soldiers asked, but I didn't bother about him, I walked towards the kitchen. Both of them followed me right away and pulled their guns. This scream couldn't come from the rest of the house because I checked it. I didn't find anything or anyone that indicated that he was here. I tried to think of what I left out and didn't inspect and then it hit me. In the back of the kitchen I saw a small door that probably led to the basement. I had totally forgotten to check the basement. Every basement was the perfect hiding spot. I opened the door to the basement and there was nothing but darkness around me. I searched for the light switch and turned the light on. Before I went down the stairs I ordered one of the soldiers to call for backup from the base, that needed to be here as soon as possible; we did not know what we were dealing with here. One of the soldiers left the kitchen and walked outside. The whole basement was now lit up and we could see. With my gun in my hand I walked down the stairs and the soldier followed me. I couldn't stand this uncertainty any more, I knew that this scream was Sarah's and I wanted to find her as quick as possible. With quick steps we walked down the stairs and we stopped in the middle of the room looking around; we couldn't see anyone. In front of us in the left corner we saw the boiler and the barrel for the heating petrol. Not interested in that I turned and looked around the room. I saw a tool bar with all kinds of tools; from a simple screwdriver up to wrench, from a drill to a grinder. It was all organized in order as if they were just waiting for the owner to use them. Under there was a cabinet with two closed doors which I walked too. I told the Soldier to give me back cover and opened the doors. I aimed my gun inside the cabinet but saw nothing apart from empty gas cans. Frustrated I turned and walked away from the tool bar. Apart from the washer and drier that were standing to our right, nothing else was in the basement. I looked at a poster that caught my eye, on the wall and started walking towards it. It showed a group of soldiers that was kneeling in front of a tank smiling into the camera. The poster was huge; it must be about one meter twenty wide and one meter ninety high. It was one of these huge posters they would advertise the military with, to get young people interested. I turned around and looked at the soldier.

„ Where did the scream come from, Sir?"

I was asking myself the same thing and rubbed my chin with my right hand. I could not imagine where the scream was coming from. Did I, maybe, imagine it that it came from this house? I was so sure that it came from this house, but I couldn't find out where it came from.

„ I have absolutely no idea, Soldier, where it came from. As you can see, we couldn't find anything. Apart from that I checked the whole house and found nothing. This silence in this house is killing me, you know that?"

„ Yes, Sir. I absolutely understand."

„ Let us go upstairs and wait for back up. When they come we will tear this place apart if we have to!"

With these words we turned around and started to walk up the stairs. When we arrived upstairs the soldier went out first because I wanted to turn off the lights. After I turned them off I stayed there for a minute on the last step thinking about everything. They must be somewhere here in the basement. Maybe it was better to wait for the others; they knew how to search a house properly. I just wanted to leave the basement, when I looked at a bright frame on the wall in the basement. I was curious so I turned on the light. In the place of that frame was now the poster hanging on the wall. Quickly I turned the light back on and I could see the frame again. Silently I called the soldier to stand next to me and look at what I was seeing. Whispering I told him to look at the frame on the wall and to watch closely what was about to happen. I turned the light on, turned it back off and then on again. The soldier whistled.

„ Sir, What could that be?,, he asked me.

„ I am sure soldier and if we would bet, I would bet on the possibility that there is a lamp behind the poster. Let's go down and check the poster one more time."

Slowly we walk down again and stood in front of the poster. With both hands I felt the poster but couldn't find anything out of the ordinary. It looked perfectly normal and I wandered how this frame appeared. We didn't speak a word to each other and the soldier continued to check the poster, when suddenly we heard noises on the other side of it. We stopped moving and I put my ear on the poster and definitely heard something behind there. I couldn't hold myself any longer; I needed to know what was behind there.

„ Help me Soldier to take this poster of the wall. Quick. I don't want to waste any more time. This is a matter of life and death."

With both hands we took the poster of the wall and, at first, we couldn't see what was in front of us. A few minutes late we understood that it was a hidden door. This cunning bastard, build a hidden door in the wall and put the poster in front of it so no one could see it. The door behind the poster was a metal door that was plastered to look like the wall, so that no one would notice. He just put the poster in front of it and that was it. A damn safe hiding spot. Who knows how long he was in there without anyone finding him. Panic rose inside of me and all I could think of was Sarah and that scream. As long as I held my ear to the door I couldn't hear anything. Was this a good or a bad sign? I didn't want to wait any longer, so I pulled my gun and stepped away from the door. The soldier did the same and together we tried to ram the door open. We tried several times, but nothing happened. The only thing we could hear is furniture being knocked over and a few seconds later we smelled gasoline that was running out the door and we could hear an evil laugh from the other side. And then, nothing but silence.

CHAPTER 45

He rammed his knife deep into her abdomen. The scream she let out ran through his body like lightning. He was still sitting on top of her and tried to get his thoughts back together. He was breathing heavy. His hands were still on the knife and he was staring at her. His hands were covered in blood that was still coming out of the wound. He held his hands up and looked at them as if he saw blood for the first time. With slow movements he stepped off the dead woman and left her there on the table. He didn't give her one more look. While he walked to a sink that he had installed in the room, wild feeling rose inside him. He did it again; he killed his mother and it felt great. He felt like God because he punished her for her actions once again. Breathing heavily he inhaled the smell of blood in the room. He stood in front of the sink so that he could wash his hands. He took a piece of soap and washed and rubbed his hands clean. Lost in his thoughts he was thinking of what to do with the body when he heard someone opening the normal basement door and speak loud. Could it be that they found him? Quickly he turned the water off and stood still for a few seconds. He thought he was hallucinating, when suddenly the door was rammed from the outside. Startled he walked a step back from the door and stood still. Fortunately he had put in a metal door when he build that room here. It was not so easy to open or break. A smile appeared on his face and he could imagine the detective trying to open the door from the outside. He would have trouble opening this door and he wouldn't manage to do this any time soon. Now it was time for him to disappear and quickly he turned away from the door. As he turned around he bumped into the small table with his tools and knocked it over making a loud noise. The small bottles rolled under the ping pong table and he left them there. He didn't care about the table and he grabbed his gun. With his suitcase and his gun he made his way through the tunnel when he saw a gasoline can that was standing in one corner and he stopped. Immediately he put his suitcase down and walked to the can. It was a five liter can, the sort you keep in your car in case you run out of gas. He took the can in his hand and shook it; it was half full. He opened it and threw some on the floor; he walked to the metal door. He poured the rest of it in front of the door and on the walls around it. If he was lucky everything would go up in flames and he would have time to escape. After he finished he threw the can on the floor and searched for a lighter in his pockets, but he couldn't find anything. Irritated he looked around in the room and saw a box of matches and held it in his hand. With shaking hands he tried to light the first match but it went out immediately. The same happened with the second one and he started to swear like wild. The matches were wet; this is why they wouldn't light. With the third match he had luck and it lit immediately. He held it in his hand for a few seconds, so that it would burn until the middle and would not go out again, then he threw it in the puddle of gasoline. When the match hit on the gasoline it went immediately up in flames. Quick he turned away from the door, took his suitcase and walked towards the tunnel. He looked into the room one last time and saw that the flames where filling it quickly and an evil laughter came out his mouth. With quick steps he walked along the tunnel and tried to get to the end of it as quick as possible. When he got transferred five years ago to this base and he rented this house, he had a good look at the houses blue prints. As the housing estate was next to a forest he got the idea to build this tunnel so he could come and go without anyone seeing him. He made the effort to build the torture room and the tunnel leading out of it into the woods. At first he thought about getting a contractor to build the room so he could finish then the rest, but he would probably ask too many questions. So he decided to build it himself. It took him months to finish the room and another four months to finish digging the tunnel. The room and the tunnel were not meant to look nice they were there to serve him and his needs to play around and escape unseen. To bring his victims in and out the house without the neighbors seeing him. Now he was happy that no one found the door to the tunnel in the woods. Of course his neighbors were jogging or walking in the woods and this is why he always had the trap door covered with tarp and leaves so that it was not visible. It was not easy to walk in the tunnel with the suitcase in his hand because the tunnel was not that wide or tall. He had to hold his suitcase behind his back so that he could walk faster but got stuck in the tunnel many times. It was not so far away now, and then he would get to the door and be free. Free to begin a new life.

CHAPTER 46

With joined forces we tried to open that door and rammed our shoulders against the door, but nothing happened. Suddenly we saw the gasoline flowing out under the door and then we could smell that it went up in flames. Smoke was coming out of the door and slowly filled the basement. Panic rose inside of me and a yelled at the Soldier where the hell the rest of the troops where and he just raised his shoulders. As if I had some sort of magic powers, we heard heavy steps above as and soon they were walking down the stairs. I didn't have to explain much because the smoke was filling up the room and we could barely breathe without coughing.

„ Quick. We need to break down that door to put out the fire on the other side, otherwise the roof will fall on our heads!" I yelled at everyone.

„ Who is behind that door?" the officer asked me.

„ We have no time for questions you idiot. Don't you see? The fire is spreading on the other side and it will come over to us when we don't do anything quick!"

The officer ordered his men to ram the door but even they could not break it. The smoke got thicker and thicker and I didn't want to lose any more time. I remembered the crowbar that was in the back of my car and left the basement to run to my car. I opened the trunk and got the crowbar. I looked around and saw the Jeeps of the military police that were standing there and walked towards them. I sat in one of them and talked into the radio quick.

„ Listen, Officer. Here is Detective Man. Me and my men are now in the house of Colonel Silk. The Colonel set the house on fire and ran away. We believe, no, we are certain that the victim is injured in the basement.

Send us the fire department, an ambulance and more back up to catch this son of a bitch. He cannot be so far away he must still be around here."

„ Yes, Sir. I understood. Should I inform anyone else about this?"

„ Yes, call General Pilot inform him about everything."

I also told him to get in contact with my boss and that the base should be on alert and standing by. I had no time for further explanations and left the Jeep to get back to the basement. When I arrived I saw that the men were still trying to break the door open, but they did not succeed. They had broken the basement windows to get the smoke out the room and have more light. I stood next to the door and put the crowbar between the door and the door case. With joined forces we pushed the crowbar and we heard a crack. This made us push even harder and suddenly the hot metal door opened in front of us and we could see how the flames had gone up the walls. I laid my arm over my eyes to shield me from the heat and I had to squint to look into the room. Through the flames I could see a table and on there was a person. I was sure that this person was Sarah and wanted to walk into the flames to get to her, but they tried to hold me back. Like wild I tried to free myself and I started shouting at them to let me go. They let me go and I walked into the flames and entered the room. I felt the flames on my clothing but I didn't care. The only thing that mattered was Sarah. Quick I walked to the table and bent over her. Frightened I laid my hand on her neck to feel her pulse to see if she is still alive. I felt a slow pulse; that was bad. I looked down and saw the knife that was still inside her abdomen and felt the need to take it out. I didn't, because I knew that it would make everything even worse. I heard sirens from afar and I was hoping that the ambulance would arrive first. The men tried to come behind me into the room but the y couldn't get forward easily because the flames spread into the basement as well. They were constantly shouting at me to get back out. I felt that my clothes were on fire and my legs started burning when suddenly they threw water and got my wet from top to bottom. The fire department was here and the ambulance at the same time. They saw the fire from the street and had thrown the water hoses from through the windows that were broken. The soldiers grabbed the hoses and started without delay to put out the fire. They started spaying water on me and into the room and in a few minutes the fire was put out. With the corner of my eye I could see the men from the ambulance come down the stairs.

They came into the room quickly and the stretcher on the ground in front of the table. I had cut the ties of her hands and legs to make it easier for the men to take her carefully from the table and lay her on the stretcher. They covered her with a blanket to keep her warm. I left the basement with the men and escorted her to the ambulance. When we were outside I could take a better look at Sarah and my breath stopped. Her face had turned blue; the Colonel must have beaten her like wild. He would pay for that! I wouldn't let him get away with this. They put the stretcher into the ambulance and put a drip on her at once. They started cleaning the wounds and both stopped at the knife. They were not sure what they should do, even the doctor was not sure if that would complicate things a lot. They put a tube through her nose to make it easier for her to breath. As she had a very low pulse they gave her a shot to keep a heart going and connected her to the heart monitor to watch her pulse. I was constantly coughing from inhaling all that smoke. They wanted to take care of me too and as soon as they came to me the monitor sounded the alarm that Sarah's heart stopped. Immediately they turned to Sarah again and let me go; they tried to revive her and threw me out if the ambulance. They tried to bring her back and the doctor shouted at the driver to start the ambulance and drive to the hospital at once. They closed the doors quickly and drove off with the blue light. I just stood there in the driveway and hopped that they could save her. I looked around and realized that the whole street was full of curious people and the soldiers needed to keep them back so that they would not come near the crime scene. Everywhere the same. Where there was something to see sensation seekers were not far away. I was sick of them and turned around. A soldier appeared next to me who was helping me earlier to open the door and he stood in front of me. He wanted to give me the report of what happened while I was gone, but I stopped him raising my hand and asked him for a cigarette. I had seen the Marlboro packet in his shirt pocket. Without hesitating he pulled the packet out, offered me a cigarette and gave me his lighter. As soon as I lit the cigarette this terrible cough came back. Like wild I was coughing and slime was coming up in my mouth and I spit in the driveway. When I calmed down from the coughing I let the soldier give me his report.

„ Sir, the fire was put out successfully. We have everything under control but I believe that you should come and have a look for yourself!"

„ What did you find in that basement?" I asked him and kept sucking on my cigarette.

„ Apart from the small room we examined we found another door that was locked from the outside. We managed to break it open and saw that it led to a tunnel."

„ What tunnel?" I asked not believing what I heard and started walking towards the house to go into the basement again.

When I arrived in the basement my shoes sucked up the water that was on the floor from the firemen when they put out the fire. Slowly I walked into the small room where we found Sarah. I stepped into the room and looked around. I saw the small table that Silk must have knocked over and saw all the tools that were laying on the floor. I became goose bumps and I was glad that Sarah was not found even worse than she was. I bend down under the table and found one of the tongs that were there and took it in my hand. Dried blood was on that and a piece of fingernail was stuck on the tong. I felt sick, because I could imagine what this sick bastard did with all these tools. I looked at the ping pong table and found the small bottles that fell down and took them in my hand. Unfortunately I couldn't read the labels because the water had damaged them. Then I stood up again and looked around, apart from the sink I couldn't recognize anything else. Behind me must have been a couch but the fire destroyed it completely. I looked at the men that were standing in front of the door that they found, which led to the tunnel the soldier told me about. Curious I walked over there and the men opened the way for me so that I could inspect the tunnel closer.

„ What do we have here?" I was talking more to myself than to the other soldiers.

The tunnel was completely dark and I couldn't see a thing. I asked for a flashlight and I was given one at once. I turned it on and looked inside the dark tunnel but after ten meters I couldn't see anything. I must be a long tunnel and I was not sure where it was going. I was just about to say that we should form a group to follow the tunnel, when I saw a light coming my way. I pulled my gun and aimed at the figure that was coming closer but he shouted to us not to shoot. A few minute later a soldier appeared in front of us with sweat running down his face that needed a few moments of rest. As I was os nervous and couldn't wait I urged him to tell me what he saw.

„ Well, Soldier, speak. What did you find?"

„ Well, Sir. As I calculated the tunnel must be about one hundred twenty meters long. I got to the end of it but couldn't get any further!"

„ Why not soldier?"

„ Because at the end of the tunnel there was a trap door that was locked from the outside. I tried to open it but I couldn't make it so I came back to inform you about it."

„ Well done, Soldier. Now inform us about the tunnel, how was it build, because from what I could see it is full of dirt and soil."

„ You are right. Someone dag the tunnel by hand. It is not a professional job, along the way you trip on tree roots that are all over the place. At some points you need to dunk and at some points it gets so narrow that you have trouble moving along."

I thought about what he said and looked at my watch to look at the time. From the time we found the door fifty minutes had passed. If I could believe the soldier's words it was not easy to get through the tunnel, which means that Silk must still be around here. I thought about a plan quick and decided to go with it.

„ I need four men to go inside the tunnel. The rest of you take a car and seal off the area. I don't want anyone to go in or out this residential area. Did you understand?"

„ Yes, Sir!" the soldiers answered and were already out the basement.

The four soldiers stayed with me and we talked about how we would proceed. We decided to take the crowbar with us and that we would try to break the door open. One after the other we turned on the flash lights and went in the tunnel.

CHAPTER 47

He tried to get through the tunnel as quick as possible without wasting another minute; it was a matter of life and death now. It was not easy to get through the tunnel. Every now and again he tripped on these stupid roots and stones and could barely hold himself from falling down. Sweating he pushed himself to go further and cursed that he didn't get a carryall instead of a suitcase. The only thing he really needed anyway was the false papers, the cash and his credit card. New clothes he could buy later. The only thing that mattered to him was to get out of this in one piece. He must have been half way along the tunnel and he couldn't wait to come to the end of it. Again he tripped on a root and this time he couldn't hold himself and fell down on his face. When he fell he hurt his knee and he could hear a cracking sound. For a few seconds he laid there exhausted and tried to get his breathing back on track. He was panting and breathed frantically in and out. He got dizzy and started swearing at himself. He wanted to get up again but his left knee was hurting badly. From the fall he must have broken it and now it hurt like hell. One last time he took a deep breath and he continued his way. He must have injured himself worse than he thought. Slowly his powers were leaving him and he forced himself do move along. If he only would be that smart to take his painkillers with him, but he could stop at a drug store later and get some. Sweating from the pain he took his suitcase and continued along limping. He was coming forward slowly but he had no other choice but to get out of this tunnel. Finally he reached the end of it and stopped for a minute. He listened inside the tunnel but no one was following him. He desperately needed to rest for a few minutes; his knee was killing him. Panting he stood against the tunnel's wall and tried to catch his breath. Again he tried to

239

hear if anyone was coming after him but he couldn't hear a thing. That calmed him down a little and he was breathing a little better. He searched for the keys in his pocket and found them. He held the key chain up but he couldn't see a lot in the dark so he turned on the flashlight. After a few seconds he found the key and tried to open the lock. From the stress and the pain his hands were shaking and he only managed to open it the second time he tried. He heard the click he wanted so that he understood that the lock was open. He let the lock fall on the floor without giving it another thought and opened the hatch carefully. He needed to make sure that no one was around to see him. He opened the hatch just a split and he saw that no one was around. So he pushed the door open with his strength he had left and slowly he left the tunnel. With the gun in his hand he checked the surroundings and again he couldn't see anyone. He let the suitcase on the floor and went back to the hatch to lock it from the outside. He had left the lock there from when he opened the hatch to go in with Sarah. After he was done locking the door he took the key chain and threw it as far into the woods as he could and didn't bother about it again. He wouldn't need them, ever again. With the suitcase in one hand he walked as fast as the hurting knee let him into the woods. He didn't have to walk far, he had his car parked nearby, but with his knee, he only moved slowly. As he was coming closer to his car, he heard voices coming closer. With a brisk movement he wanted to hide behind a large tree, but his knee made it difficult for him. With this movement his knee snapped due to his weight and he fell hard on the ground. As if this wasn't enough he hit his head on a tree root and everything around him went dark. He tried to fight it but he passed out. not moving he laid on the ground.

CHAPTER 48

We went into the tunnel one after the other and followed him as quickly as possible. The soldier was right with his description of the tunnel and we had to be careful not to fall on each other. While we were walking along the tunnel I imagined how the Colonel dug up this tunnel and what his thoughts must have been. He must have a concrete idea where the tunnel was leading to and where it would end. But now for real. Where did this tunnel end? Would we fall into a trap, or would we land somewhere in the open? If that was the case it meant that he slipped out of our hand s again and that the state police must continue looking for him. I would be off the hook then and could enjoy my peace. I was so lost in my thoughts that I didn't see a root and tripped. I caught myself at the last minute and didn't fall. While the other men were walking I stood a moment to have a look around. He had really made quite the effort with this tunnel. It was astounding how he had thought of all this and made it happen. Everything, the plastered metal door, the torture room, the tunnel, they were all well thought through. From this I could see that this man was mentally really sick. But this was no excuse to torture and murder all these young girls. After digging the tunnel he didn't work on it further, it was only an entrance and an exit. Left and right of them were walls of dirt where you could see that you were under the face of the earth and also the uncertainty of not knowing where this tunnel led to. I escaped from my thoughts and followed the other men. There were not far away and after a few meters I met them. We still walked a few meters when the leader said that we arrived at the hatch. Since the tunnel was really narrow we couldn't stand next to each other so we needed to wait for the guy in front to break the lock hat was on the outside. Then we could get out of the tunnel. I heard as the first man was talking to the one behind him to put the crowbar in together. With all their strength they tried to open the hatch but they couldn't. The third guy tried to fit in there as good as possible and together they tried to open it. With joined forces they pushed and we could hear the lock breaking and the hatch opening to the outside. They stopped to collect their strength and one more time they gave it a good push and the lock busted open. With the hatch being open, they all pulled their guns out and the first soldier exited the tunnel. I turned my flash light out and put it back in my pocket. As we could see we got out in the open so we wouldn't need a flash light. We needed a few seconds to adapt to the daylight and then we all came out of the tunnel. We gathered around the exit with our guns ready, we looked around and saw that we were in the woods behind the houses.

„ What now, Sir?, one of the men asked.

„ We will search the woods. Maybe we would find a clue where he went. We should ask for back up first so that they could help us find him."

„ Yes, Sir!" the men answered and one of them pulled his cell phone out to call the men that were still in the house. He gave them a quick report and the location we were.

I waited for him to finish when I saw the red truck that was parked not far away from us. It must be the car the witness saw in front of Sarah's house. I gave the soldiers a sign to follow me carefully. We all walked to the car watching the surroundings as well. When we arrived we had a closer look at it. The driver's door was unlocked and there were no license plates on the car. I looked at the back and saw Sarah's white carpet on it; immediately I knew that this was the car he kidnapped her with.

„ Since the car is still here, the Colonel must still be around her. I couldn't imagine that he was on the ran on foot. Keep your eye open and if you see him move you are free to kill him, except if he turns himself in. Be careful this man is dangerous and he is capable of anything. Is that clear?"

„ Yes, Sir!" the men answered and spread in the woods.

I wanted to have a closer look at the car and stayed behind.

Slowly he woke up again and opened his eyes. His head and knee where pounding in pain. How could he be so careless, he asked himself while trying to sit up. He had just sat up when he heard voices not far from where he was. One voice he heard was familiar and he stretched to see. He could see five armed men standing around the hatch talking to each other. At once he dunk again and started looking for his gun; he lost during the fall. He searched in the leaves and found it quick. Slowly he was limping from one tree to the other so that the men would not see him. he was glad that he knew this part of the woods so good. If he would be lucky they wouldn't see him at all. He watched them and saw that they had found his car and that they spread out to find him. He was laughing, if only they knew that he was so close. He could see the car clearly from here and he could see that they were inspecting it quick. Then he saw how the four soldiers left the Detective by the car and walked away into the woods. Now was his chance to kill the Detective. He didn't have to lose anything anyway; they found the room and the tunnel. They already knew that he was behind everything. Now he would have the chance to kill this Detective. He slowly walked through the trees on a path. Carefully he sneaked up to the car and was standing now exactly behind the detective as he was bending in the car to examine it. This stupid man didn't even hear him walk up to him and now he was standing behind him. He could just shoot him in the back and walk away. But he wanted to see the look in his face doing it. Only a coward would shoot him in the back; not he. Quick he held his gun against the detective's back and said:

„ Well hello, Mr. Man. What are you doing in my car?" he asked with a squeaky voice.

I froze and couldn't believe that this bastard surprised me. I was a fool for not being careful enough and hear him sneak up on me. From the windows I could see that the soldiers were already too far away in the woods searching for him.

„ Hello Colonel. I was just around and thought I could pay you a visit. We should have a quite conversation us two, don't you think? I answered him as I came out of the car.

I was still with my back to him but I wanted to change that. So I turned around and had the man facing me that tortured and killed so many women. Fortunately I had still my gun in my hand and now we were both aiming at each other.

„ Yes, I think it is a great idea, although I don't see what we should talk about!" he answered.

I got goose bumps with these words and I didn't let him out of my sight. We were both in a strange situation and as I could see he was capable of anything. If necessary I will just kill him here on the spot. I was amazed that he didn't shoot me in the back.

„ What do you think about you giving me your gun and turn yourself in. This would be the best call for both of us. You know that we know all about you anyway so don't make it harder and turn yourself in. Give me your gun."

„ You are so sure that I would turn myself in. Did you forget that the soldiers are in the woods looking for me and that it would be easier for me to just kill you here and drive off in my car. The car is here, I have the keys, so the only thing these soldiers are going to see is the dust of my car."

„ Yes I know that you could do that, but you are not going to. Deep down you know that you want me to catch you, otherwise you wouldn't leave me that note on the mirror. Or not?"

While I was telling him my thoughts I saw that another Jeep from the military police was coming towards us. The Colonel couldn't see them because they came from behind his back. They must have seen us because they stopped the car and stepped out of the car. I didn't want him to see them so I moved a little bit so that he would focus on me. It seemed to work; when I moved he moved to and stood in front of me without seeing them.

„ I kidnapped the doctor only to make you see what I am capable of. Of course I wanted to get back at you, and as you saw, everything went as planned. You cannot imagine how sorry I feel about your girlfriend but you must understand, I needed to finish what I started!" he said and an ice cold smile appeared on his lips.

Exactly in this moment I could just shoot him, but I was still a Detective of the military. Oh God how good it would feel to kill this bastard myself. With the corner of my eye I could see that the men had moved closer to us and had gathered behind him. Without making a sound they were standing there all aiming at Silk, keeping an eye on him. I tried to give them a signal to grab him. The Colonel must have noticed that because quickly he turned and stood now next to me holding his gun at my head. Everything went by so fast that I couldn't react; now he was holding me by the neck. He was really strong; looking at him you wouldn't think so.

„ Don't move or I will shoot this pig!" he threatened the soldiers.

The soldiers froze but were still aiming at him not leaving him from their sight. They were nervous and were not quite sure what to do now and looked at me. I dint want to see him slip through my fingers again and shouted.

„ Shoot this bastard!"

„ Shut up Mr. Man, or do you think, that I would not take you in my car as a hostage to leave here and throw you dead out of the car?"

„ What are you waiting for men? Shoot him and don't mind me!" I ordered the soldiers.

While I was talking to them, Silk pulled me closer to the car and used me as a shield. The soldiers were not sure where they should aim at on the Colonel and when they should pull the trigger and so they hesitated even longer. The Colonel sat in the car and used me still as his shield and had no intention of letting me go. I tried to break free of his hands and I almost did it. The Colonel had started the car quick and wanted to kick me away when I got free. I pointed my gun at him and pushed the trigger exactly the same moment he did. I felt a pain like fire in the right side of my body and I felt dizzy. The only thing I can remember is aiming at him and shooting at him.

CHAPTER 49

Deep in my subconscious I could hear a rhythmical beeping sound. I tried to open my eyes but my eyelids were so heavy I couldn't lift them. I had to be in a hospital, I could smell the smell of disinfectant in my nose. I tried to remember what happened but it was impossible. It was like I had amnesia. My throat was dry and I had to swallow to wet it a little. Slowly I opened my eyes and needed to some time to adapt to the light in the room. What day was it? How long was I in here? Next to me I heard a familiar voice talking to me. When I finally opened my eyes, I saw Jack, my boss, sitting in a chair next to me. Slowly my eyes adapted to the light and I could see that I was connected to a heart monitor. And that I had a drip in my left arm and that my right leg was in plaster. How did I do that? I couldn't remember.

,, How are you, John?" Jack asked.

,, Feel like a train hit me!" I answered silently and started coughing that made me hurt all over.

Jack stood up immediately and offered me a glass of warm water with a straw putting it in my mouth. I sucked on the straw and immediately felt better. The cough stopped and I thanked Jack.

,, Thanks, Mum" I teased him. '' Tell me please what happened and I am laying here in the hospital!"

,, Don't you remember?" he asked me.

,, I only remember that the Colonel shot me and that I shot back. What happened then, I don't remember."

,, It is ok John. If I had lost so much blood like you, I wouldn't remember either. As we found out by asking the soldiers that were with you at the scene, the colonel wanted to get away in his car. It is correct, he did shoot at you and you shot him back; you missed him but he didn't. As soon as he shot you passed out and when he tried to drive of the soldiers started shooting at him like crazy. They put a lot of holes in his car and of course he didn't escape; he was shot numerous times. As a result of that, the Colonel drove in reverse and before hitting a tree he drove over your leg. He was dead at the scene. Congratulations. You put an end to this case."

„ Yes, but with what price? Where did this fucking bastard shot me? I haven't talked to any doctors yet."

„ The Colonel shot you in the right side of your abdomen and put a hole in your liver. Luckily the bullet went straight through and exited in the back. You were really lucky; the ambulance came really quick to the scene. They brought you straight to the hospital and were operated on as soon as you got here. I have talked to the doctor the operated on you and he said you need to be careful for a few month and with the proper diet your liver will be as good as new."

„ Thank you for your comforting words my friend!, I answered him in pain. Now I knew why I had this bandage around my belly. For a while we were just sitting there, without saying a word. This whole story could have ended so much worse, if the Colonel aimed a little better. I got goose bumps only thinking about it. Jack must have noticed and padded me on the shoulder.

„ Now everything is ok my friend. Rest a little so that you get some strength and get back to being you. I will go in my office and will come by later to check on you."

I didn't want to let him go so easily, I had one question that really burned on my tongue. What happened to Sarah? Was she still alive? Was she dead and he didn't want to tell me, I had to find out and so I asked him.

„ What happened to Sarah? Is she alive? I asked him.

Jack turned slowly back to me and looked at me. I saw that he tried to find the right words and he was struggling.

„ Come on, tell me!" I said and had that terrible feeling in my stomach making me feel sick.

„ John, it doesn't look good for her. The stab wound in her stomach that this bastard did to her nearly killed her. She is now in a coma and no one can say when she will wake up or if she will. The smaller wounds will heal quickly, but this large wound will take a long time before it will heal;

he did great damage to her. She was flown to the Columbia University Clinic and was operated straight away. She had lost a huge amount of blood and the operation was very difficult. If you had found her just fifteen minutes later it would be too late for her. John, I am so sorry for the girl. I really liked her. You must believe me."

„ Don't talk about her like she is already dead. I dare you." I answered him.

„ John…!" he started but I didn't let him continue.

„ It's ok. Let's change subjects. I am sure that you have my resignation letter on your desk, or not?"

„ Yes, I do actually. Are you sure you want to do this? I think it would be better if you would think that through and when you will be better we can talk about it. What do you think?"

„ I have thought about it and to tell you the truth I have been meaning t write this letter since the first day I arrived in Ford Creek. This case and Sarah have nothing to do with this decision. Do you understand? I could not do this any longer!"

„ Yes, I understand what you are saying. So we will see us in few hours. I will come by."

With these words he left the room. I was quite sure that he already found my replacement. But I didn't care. The only thing I cared about now was my life and what do to with it. Exhausted I laid on the cushion and slept tight.

A terrible storm was building up and I couldn't wait to sit on my terrace and look at the spectacle. I went to the fridge and got a couple of beers to take with me on the terrace. My wound from the shot and the operation still hurt me. Especially when the weather changes like that. It has been four months since I was shot and slowly I went back to normal again. I had strict orders from to doctor to relax. I had quit my job and had just got my compensation from the army from which I wanted to open my own private investigators office. With the beer in my hand I walked on to the terrace and sat slowly in the swing. I pulled the cushions behind my back and sat back opening a can of beer. With a large sip I drank all of it. It was very hot today and it was unbearable. Sweat was running down my back. I smashed the first beer can and opened the second one. I took a small sip and put it back on the table. I could hear thunder from far away and the sky became darker. It was about four o'clock in the afternoon but it looked like evening. I sat back in my swing and took some papers in my hand. I looked again at the lease to my office that I wanted to open. I took a pen and signed it. Then I put the papers on a table next to the swing on the terrace.

Once a detective, always a detective. The only difference was that I would be my own boss now. I was retired for four months now and it was about time to start working again. I thought about my last case and immediately I thought about Sarah. Five weeks had passed since my last visit. Then she was still in a coma. The doctor couldn't say when she will wake up from it. I had visited her three times in the hospital and had a good look at her wounds. The smaller stab wounds the Colonel had made her had healed up well, only the large one under her breast that had left a scar. The doctor had told me that the operation was successful and that she would have no damage from it. Except that she couldn't have any children because they needed to take out her uterus. Due to the stab wound he had damaged the uterus so bad that they needed to take it out. Due to losing so much blood it was normal that she was in a coma. We only had to wait for her to wake up. I begged the doctor to inform me a soon as something changed with her situation. With the thought if Sarah I sat back in the swing and took another sip of beer. Suddenly thunder and lightning started to come closer and the first raindrops fell on the ground. The wet soil had now a great smell to it. I took a deep breath and enjoyed it. After a while the raindrops became more and it started pouring. The rain was falling so fast that small ponds of water were forming on the ground. You couldn't see very far in this rain. I tried to look out on my land, that was many hectares big but it was impossible to see anything. It seemed as if a car was driving up my driveway coming to the house, but I could be wrong. A strong wind came and took the papers from the table blowing them on the terrace and I stood up to catch them. I gathered them again so that I wouldn't lose anything; I walked inside the house so I could leave them on the coffee table and walked out on the terrace again. As I sat back into the swing I looked down to the driveway and I could really see a car parking in front of the house. I looked closer to recognize the persons that were getting out of the car, because due to the heavy rain I couldn't see clearly.

The person next to the driver got out of the car and stood there in the rain. She looked at the house and was not sure what to do next and continued standing in the rain. Slowly I walked down the steps of the terrace that led to the driveway and as she saw me walking down she walked to me. She looked familiar, but I couldn't see clearly as she was walking towards me. This was impossible. It was Sarah that was walking up to me. I couldn't believe it and we walked to another. We stopped with almost one meter distance between us and we looked at each other with mixed feelings. We were both staring at each other completely wet. I couldn't hold myself any longer and walked towards her. We were still staring at each other, without saying a word. I held my hands up to touch her and I still couldn't believe it was her. She came a step closer and we fell in each other's arms. Minutes passed until we could let go of each other and now she was standing in front of me. I had to kiss her, so we stood in the rain kissing passionately. I wanted to say something to her, I had so many questions but she just put her finger on my lips and so we stood there looking at each other. The driver's door opened Jack my ex-boss looked out of the car. He just waved at me and I waved back. Quickly he got back in the car; he didn't want to get wet and started the motor. He turned the car around and drove off. We looked at him while we were still in the rain hugging. When the car was gone I looked Sarah in her eyes and said to her:,, Shall we?" . She nodded and hand in hand we walked to the house. Before the stairs I stopped her. When she tried to say something I just picked her up and took her in my arms. With Sarah in my arms I walked in the house, entered with the right foot the door and took her all the way up to the bedroom.

Printed in the United States
by Baker & Taylor Publisher Services